THE SUPREME FICTIONS OF

JOHN BANVILLE

GW00633981

MANCHESTER
UNIVERSITY PRESS

THE SUPREME FICTIONS OF
JOHN BANVILLE

Joseph McMinn

MANCHESTER
UNIVERSITY PRESS

MANCHESTER AND NEW YORK

distributed exclusively in the USA by St. Martin's Press

Published by Manchester University Press
Oxford Road, Manchester M13 9NR, UK
and Room 400, 175 Fifth Avenue, New York, NY 10010, USA

Distributed exclusively in the USA by
St. Martin's Press, Inc., 175 Fifth Avenue, New York, NY 10010, USA

Distributed exclusively in Canada by
UBC Press, University of British Columbia, 6344 Memorial Road, Vancouver, BC, Canada V6T 1Z2

British Library Cataloguing-in-Publication Data
A catalogue record is available from the British Library

Library of Congress Cataloging-in-Publication Data applied for

ISBN 0 7190 5397 8 *hardback*
ISBN 0 7190 5698 5 *paperback*

First published 1999

06 05 04 03 02 01 00 99   10 9 8 7 6 5 4 3 2 1

Typeset in Charter
by Northern Phototypesetting Co. Ltd, Bolton
Printed in Great Britain
by Bell & Bain Ltd, Glasgow

IN MEMORY OF

MY FATHER

What makes the poet the potent figure that he is, or was, or ought to be, is that he creates the world to which we turn incessantly and without knowing it and that he gives to life the supreme fictions without which we are unable to conceive of it.

Wallace Stevens, *The Noble Rider and the Sound of Words*

Contents

Figures

Preface

THIS study of Banville is a completely revised version of my earlier work, *John Banville: A Critical Study* (Dublin, Gill & Macmillan, 1991), an attempt to bring it into line with subsequent developments in Banville's fiction as well as the significant growth in the critical literature on that fiction. A palimpsest of sorts, it retains and extends the original structure of the earlier study, but does so from a new introductory perspective, one which tries to place Banville within the contexts of the theory and practice of postmodernist writing. That perspective, while it retains faith in some of my original observations on Banville's fiction, has been substantially modified by watching, and trying to keep up with, the remarkable adventurism of that fiction, especially since the publication of *The Book of Evidence*, the last novel considered in my original study. With the appearance of that remarkable novel, it was clear that Banville had opened up a new mythology about imaginative knowledge, one that was inspired by the idea and the metaphor of pictorial art. That mythology, as I have tried to show and explain, had been lurking in Banville's fiction from a very early stage, and suggests that students of Banville's intertextuality should look within as well as without the novels for inspirational leads. Another significant change in that perspective is the emphasis on the gendered nature of fantasy in this fiction, a feature I originally thought of as incidental, but which now strikes me as fundamental. Much criticism of Banville has been so preoccupied with his literary and intellectual allusiveness that it has perhaps neglected an underlying dramatic pattern which questions the relation between masculinity and intellectualism - this is a series of fictions in which men fantasise about women and despair of their own sensuality.

These reconsiderations have entered into all rereadings and revisions of my original chapters, giving a clearer picture, I hope, of the growth and development of certain motifs in Banville. The present work has also allowed me to acknowledge and integrate the substantial growth in critical studies of Banville, studies which have helped me to look afresh at the novels, and to revise earlier observations and judgements. The current bibliographical checklist on Banville's fiction shows a dramatic increase on that which was available a decade ago, and reflects the international character of Banville studies.

I would like to thank Fergal Tobin and Jonathan Williams, who first encouraged my work on Banville; Declan Kiberd and Kevin Barry, who gave decisive support to the idea for the present study; Matthew Frost, my editor, for his responsive and enthusiastic attention to the work at all stages; Tom Kilroy, who read early drafts of chapters and offered several valuable critical suggestions; my colleagues in the Staff Research Seminar at Jordanstown, Ronnie Bailie, Bill Lazenbatt, Gerry Macklin, Kathleen McCracken and Andrew Thacker, who subjected several of my ideas about Banville to rigorous and constructive scrutiny. My thanks also to the following, who helped in a variety of ways: Bruce Arnold, Janet Campbell, Debbie Mitchell, Paul Parkhill, Monika McCurdy, George Steiner and Rob Walker.

I gratefully acknowledge the assistance and support of the library staff at the University of Ulster, Jordanstown, and thank the following for permission to reproduce works in their collections: Bildarchiv Preussischer Kulturbesitz, Berlin; Her Majesty Queen Elizabeth II, Royal Collection, Windsor; The Fogg Art Museum, Cambridge, Massachusetts; Mauritshuis, The Hague; Musée du Louvre, Paris; Museum of Fine Arts, Budapest; The National Gallery, London.

Finally, my thanks to my wife, Edna, for her unswerving support from beginning to end.

Joseph McMinn
Belfast

Introduction

When I heard the learn'd astronomer,
When the proofs, the figures, were ranged in columns before me,
When I was shown the charts and diagrams, to add, divide, and
    measure them,
When I sitting heard the astronomer where he lectured with much
    applause in the lecture room,
How soon unaccountable I became tired and sick,
Till rising and gliding out I wander'd off by myself,
In the mystical moist night-air, and from time to time,
Look'd up in perfect silence at the stars.
        Walt Whitman, 'When I Heard the Learn'd Astronomer'

ALL OF Banville's novels read as variations upon a premeditated theme, which I take to be the life of the imagination. From his earliest fictions, it seems that Banville always knew where he was going: the stylistic challenge was to find, or borrow, metaphors and mythologies which would best serve that sense of purpose. This study hopes to show how a single story is told throughout Banville's work, each fiction experimenting with an increasingly refined metaphorical aspect of that story. Much of the originality of Banville's fiction comes from the way he engages with, and then rewrites, some of the myths of romanticism and modernism, a form of creative dependency which is structured and inspired by an imaginative and elaborate use of allusion and quotation.

This preoccupation, and this method, suggest that Banville's fiction, like so much of postmodernism, is driven by a deep attraction towards the legacy of romanticism, most crucially in how the imaginative faculty acts as a quasi-divine agent of knowledge and perception in a fallen world, one which is marked by a sense of loss and exile.[1] Fredric Jameson has noted this strong nostalgic impulse in a great deal of postmodernism.[2] Banville's work is self-consciously and adventurously in touch with contemporary theory about fiction, aware of the influence and the inheritance of the poststructuralist revolution in thought about the constructed and fictive nature of subjectivity and its language, and of its philosophical challenge to the optimism and reason of Enlightenment humanism. While it shares many of the narrative features of what is seen as postmodernist fiction, it has created its own very distinctive mythology about the postmodern consciousness and its relation to the history of ideas about the imaginative faculty.

In my earlier study of Banville I quoted Georg Lukács's view of the modern novel as 'the epic of a world that has been abandoned by God'.[3] This characterisation of the nature and condition of the modern novel still offers, I believe, a suggestive perspective on Banville's kind of fiction, especially on the importance which that fiction attributes to the power and the necessity of the imagination. Most of his leading characters are engaged in an intellectual and emotional conflict with a violent and senseless world in which they feel like strangers or aliens: in nearly every novel the imaginative life of those characters, usually presented in a dramatic form of self-consciousness, even self-delusion, is the subject of the essential drama. Since all of those characters are men, who are almost invariably fascinated by images of women, this fiction is an anatomy, and a pathology, of a distinctively male psyche. If there is a romantic quest here, I suggest that it turns upon the search for a lost unity, notably in the masculine personality, between the imaginative and the rational faculties, or between body and mind. Patricia Waugh, addressing Jameson's diagnosis of postmodernism as the schizophrenic condition of late capitalism, suggests that the divided self of postmodernism and the autonomous transcendent self of Enlightenment humanism are products of the same cultural tradition, which equates rationality with patriarchy:

> [The] 'schizophrenia' of Postmodernism can be seen as a fin-de-siècle parody or caricature of a dualism inherent in the Western tradition of thought where the self is defined as a transcendent rationality which necessitates splitting off what is considered to be the irrational, emotion, and projecting it as the 'feminine' onto actual women. It is to see T. S. Eliot's 'dissociation of sensibility' from a feminist rather than a High Tory position.[4]

The typical Banville protagonist is deeply damaged, split between what he can understand and what he can imagine, between being and potential. Only 'supreme fictions' offer some form of relief and understanding, some way back to a sense of original harmony.

These 'supreme fictions' are an idea, or a myth, which Banville borrows from the modernist poet Wallace Stevens, specifically from his classic poem *Notes toward a Supreme Fiction* (1942).[5] A 'late Romantic poem', according to Harold Bloom,[6] *Notes* is an elaborate and most testing exploration of the creative necessity for imaginative perception in an age where excessive abstraction, of the worst kind, has diminished the human ability to perceive beauty. If we are to understand Banville's aesthetic, we would do well to see how Stevens's celebration of the imagination, and of the vitality of fiction, provides a historical link between romanticism, modernism and the postmodern mythologies of Banville's novels. As Denis Donoghue points out, these extreme claims for the transcendent, the divine, powers of the imagination derive from the romanticism of Coleridge, 'a late theology of the creative Word', through which humanity takes over the divine creativity once solely, or exclusively, associated with God.[7] Donoghue offers the following gloss on Stevens's variation upon Coleridge:

> Notes toward a Supreme Fiction: supreme, meaning 'fully answerable to man's needs and desires', leaving no ache behind; fiction, meaning a structure of man's invention, corresponding not to an impersonal, objective reality but to the nature of the inventor; great because he is great.[8]

This humanistic aesthetic, which displaces God in favour of humankind, while retaining the divine attributes of the displaced centre of inspiration, is a crucial part of the narrative drama in Banville's fiction, notably in the scientific tetralogy, where it is made clear that there may be a demanding and confusing emotional as well as intellectual price to be paid for the elevation of the human to such godly heights. The creative individual, scientist or artist, may exhibit something divine or wondrous in the life and work of the imagination, something which proves a transcendent link with divine creativity, but there is a concomitant sense of loss, isolation and confusion. Much of the power of Banville's scientific tetralogy comes from its direct and sympathetic engagement with this philosphical and historical contradiction.

In a fallen world, a world which has abandoned, or been abandoned by, God, humanity is left to its own imaginative devices or, as Stevens has it, to its supreme fictions. This legacy provides the dramatic landscape for Banville's fiction. His versions of that legacy are attracted to its dual character, its possibilities and its dangers. For the writer, a supreme fiction may achieve the status of a self-enclosed, self-referential world, a parallel cosmos, in which the artist is a little god. But the supreme fiction must be realised, achieved, through a language which does not always obey the divine imperative. This is where I think Banville moves beyond the romanticism of Coleridge and that modernist version of it in Stevens and Rilke, creating his own postmodern myth of the imagination's struggle with an estranged world and a diminished perception, while retaining sympathetic faith with their idealism and their humanism.

A recurrent theme in Banville, one which finds a multitude of metaphorical forms, is that of a highly sensitive, imaginative consciousness trying to translate itself into a language adequate to its troubled sense of self. While it is indebted to the romantic inheritance and the humanistic legacy of the Enlightenment, Banville's fiction is incapable of a simple or innocent faith in either. One of the several studied contradictions about this body of work is its sceptical regard for its own ideals. The imaginative faculty in Banville's fiction is a complex and deceptive presence, as much a form of delusion as one of revelation, a source of great confusion as well as rare sublimity.

Texts as well as characters can lose their innocence, and Banville's novels are primarily attempts by the subjective consciousness to understand the nature and consequence of that loss. They are also driven by a provisional faith in the ability of the imagination to construct, or conjure, fictional accounts of the past which offer some form of aesthetic comfort. Nearly all of Banville's narrators are writers, each one of them engaged in a self-conscious attempt to produce a narrative which reinvents the past while demonstrating the writer's seduction by the fictive possibilities of language. This is a fiction moulded by a nostalgic imagination, a series of autobiographical fantasies, but it is also one which confesses an incurable sense of confusion with the very process of recollection. That process is complicated by the way imagination controls memory, so that any certainty about the precise, factual nature of the past seems like a grand illusion. All too often, the narrators feel that their stories, and their language, can only issue in a fantasy that the past can never be retrieved or understood, merely rewritten. There is no way back to the past, only a story which leaves the writer stranded with a fiction. In *Birchwood* , Gabriel Godkin is the first of many narrators to articulate this sense of the necessary, inevitable limit to such accounts:

> We imagine that we remember things as they were, while in fact all we carry into the future are fragments which reconstruct a wholly illusory past. That first death we witness will always be a murmur of voices down a corridor and a clock falling silent in the darkened room, the end of love is forever two spent cigarettes in a saucer and a white door closing. I had dreamed of the house so often on my travels that now it refused to be real, even while I stood among its ruins. It was not Birchwood of which I had dreamed, but a dream of Birchwood, woven out of bits and scraps.[9]

As an exemplary Banvillean narrator, Gabriel seems to understand the nature of his ignorance, and to sense the mysterious and elusive forms of knowledge permitted by the imagination. The past reveals itself only through silent synecdoche, images which belong to, but never explain, the past. Experience can be retold and recalled, but never truly understood with any certainty; but the imagination can, and must, reconstruct it, and this will always be through poetic image. Objective knowledge gives way to subjective impression. The compulsive, confessional style of such narratives emphasises their fatal attraction towards the past, knowing, or hoping, that an imaginative version may yield, or retrieve, some consolatory image of order and beauty out of what is almost invariably a history of violence and chaos. Few of Banville's narrators trust their own faculties or abilities, and their stories are as much about this epistemological unease and doubt as anything more objective. This is a sustained narrative drama about the divided self, one which is caught between past and present, dreaming and writing: in Seamus Deane's phrase, it is 'a war of attrition between imagination and time'.[10]

This defining and distinctive motif of a divided self, one caught between, and fascinated by, opposed forces and forms of knowledge, has equal relevance to Banville's own position in relation to the competing claims of history and fiction. If we think of Banville's work as a series of 'supreme fictions', the implied tribute is to an achievement which has gone beyond history and historical narrative, having attained a kind of parallel, superior reality, one which is not governed by any acknowledgement of, or respect for, time and circumstance – an independent republic of fiction. It suggests, perhaps misleadingly, an escapist art, one which is determined and content to leave history behind in favour of the freedom of fantasy. A close examination of

Banville's work shows, however, quite a different pattern, one in which fiction itself has a history, and where history may often become a kind of fiction. Banville does not offer fiction as an alternative to history: rather, his interest lies in the difficulty of understanding the difference, or the relation, between both forms of perception.

A brief glance across the range of Banville's fiction confirms its attraction towards various kinds of history, literary, scientific, political and artistic. Some texts, such as *Long Lankin* or *Birchwood*, revisit traditional literary genres which fictionalise history; the scientific tetralogy, from *Doctor Copernicus* to *Mefisto*, is based largely upon Banville's reading of astronomical history, for which he provides his own bibliography of historical sources; *The Untouchable* is based on his researches into the politics of the Cold War, especially the role of the master-spy Anthony Blunt; novels such as *Athena*, so radically fictional, are deeply grounded in Banville's knowledge of the history of art, largely aided by such classic authorities as E. H. Gombrich. It is also noteworthy, though little has been said about it, that the best-known character in Banville, Freddie Montgomery, the narrator of *The Book of Evidence* and, in reinvented forms, of *Ghosts* and *Athena*, is based on a contemporary criminal figure in Ireland, as is 'The Da' in *Athena*. (Aside from *Doctor Copernicus* and *Kepler*, every fiction by Banville, including the plays, draws on an Irish historical landscape.) History, old and new, seems to supply Banville with most of his fictional requirements. The obvious point to be made here is that even such a decisively fictional, non-realistic body of work such as this moves towards, rather than away from, the objective world for its fictional strength. Banville's 'supreme fictions' contest, rather than evade, history, looking at the ways in which they reflect upon each other, and how this mutual reflection confuses any old certainties about the secure and knowable differences between the real and the illusory.

Linda Hutcheon is one of very few critics who have tried to theorise Banville's fiction in relation to postmodernism, doing so on the evidence of the early narratives in the tetralogy, *Doctor Copernicus* and *Kepler*.[11] She proposes the category of 'historiographic metafiction' as one which captures the dynamic relation between history and fiction in Banville, and which illustrates a generic similarity between his work and that of other writers in the postmodern literary world, such as Nabokov, Fowles, Doctorow and Eco. Historiographic metafiction, according to Hutcheon, is perhaps best understood as the opposite of the kind of realist approach analysed and championed by Georg

Lukács in his classic account, *The Historical Novel* (1937).[12] Whereas Lukács saw and recommended characters in the nineteenth-century novel, that by Scott or Dickens, as representative of their class and age, Hutcheon notes that the central characters of this kind of postmodern fiction are, or tend to be, 'ex-centrics, the marginalized, the peripheral figures of fictional history'.[13] Postmodern novels reject what Hutcheon, drawing on the theoretical work of Lyotard and Foucault, calls 'the master narratives of bourgeois liberalism', continuing a postmodern history of the deconstruction and unmasking of Enlightenment humanism. Although there is much in Hutcheon's attempt to classify and categorise this kind of fiction which helps us to understand Banville as part of an international trend in fiction (and which shows how attuned Banville is to the theoretical world), her defence of postmodernism as a kind of fictional liberation movement does not capture the deep sense of critical sympathy in Banville for those, like Copernicus and Kepler, who dreamed of metanarratives and unifying visions. Banville can deconstruct with the best of them, but there is never the feeling in his work that the exposure of constructed myths about identity and nature is a simple cause for celebration. Quite the opposite, I would suggest. There may no longer be any hope of a convincing master narrative, but most of Banville's characters wish there were.[14] If the past is a series of deceptive, elusive, finally unknowable fictions, if history is a kind of supreme fiction, this rebuff to intellect may come as a terrible shock; but knowledge of a different kind offers itself, self-knowledge of an imaginative kind. This is largely the script of *The Newton Letter*. Various histories present themselves for imaginative scrutiny in Banville, Irish and European, familial and personal, and suggest a kind of thematic continuity throughout this fiction, whether it deals with astronomy or with art. The writer-protagonist in nearly every story is trying to construct a version of the past which accepts its mysteries while trying, at the same time, to make a fictional virtue out of them. If there is no truth, there is always the possibility of some consoling revelation, some glimpse of beauty, what Donoghue calls, in his study of this kind of imaginative yearning, 'a gratifying presence'.[15]

The tradition of the modern Irish novel, seen in relation to postmodernist trends in fiction, offers a complementary perspective on Banville. In suitably, and predictably, 'modernising' terms, Banville has dismissed the influence and the appeal of that tradition, although he accepts that it has probably determined and shaped his fictional dissent.[16] Richard Kearney sees Banville's work as part of 'the critical counter-tradition of Irish writing', a tradition which sets itself against realism and naturalism, sharing 'the post-Joycean obsession with the possibility/impossibility of writing, and more particularly with the problematic rapport between narrative and history'. This counter-tradition, argues Kearney, was initiated by Joyce and Beckett, developed by Flann O'Brien, and includes several contemporaries of Banville, notably Aidan Higgins and Francis Stuart, all of whom share, according to Kearney, a 'common crisis of imagination' which is reflected in an 'obsession with the crisis of narrative'.[17] Seamus Deane's view, one which, like that of Kearney, is based on Banville's early work, sees a very similar pattern of influence and congruence:

> What we meet in his work is another version of that brand of self-consciousness which has been such a distinctive feature of one tradition (and that the major one) of Irish fiction which includes Joyce, Flann O'Brien, and Beckett on one level, and accommodates a variety of people, from Jack Yeats to George Fitzmaurice to Aidan Higgins on another. All of them are at times masters of the boredom which comes from self-contemplation, solipsism carried to a degree of scientific precision, some of them are equally at times mastered by it.[18]

Deane goes on to make the point (an important one, I think) that this kind of introverted fiction is based on a deep disillusion with politics, an irrational force which both attracts and repels the narratives. For Joyce's Stephen Dedalus, history is a nightmare from which he is trying to escape; for Banville's characters, something very similar is true, from the world of the Greek colonels in *Nightspawn*, through that of the Irish famine in *Birchwood*, to the Cold War in *The Untouchable*. War and its violent energies, its release of obsessive, destructive passions, fascinate the hypersensitive minds of Banville's narrators, forcing them to contemplate a world of terrifying action which they both loathe and envy. In *Doctor Copernicus*, the Grand Master of the Teutonic Knights, Albrecht, with characteristic rhetorical anachronism, remarks to an appalled Copernicus that the astronomer and the soldier have a common interest in power: 'You and I, *mein Freund*, we are lords of the earth, the major men, the makers of supreme fictions.' In *The Untouchable*, Victor Maskell, hearing of another massive IRA bomb in London, writes, 'We should have been like that. We should have had no mercy, no qualms. We would have brought down a whole world.' Here we have two versions of the intellectual's view of power and politics, one sympathetic, the other ironic, neither character capable of denying the pressure or the attraction of a political world, so certain of itself, which leaves them feeling exiled and impotent.

Banville's fiction is dominated by intellectual figures who discover that they have misread the world, and now have to rewrite it. The most striking irony of that fiction is to be found in the dramatic conflict between the intellectual ambition of his narrators and the sensuous, lyrical resolution of their tales. These are self-conscious memoirs, not just in the conventional postmodern way in which they draw attention to their own narrative efforts, but in the way their reflective cast of mind regards the competing powers of intellect and imagination. Most of these narrators come to realise, too late, not just that a certain kind of abstraction has blinded them to the sensuous world about them, but that they have denied or repressed a kind of knowledge available only through a poeticised imagination. The progress of Banville's fiction shows a continual reworking of elaborate, structured myths, or metaphors, through which this belated recognition can be staged.

Just as every fiction by Banville may be seen as a poetic analogy for the conflict between versions of reason and imagination, so too does each narrator reinforce and develop a variation of the obsessive, egotistical male intellect, one which is usually, but not always, humbled by the poetic revelations of his own narrative. A Banvillean narrator is a learned man, conscious of his former intellectual talent, a gift now seen as decisive in his fall from knowledge. The astronomers, Copernicus, Kepler and Newton, are the prototypes for this figure, but subsequent characters suffer from a similar epistemological confusion and humiliation. Gabriel Swan, the childprodigy of *Mefisto*, ends what he calls his 'black book' with an admission and a realisation: 'About numbers I had known everything, and understood nothing'. At the end of *The Book of Evidence*, Freddie Montgomery, one-time university lecturer in statistics and probability theory, believes that 'failure of imagination' was his real crime, 'the one that made the others possible'. In *Athena*, Freddie, the born-again art scholar, realises that he could not tell the difference between the real and the fake pictures, or that between authentic and false friends. Victor Maskell, the narrator of *The Untouchable*, may be the exception that proves this fictional pattern. He concludes what he calls 'this fictional memoir' by noting how many things he misunderstood and misread, but he feels no diminishment of his heroic self-image. Unlike most of Banville's narrators, Maskell remains defiantly untouched by delusion or regret, a latter-day Stoic who still believes in the superior reality of neoclassical art.

The two great issues which dominate Banville's work, and to which he continually returns, are Science and Art, both of them offering rich narrative possibilities for an exploration of a patriarchal personality and its intellectual pretensions. Those 'high cold heroes' of the scientific tetralogy who, in the words of the narrator of *The Newton Letter*, 'renounced the world and human happiness to pursue the big game of the intellect', are followed by a series of narrators who are obsessed with a very different, complementary system of representation, that of painting. Having taken the motif of science as far as possible, Banville chooses to substitute image for number, sensuous silence for abstract harmony. This decisive and ambitious shift in design opens up a new series of metaphors for the drama of the imagination, this time engaging directly with male fantasies about women, and the seeming superiority of a speechless art over one buried in language. The novels which follow the tetralogy are, in a sense, a feminine counterpart to the earlier fictions dominated by 'those great, cold technicians':[19] the narrator remains male, but this time he contemplates the supreme fictions of an art which, like the feminine myth it seems to embody, is resolutely mute and self-contained. In the trilogy narrated by versions of Freddie Montgomery, *The Book of Evidence, Ghosts* and *Athena*, and in *The Untouchable*, we listen to the testimonies of artful voyeurs, men whose imagination is fixated upon pictures. If we could X-ray this sequence of fictions, we would detect the mythical shadow of Pygmalion, the artist in love with an ideal form of beauty, one which threatens to come alive.

This characterisation of Banville's subject-matter, a tetralogy on Science followed by a trilogy on Art, while it reveals an obvious sequence of interests and images, conceals a significant interaction between the two series of novels. The idea of using paintings as a vehicle for the workings of the contemplative imagination is also found in the tetralogy on science, as if Banville had seen its fictive potential long before he chose to exploit it, leaving it in the narrative margins of the novels about star-gazers, who later metamorphose into image-fetishists. Banville's work, as Rüdiger Imhof has so meticulously demonstrated, is richly intertextual, as is so much of postmodernist fiction, but it also has a noticeable habit of quoting itself, of moving forwards with an image or an idea taken from an earlier work.

The embryonic fascination felt by Banville's narrators for the imaginative eloquence of certain pictures, usually idealised representations of women, even predates the tetralogy, as can be seen in *Birchwood*, where it is strongly linked to Gabriel's search for Rose, his fictional sister. Gabriel's most prized possession is a jigsaw 'of over two thousand tiny wafer-thin pieces'. One day, in the company of his demonic brother, Michael, he finally assembles the work, which reveals 'a glorious gold and blue painting of a Renaissance madonna'. Michael deliberately upsets this delicate construction, leaving Gabriel to lament, not his wasted effort but, more philosophically, 'the fragility of all that beauty'. This proto-aesthete already has the makings of a Freddie Montgomery.

In the tetralogy itself, there begins a series of allusions to the art-world, romantic and humanistic in spirit, which helps to characterise and define the imaginative life of the narrators and protagonists. One of the most significant of these references involves Kepler, probably the most sympathetic figure in Banville's entire work. A scholar of deep religious faith, Kepler believes in the inspirational and consolatory power of heroic art, carrying with him on all his travels a copy of Dürer's *Knight with Death and the Devil*, an engraving which for Kepler embodies 'an image of stoic grandeur & fortitude'. This icon of 'manly' resolution is one which will reappear fourteen years later in *The Untouchable*, to strengthen Victor Maskell's self-image as a worthy successor to the Stoic ideal.

But it is in *The Newton Letter* that Banville's experimentation with the trope of art is first explored, not just as incidental allusion or reference, but as a distinctive, almost inevitable, feature of the narrator's crisis of imagination. Addressed to Clio, the Muse of History, the novella opens with the anonymous narrator's admission that he has lost faith 'in the primacy of text', that words distract rather than reveal his thoughts. In trying to recall and describe the woman he truly loved, Charlotte, he writes about the futility and inaccuracy of his efforts to imagine her, but is still able to suggest, by way of pictorial analogy, how his imagination might bring her back to life:

> Perhaps call it concentration, then, the concentration of the painter intent on drawing the living image out of the potential of mere paint. I would make her incarnate. By the force of my unwavering, meticulous attention she would rise on her scallop shell through the waves and *be*.[20]

Disillusioned with the power of language, the narrator envies the magical arts of the painter, a kind of aesthetic necromancy which would will Venus into being, like Botticelli's triumphant *Primavera*, an image of fertility which mocks the narrator's sense of impotence. The constant fear of women felt by Banville's narrators is matched only by a fascination with them: this defining anxiety forms an essential part of the psychological, sexual and emotional life of these writers, a feature confirmed by the fact that almost every novel ends with the unsettling and threatening season of spring.

The imaginative progression in Banville's fiction from a mythology of science to one of art is also featured in the autobiographical fictions of Freddie Montgomery and Victor Maskell, both of whom turn away from the discipline of mathematics towards the world of art scholarship. Much like their astronomical counterparts, they see scholarship as a refuge from a violent world, an ordered landscape of the imagination in which they can act out their invented lives as aesthetes, roles made all the more necessary by their personal involvement with violence, criminal and political. Freddie believes, as we have seen, that his brutal murder of an innocent woman was the effect, and not the cause, of an inadequate and impoverished imagination; he also believes that the contemplation of women in paintings will somehow restore his understanding of real women. In each novel of the trilogy, Freddie is obsessed with a woman and a painting – Josie Bell and the *Portrait of a Woman with Gloves* in *The Book of Evidence,* Flora and *Le Monde d'or* in *Ghosts,* A and *The Birth of Athena* in *Athena* – but the trilogy charts his growing uncertainty about the necessary difference between art and reality, authenticity and fakery. Freddie's imagination is so over-stocked with images and analogies drawn from the world of art that he can only contemplate actual women as artistic objects which have somehow, mysteriously, escaped from the frames which usually contain them. Life imitates art in ways which leave Freddie convinced that everything, including the women he adores, is an invention, a fiction scripted by some invisible, unknowable artistic deity. Art has robbed Freddie of his senses, and his three solipsistic narratives show an imagination rich with fantasy but utterly baffled by his own fictions.

Although Victor Maskell, the narrator of *The Untouchable,* shares several characteristics with the gallery of Banville's narrators – their intelligence, their hyperactive imagination and their fear of intimacy – he is also an unprecedented figure in an important respect, one which seems to determine an alternative ideal in matters artistic. Maskell's preferred object of desire is male, not female, his homoeroticism a seeming reflection of his love for Poussin's art of male stoicism. He likes to think that his sexual preference and practice exempt him from the misogyny which he believes is at the root of men's desire for women: he pities women who fail or refuse to realise 'how deeply, viscerally, *sorrowfully*, men hate them'. The supreme connoisseur of duplicity, an Irishman pretending to be an Englishman, Maskell is both a family man and a secretive homosexual, Keeper of the Queen's Pictures and a Russian agent, academic and ideologue. Like Freddie, most of his emotional life is devoted to artistic objects, his prized possession being Poussin's *Death of Seneca*, a representation of principled suicide. Maskell is probably the coldest of all Banville's characters, someone who believes that 'things, in their silence, endure so much better than people.' His cultivated aesthetic of supreme detachment from the world of the emotions and the senses is in marked contrast to Freddie's rapture in the presence of those romantic, mysterious images of Vermeer and Watteau.[21] Everything 'natural' is rejected by Maskell in favour of the fictive. The irony of his tale is that the master of deception is himself finally deceived, having failed to appreciate that others excel him in acting out roles which he misread and misinterpreted. This is the final, almost inevitable madness of a mind which rejects all appearances as deceptive, which believes that everything is a kind of theatre, that nothing, not even the mask, can be trusted.

The Untouchable is probably the darkest version of that theatrical conceit which plays itself throughout Banville's fiction, a conceit which suggests, not just the element of performance in text and character, but also the sense, held by so many of Banville's narrators, that the world about them is a 'staged' imitation of Nature. The invention of a new identity, often a necessary fiction brought about by a need to escape the clutches of the past, can bring a revitalised sense of liberation and possibility, but also a sense of having lost any original authenticity. For Gabriel, in *Birchwood*, his flight from the madness and cruelty of home brings him to Prospero's circus, where he acquires an anagrammatic version of his author's name, Johann Livelb, and happily performs his role in entertaining audiences only too willing to be deceived. He recalls those days as the happiest of his life: 'Never had I felt such freedom'. Freddie Montgomery, of course, is a supreme thespian, self-consciously aware that he must impersonate the humanity he does not naturally possess, delighted with the style and success of his performance. Looking back on his days of freedom, he writes, 'What an actor the world has lost in me!'[22] In *Ghosts* and *Athena*, Freddie is obliged to reinvent and rename himself, eventually deciding on Morrow, a new surname chosen, as he puts it, 'for its faintly hopeful hint of futurity, and, of course, the Wellsian echo'.[23] Victor Maskell goes through the most complete, and ultimately the most alienating, series of constructed identities, realising that a great spy leads a life that is an uninterrupted performance, forever looking at the world from behind a false front. A lifetime spent acting renders meaningless, or at least problematic, any notion of authenticity. The ability and the power to deceive breed a special kind of pleasure, what Maskell calls 'the aphrodisiac properties of secrecy and fear', as well as an addiction to performance which eventually eliminates any sense of a fixed, stable identity.

Banville explores this deceptive and illusory dimension to contrived identities with great psychological and stylistic imagination, one that is sometimes sympathetic, sometimes clinical. Characters like Freddie and Maskell produce exhilarating textual performances, as contrived and as theatrical as their personalities. Both are aware that their dramatic, and dramatising, style is marked by constant use of analogy to describe or capture the protean identity of others, a narrative habit which cannot resist the comparative gesture. As Freddie puts it, in *Athena*, 'Ah, this plethora of metaphors! I am like everything except myself.' There is, it seems, an epistemological price to be paid for such imaginative daring: nothing is known or understood in itself; everything is always part, a dependent part, of a rhetorical construction, usually drawn from other fictions. Knowledge becomes part of a theatrical design, and all gestures and expressions of meaning are a kind of mimicry. In the early pages of *Ghosts*, Freddie recalls the moment when he was released from jail, when everything 'looked like an elaborate stage-set, plausible but not real'. Life is so dependent upon, so interchangeable with, artifice that it appears to have no authentic character of its own, only one drawn by comparison with fiction.

This sounds like a supreme fiction taken to its imaginative limits, a point reached by a subjective consciousness no longer able to distinguish between reality and fiction. The characteristic mood of this kind of conclusion to an obsessive monologue is one of disappointment and confusion, rather than anything approaching the tragic, as if the narrator had exhausted imaginative resources. The mood is quite different in the tetralogy, especially in those two works which do not take the form of a confessional monologue, *Doctor Copernicus* and *Kepler*. Their shared sense of a supreme fiction is closest to that version of textuality associated with Derridean theory, whereby a text is merely a fictional structure, a discourse with no meaningful or knowable external reference. Copernicus accepts his failure to discover and represent the nature of the planetary order, and tells his disciple, Rheticus, that his lifetime's work is 'merely an exalted naming' – nothing more, nothing less, as Declan Kiberd argues, than a new discourse.[24] The stars, he realises, do not care what they are called. Kepler's final contribution to astronomy is a science-fiction novel, a futuristic fantasy inspired by his dreams of those other worlds whose movements he had once tried to calculate. Both scientists experience a shocking crisis of knowledge and belief; both novels achieve an epic sense of intellectual daring, a Faustian effect of admiration and pity.

To characterise Banville's work as a series of fictions about epistemological conflict offers a useful critical abstraction, but a kind of abstraction which those fictions challenge. This is a highly intellectual fiction which is both delighted and appalled by its own ingenuity. At the heart of the stylistic bravura there is a sense, a regretful and envious one, of Nature's indifference to such a display, of a superior order which silently and ironically observes the manic efforts of the modern consciousness to find an authentic sense of self, even one based on fictions. The romantic, humanistic strain in Banville is there from the earliest fictions, as we see, for example, in *Birchwood*, where an exhausted Gabriel Godkin resigns himself to the confusion of his condition:

> Spring has come again, St Brigid's day, right on time. The harmony of the seasons mocks me. I spend hours watching the sky, the lake, the enormous sea. This world. I feel that if I could understand it I might begin to understand the creatures who inhabit it. But I do not understand it. I find the world always odd, but odder still, I suppose, is the fact that I find it so, for what are the eternal verities by which I measure these temporal aberrations?[25]

In many ways, these self-conscious reflections upon the absence of absolute, or universal, forms of knowledge, this bemused wonder in the face of Nature's confident, serene rhythm, offer a paradigm for the rest of Banville's fiction. Over two decades later, in *The Untouchable*, Victor Maskell, writing his own testament in the refuge of his apartment, echoes Gabriel's wistful sense of exclusion:

> Too much brooding, here, under the lamp, just me and the scratching of my pen, and the distracting noise of the birds in the trees outside, where spring has come to a frantic head and toppled over into full-

> throated Keatsian summer. Such rude good weather strikes me as heartless; I have always been prone to the pathetic fallacy.[26]

Banville's fiction, it seems, has its own stylistic version of Nietzsche's *die ewige Wiederkunft*, the eternal recurrence of certain forms of thought and perception.[27] Without this motif of lost innocence, of envy and admiration for a natural order which defies explanation but which occasionally offers intimations of outstanding beauty and harmony, the fiction would be simply clever, and without that vital mythical dimension which gives it the sense of a modern fable, one about the loss of a defining form of humanity. Like so many of its characters, Banville's fiction works with a divided sense of self, intellect struggling for definition and knowledge, imagination yearning for wholeness of being.

Joseph Riddel sees similar contradictions in the work and achievement of Wallace Stevens, the poet who has inspired so much in Banville's exploration of fictionality and the modern consciousness:

> He is and is not an intellectual poet ... He is a romantic, but disconcertingly impersonal; a traditional poet, yet experimental; an imagist, but also a symbolist of sorts; a lyrical and meditative poet who wears equally well the masks of clown and pedagogue ... The experience of his poetry, even at its most militantly anti rational, is within the mind rather than at the tip of the senses.[28]

As I have said before, and elsewhere, Banville is best approached as a poetic novelist for whom ideas are vital, but for whom metaphor is supreme. This is a postmodernist body of work, energised by its awareness of the history of narrative and representation, of the intimate and incestuous relation between theory and fiction, of the radical possibilities of the novel form. What is perhaps most remarkable about Banville's work is the way it depends upon such an awareness for its design and yet suggests that, ultimately, the quality of style in narrative performance is the real consolation, the only durable form of knowledge. It reads as a profoundly pessimistic fiction, dramatising a series of figures whose minds betray them, but whose accounts of that betrayal display exquisite imaginative power and invention.

I

Long Lankin

The role of objects, is to restore silence.
Samuel Beckett, *Molloy*

JOHN BANVILLE's first published work, *Long Lankin* (1970), is an unusual assembly of fictions. It is arranged in two parts: Part One is a series of nine short stories, while Part Two is a novella, entitled 'The Possessed'. The title of the collection is taken from an old Scots-English ballad, 'Long Lankin', or 'Lamkin', the story of a horrific murder. Intent on revenge against a former master, Long Lankin steals into the house while the master is away and, with the help of a treacherous nurse, sadistically murders the baby of the house:

'Where's the little heir of this house?' said Long Lankin.
'He's asleep in his cradle', said the false nurse to him.
'We'll prick him, we'll prick him all over with a pin,
And that'll make my lady to come down to him.'

The mother hears the screams of the baby and the appeal from the nurse, and is lured to her own murder:

My lady came down, she was thinking no harm
Long Lankin stood ready to catch her in his arm.
Here's blood in the kitchen. Here's blood in the hall.
Here's blood in the parlour where my lady did fall.

It is a shocking tale of calculated cruelty and ritual slaughter, all the more horrific because there is scant, if any, evidence of any motive for such evil.[1] Motiveless violence against innocence is a theme which reappears in Banville's later fiction, most notably in the character of Freddie Montgomery in *The Book of Evidence*.

None of these stories deals directly with the character of Long

Lankin. Instead, Banville uses the violent pattern of the legend to structure and unify a series of tales set in contemporary Ireland. The tale of Long Lankin is used to create and sustain an atmosphere of foreboding and anxiety for a series of psychological fictions. All the stories, and the novella, re-enact the drama of Long Lankin's violent and cruel intrusion. Banville himself has commented on his original intention:

> The stories, all nine stories, have each a cast of two characters closely involved with each other – they are in love, they are married, they hate each other, whatever – whose relationship is destroyed, or disturbed in some radical way, by the interference of a third character, the Long Lankin, or interloper figure.[2]

The imaginative intention is clear and dramatic. How effectively, though, is the original horror story translated into a modern psychological form?

The opening story, 'Wild Wood', is one of the most successful evocations of the kind of primitive mystery and fear suggested by the ballad. Two boys have stolen away from school, and are found sitting by a fire in a wood. One of them, called Horse, 'a strange wild creature who rarely spoke and never smiled', cuts wood for the fire with an axe. Suddenly a third boy appears and tells them of the savage murder of an old woman-shopkeeper during a violent intrusion in which, mysteriously, nothing was stolen. Horse listens but says nothing. Then, leaving his axe by the fire, he walks off into the wood, leaving the two frightened boys alone with the echo of their calls. It is a carefully told story, dependent on mystery and suggestion for its eerie effect. The brooding character of Horse, the primitive setting, the implied connection between Horse's axe and the inexplicable murder - these are the main elements of a convincing atmospheric tale. Most effective is the suggestion that behind the story is a story withheld.

As with Joyce's *Dubliners*, there is in *Long Lankin* a clear sense of stylistic purpose and conscious formal arrangement.[3] Banville's stories, however, do not foreground a social or a political condition. They are more concerned with the psychology of fear: these are studies in modern melancholia, or what later characters in Banville call 'accidie', a kind of social torpor, or listlessness, which finds remarkable over-compensation in a hyperactive imaginative life. Such a condition does not always lend itself easily to dramatisation, and several of the stories, however carefully written, merely contrive or assert despair and dread without creating a convincing dramatic situation.

Two of the most convincing stories are 'The Visit' and 'Summer Voices', both of which deal with childhood. The first of these is about the fragile freedom offered by imagination. A small girl living with an old aunt waits anxiously for a promised visit from her long-absent father. While waiting, she encounters a travelling magician named Rainbird who delights her with fabulous tricks and then takes her for a hair-raising spin on his bicycle. She returns to the house for the expected visit, now determined not to see her father, but is dragged screaming to pay her respects. The primitive emotions of this story have a dramatic and psychological coherence uncomplicated by the brooding consciousness of other stories in the collection. Rainbird, the unexpected intruder, represents a delightful form of imaginative release from the tension of ambivalent expectation. The father, paradoxically, becomes an unwelcome and sinister intruder. The same girl reappears in 'Summer Voices', this time with a brother. The two set off from their aunt's house to keep a secret appointment with an old man who has promised to show them a corpse washed up by the sea. The girl enjoys her brother's fear as much as she enjoys the grotesque surprise. Once they get home and prepare to go to bed, the recollected image of the corpse suddenly terrifies the girl, and she pleads for the brother's comfort and physical reassurance. He coldly ignores her and she goes to bed alone, terrified and weeping. The boy's earlier humiliation is revenged. The sinister quality in these two stories comes partly from a fusion of cruelty and innocence. As we shall see later, there is always something creepy about Banville's children, who seem more like malevolent dwarfs than little angels.

The novella that follows the short stories, 'The Possessed', is a tale of existential suffering, prefaced by an epigraph taken from André Gide's *L'Immoraliste*:

> Take me away from here and give me some reason for living. I have none left. I have freed myself. That may be. But what does it signify? This objectless liberty is a burden to me.[4]

Just as the legend of Long Lankin serves as a symbolic structure for the stories, these lines from Gide, we may assume, give notice of the existential dilemma at the heart of 'The Possessed'. The first thing we may note about the novella is the reappearance of many characters from the short stories. The central character, Ben White, has already appeared in 'Island', as have Jacob and Norman Collins in 'Persona', Julie and Helen in 'Sanctuary', Morris and Liza in 'Nightwind'. More significantly, Ben appears here with a sister, Flora, and their relationship is clearly a development of the incestuous passion hinted at in 'Summer Voices'. 'The Possessed' functions as a kind of emotional showdown for the characters introduced in the short stories.

The story is set in the wealthy home of Liza and Morris Gold, who are hosting a party for their friends. Ben, just back from a holiday in Greece, acts as the interloper in this situation, and his unexpected arrival triggers off a series of bizarre, often violent, incidents which characterise this piece of intellectual Gothic. As the final summary reworking of the Long Lankin tale, it strongly suggests a series of correspondences with the original cast, with the Golds as versions of the lord and lady of the house, Flora as the criminal accomplice and Ben as the agent of tragedy.

From the start, Ben is determined to provoke trouble among this middle-class gathering. His first victim is Colm, an earnest young accountant, who arrives at the party with Flora. Colm despises the social pretensions of the party, and is particularly hostile to the blatant theatricality of a homosexual called Wolf. This encounter produces a defence and explanation by Wolf of what he calls the 'displaced persons set':

> There is no great meaning and no great unified truth to strive after. There are only bits and pieces. Little broken things to pick up and play with. Things that can never be reassembled. Your fine upstanding world made sure that nothing could ever be reassembled once you had it broken.
>
> He paused, and his face relaxed into a smile. – And still you carry on the old lies, he went on, a dull edge of weariness in his voice. You make rules and morals and politics and gods and then you have the nerve to turn around and offer them as proofs that you are real and that a kind and personal god watches over you. That you are right and anyone who disagrees with you is lost. The awful thing is Colm that anyone who has the foolishness to disagree is indeed lost because you own the world. But for tonight you are alone and we have you in our corner. So friend prepare to suffer a little bit. (125–6)

This is a defence of decadence, all the more passionate because it is delivered in the presence of outraged bourgeois morality. Like parts of Banville's fiction itself, the purpose is to shock and discomfort. Its studied contempt for conventional morality and respectability comes, outwardly at least, from those who embody both. Bored with security and money, these characters search for some spiritual passion to enliven their empty lives. Characters like Wolf are not the most convincing or sympathetic medium for an exposure of the imaginative dullness of bourgeois society. But sympathy has little or no place in this kind of fiction, which, like its characters, prefers the dramatic effects of outrageous gestures to the banalities of conventional wisdom about the world. One such piece of theatricality is the recitation of 'Long Lankin' by one of the guests, Jacob, to the assembled company, a performance which reflects and intensifies the growing tension at the party.

The central episode of the novella is devoted to the escapades of Ben and Flora, who leave the party and drive around Dublin all night in a series of phantasmagoric incidents. The purpose of this part of the story is to create an image of a surreal underworld, typified by encounters with strange grotesque figures like the man with a car full of souvenir leprechauns or the alcoholic who carries around a public telephone in his pocket. This kind of 'Nighttown' episode will reappear later in Banville's work, notably in *Mefisto*, with equally limited success. The only scene in this bizarre episode which retains any coherent link with the theme of the story is where Flora taunts Ben with her sexuality, reminding him of their childhood passion. Ben recalls the incident behind 'Summer Voices':

> Some day I shall be drowned. From the rails of a ship at midnight or on the sunlit beach that sea will take me. That one that was lost and they took him out after a week. I recognized something in that ruined face. You laughed at the sight but I saw some rumour of the future. (157)

However clear the link with an earlier story, episodes like this become increasingly dislocated from the dramatic continuity and coherence of 'The Possessed'. Ben's utterances remain deliberately cryptic. Even Flora wearies of his studied portentousness, remarking, 'Ben, I'm tired of you and your beautiful pain.' Once back at the party, Ben asks Jacob to explain 'Long Lankin' to him:

> It's a weird song you know, he said. I got it from a fellow when I was doing that job over in Sussex. Long Lankin. Aye.
> Ben waited, and when nothing more came he asked - What is it about Jacob? What's it supposed to mean? - Ah there was a notion in the old days that a leper could cure himself if he murdered someone and caught the blood in a silver cup. Innocent blood do you see. Maybe Lankin was a leper. I don't know. (174–5)

This is a predictable anticlimax to a fiction which makes a virtue of world-weariness. The problem is that, stylistically and dramatically, the story suffers from its chronic seriousness, its cultivated *Angst*: mystery becomes obscurity, the prophetic becomes pretentious, and the initial declaration of philosophical ambition becomes a burdensome rationale for the bizarre actions of characters. Ben is more like an intellectual thug than a tormented soul.

At the end of the story, Ben confides to Mrs Gold his envy of the Greek communists – 'They had a cause. They believed in things.' Sounding increasingly like John Osborne's Angry Young Man, he voices his ambition as a writer in search of similar force of conviction:

> I think I might write a book. I could tell a story about the stars and what it's like all alone up there. He looked into the sky, but there were no stars, and he smiled at her and said – I mustn't feel sorry for myself. And anyway there are all kinds of things I could do. Join a circus maybe. (188)

These two figures of imaginative escapism, the literary astronomer and the circus entertainer, provide Banville with important metaphors for much of his subsequent fiction, suggesting that the apprentice carefully stored away these early fictional experiments, knowing that they could be of greater imaginative use at a later stage of his design.

Looking back on *Long Lankin*, Banville himself is not particularly sentimental:

> The novella in *Long Lankin* is ghastly, absolutely dreadful ... I like the stories in *Long Lankin*. I kept the style as bare as I could, and kept speculations of inner motives to a minimum.[5]

In 1984, fourteen years after its original appearance, *Long Lankin* was republished by Banville, who chose to substitute a new short story, entitled 'De rerum natura', for 'Persona', the concluding piece of Part One, and to withhold 'The Possessed' completely.[6] Without the novella, the collection of short stories seems simpler, less pretentious, more coherent. 'De rerum natura', taking its title from Lucretius' poem in praise of earthly pleasures,[7] centres on an old man who has withdrawn into the garden of his dilapidated home, consumed with delight at the intensity of nature's fertility. His pleasure is interrupted by a visit from his embarrassed son and an outraged daughter-in-law. Uncompromisingly 'natural', the old man finally persuades the son to stay with him, while the woman, scandalised, leaves the pair to their primitive fantasy. This tale of the imagination rejuvenated by the sensuous earth provides an effective coda to a sequence of stories about humankind's distorted nature.

Banville's decision to remove 'The Possessed' from the collection was possibly due to the feeling that the novella complicated the taut shape of the volume and that it was, artistically, too self-indulgent. A more mature Banville has commented on this problem of style and audience:

> It's foolish to expect readers to take you as seriously as you do yourself. Just because you've spent years of your life on something, doesn't mean you should expect them to treat it with due solemnity. They're more frivolous than that – thank God.[8]

Banville's literary sense of humour, often aimed at himself, should warn us to discriminate between earnestness and seriousness.

Long Lankin is a difficult work, but it shows serious and skilled talent in a young writer. The stories are probably best seen as experimental sketches of larger, more disciplined canvases to follow. The enduring idea in *Long Lankin* is that of the writer himself, the ambitious young dreamer, in search of an identity and a form that will represent his sense of the essential mystery of things.

2

Nightspawn

Detective stories – the modern fairy tales.
Graham Greene, 'Journey into Success'

N*IGHTSPAWN* (1971) is a psychological thriller about political espionage in modern Greece. As with *Long Lankin*, however, the genre
and the setting are not part of a realistic purpose. The thriller genre
offers a plot with promising motifs – mystery, pursuit, confusion of
identities and the need to find some kind of imaginative solution to the
mystery of events recalled – motifs which Banville assembles here for
the first time, and which he would much later deploy, with great success, in *The Untouchable*. The Greek setting of *Nightspawn* also allows
for a superficial exploitation of mythology, mostly through the names
of characters, in order to provide some kind of alllusive structure to the
tale. Stylistically, a certain degree of self-consciously contrived identification such as this is attractive to a playful formalist like Banville.
This is especially true of a writer who distrusts the conventions of a
more realistic fiction: here, as in most of his later work, Banville aims
at psychological, rather than social or historical, realism.

The chosen genre of the thriller plays the organising role of a dramatic metaphor. As Michael Denning has pointed out, this is often the
case with modern writers who turn to the formulaic conventions of
such a popular genre:

> The spy thriller is ostensibly one of the most 'political' of popular fiction
> genres. Its subject is global politics: the Empire, fascism, communism,
> the Cold War, terrorism. Yet its political subject is only a pretext to the
> adventure formulas and the plots of betrayal, disguise, and doubles
> which are at the heart of the genre and of the reader's investment.[1]

Not surprisingly, however, there is a strong parodic element in Banville's version of the thriller. Stereotypes, precisely because they are so 'far-fetched', so endearingly unreal, will always attract Banville's purely fictive intention.

Nightspawn is told by Ben White, the central character of 'The Possessed', the novella which was originally included in, then later dropped from, *Long Lankin*. As we shall see, the choice of a tormented writer as a narrator helps to explain many of the formal difficulties, the depth and the narcissism of this novel. His mournful tale seems largely the product of his obsessive personality, offered to the reader in the opening lines of the novel:

> I am a sick man, I am a spiteful man. I think my life is diseased. Only a flood of spleen now could cauterize my wounds. This is it. Hear the slap and slither of the black tide rising. The year has blundered through another cycle, and another summer has arrived, bringing the dog rose to the hedge, the clematis swooning to the door. The beasts are happily ravening in the sweltering fields of June. How should I begin? Should I say that the end is inherent in every beginning? My hyacinth is dead, and will never bloom again, but I keep the pot, like Isabella, and water with my tears in vain the torn and withered roots. What else is there for me to do? They took everything from me. Everything.[2]

This darkly cryptic opening, with its strange mixture of melodrama and romance, its echoes of Dostoyevsky and Keats,[3] puts into perspective the kind of contradictory narrative we may expect. *Nightspawn* is a fiction about a story difficult to tell, impossible to fully understand, but necessary to write. Greece, once the heart of classical culture, is now the postmodernist setting for a corrupted, nostalgic imagination.

Ben begins his tale by recalling his solitary arrival on the Greek islands, where he meets Erik Weiss and a companion, Andreas, a strange pair of grotesques. Weiss, a political journalist, is 'a tall gangling creature' with 'fearsome yellow teeth … marooned like crooked tombstones in the midst of an awkward mouth'. Andreas is a 'dark Greek gentleman with a handsome face, furious eyes, and a hideously crooked back'. White wants to join forces with these two bizarre conspirators because, as he puts it, 'accidie was my greatest fear'. (Freddie Montgomery, in *The Book of Evidence*, suffers from the same anxiety.) Political drama in a world of decisive action promises him some relief from existential boredom: becoming a revolutionary agent might provide him with something to believe in. As soon becomes clear, however, the possibility of such action seems as obscure and unreal as everything else in his life. Waiting for something to happen, Ben encounters the Kyd family – Julian, a wealthy Englishman, his putative Greek wife Helena, and son Yacinth. Tired of waiting for his conspirators, he has a violent, passionate and farcical affair with Helena. He also tries to make friends with Yacinth, who silently ignores him. Julian, Ben discovers, is involved in a parallel conspiracy with the Greek military.

The recollected plot becomes increasingly confused for Ben and confusing for the reader. Erik is murdered for betraying secrets, Andreas seeks revenge for Erik, and Ben soon realises that he is only a pawn in a complex game of shifting loyalties. He recalls trying to murder Julian, accidentally killing Yacinth, and finally taking secret refuge when the military coup takes place. He leaves the island with none of the expected pursuers on his trail. Once he recovers some peace, he begins to write *Nightspawn*.

Such a summary of events is, like Ben's story, inadequate and deceptive. An important part of the story's meaning lies not with its contrived anti-plot, but with the mind of the narrator. More precisely, the dominant theme of the novel is the problem and the burden of fiction itself. The work begins with a conviction, based on experience, of the unreliability of narrative conventions and the uselessness of commitment. It deliberately chooses a political genre to prove the inevitability of both failures. Banville himself is frank about the aim of the book: 'In *Nightspawn* I set out to fail. What was important was the *quality* of that failure.'[4] Nothing could express more clearly the self-imposed paradoxical aim of such a postmodernist fiction. It is an ingenious ambition which defies realistic gravity, but which also requires new, more convincing, illusions.

A parodic thriller seems an appropriate form of imaginative contempt for the ideological aspirations of political idealism. On this aspect of *Nightspawn*, Seamus Deane observes that such a sceptical fiction betrays a deep disillusion 'with the very idea basic to most politics – that the world is subject to improvement if not to change or transformation'.[5] It is as if Banville sets up Ben White as an artist desperate to test his characters in the public world, and then creates a plot which mirrors the madness of such a venture.

There are imaginative compensations within such a determinedly fatalistic view, and *Nightspawn* begins to reveal many of the characteristic features of Banville's special kind of fiction. One such constant feature is the tortured, sometimes overly mannered, self-consciousness of its narrator. This is a novel about a novelist trying to write a novel. We are continually reminded by Ben that he is composing, editing, lying, inventing, dreaming and memorising. In this way, Banville, through Ben, tests the many fictions of the novel form, and defies its silent assumptions by broadcasting them. Banville has described his method in this novel as 'a kind of betrayal of … the novelist's guild and its secret signs and stratagems'.[6] The arrogant narrator also enjoys teasing and provoking readers, as well as critics, those 'panting hunters of the symbol', eager to discover arcane significance. The expectant reader becomes a part of the parody. This kind of self-consciousness keeps drawing attention to the medium of the fiction, language itself, as a habit and as an inheritance, often doing so at the expense of the fiction's own narrative coherence. Repeated interruption of the narrative, whereby the medium as well as its supposed object of reference becomes a theme in itself, has a disconcerting honesty which is substituted for false promises. By denying himself any absolute knowledge, understanding or even talent, the narrator offers an alternative fiction of authenticity. This is a delicate, and a dangerous, game for any writer to play. It has a serious point to make, but such narcissistic frankness is no substitute for a persuasive fiction, self-conscious or not.

The most effective fiction within this fiction is that of a writer struggling with the disorder of memory. Ben tries to recall the past accurately, but language never seems to serve his memory faithfully:

> I am talking about the past, about remembrance. You find no answers, only questions. It is enough, almost enough. That day I thought about the island, and now I think about thinking about the island, and tomorrow, tomorrow I shall think about thinking about thinking about the island, and all will be one, however I try, and there will be no separate thoughts, but only one thought, one memory, and I shall still know nothing. What am I talking about, what are these ravings? About the past, of course, and about Mnemosyne, that lying whore. And I am talking about torment. (113)

Mnemosyne, as the Greek personification of memory, plays cruel tricks with Ben's imagination: as mother of the Muses, she plays havoc with his attempt to transfer the workings of that imagination to the written page. Most of the self-conscious effects in Ben's narrative come from this sense that the book he is trying to write is doomed. Language and its literary conventions sound like a poor, usually farcical, reproduction of an experience beyond words. As Ben remarks, 'Art is, after all, only mimicry.' Parody is, predictably, the natural expression of this painful and laughable sense of disjunction between an original and a copy.

But within the overall parody, Ben insists on the need to reinvent a past that cannot be reproduced. Again and again, descriptive passages occur in *Nightspawn* which first ask to be taken seriously, and are then exposed as a contrivance on the part of the writer to impose meaning and emotion where none was felt. For example, after a scene which recalls the growing tenderness and intimacy between Ben and Helena, we read:

> O Jesus, I can reproduce no more of this twaddle. Did she really say all that, and expect me to take her seriously? It seems incredible. And yet, what am I saying? I took her seriously, indeed I did. (93)

Once deflation is recognised as the favoured ironical device of this anti-novel, then it becomes difficult to know what or whom to take seriously. Despite its self-mockery and the games it plays with the reader, *Nightspawn* is certainly trying to say something authentic about love and grief. Although not always dramatised convincingly, the novel's ploy amounts to a view of narrative as a faulty but suggestive metaphor. Caught, like Beckett's narrators, between the urge to write and the foreknowledge of such a crafty deception, this strange narrative defends its form as something 'no better than these vague suggestions, this mixed bag of metaphors'.

This kind of fiction has an answer, or an excuse, for everything. The story fails, so the logic goes, because it was intended to; nothing is resolved, because that would be a lie; descriptions are always misleading, because they suggest a faith and understanding which were never there in the first place. Banville's experimental novel deliberately makes life very difficult for itself. Yet it obviously taught Banville important lessons about the kind of fiction he wanted to create. Ten years after its publication, Banville remarked of his first-born novel:

> Certainly it has terrible faults – its clumsiness, for instance, and its false intellectual bravado – yet I am very fond of that book, because I think it is, in a way, the most honest thing I have done. [7]

A decade after these remarks were made, Banville once again recalled *Nightspawn* with the same kind of critical nostalgia:

> Do not mistake me: the book holds a dear place in my heart. Whatever

its faults, it contains the best of what I could do. It is incandescent, crotchety, posturing, absurdly pretentious, yet in my memory it crackles with frantic, antic energy; there are sentences in it that I still quote to myself with secret and slightly shamefaced pleasure. I love the first paragraph, the first of my first paragraphs, that place of engagement where the new reader is taught anew how to read. There sounds in it too, I think, however faintly, that tragic note which is the mark of all true works of art, great and small.[8]

As his astronomers later discover, no experiment, even those which seem to end with some confusion and embarrassment, is wholly worthless: indeed, failure of a certain kind may be the path to, if not the precondition of, later success. That 'tragic note' which Banville recalls as the most valuable, the most enduring, element of this embryonic fiction was one which he later refined, with much greater success and discipline, in the novels which followed. Early on in *Nightspawn*, in one of its most characteristic passages, the ultimate value of the fictional experiment is anticipated by Ben himself:

> How tedious this is. Could I not take it all as understood, the local colour and quaint customs, and then get on to the real meat of things? But I suppose the conventions must be observed. And anyway, there are pearls here strewn among this sty of words. (36)

Nightspawn may well be, in places, a 'sty of words', but the 'pearls' represent the novelist's need for faith in the ultimate value of the experiment: like the alchemist, Ben believes that something precious and enduring will result from this disproportionate amount of dross.

Stylistically, the most enduring feature of *Nightspawn*, one which would characterise the 'tragic note' of much of Banville's subsequent fiction, is the creation of a mythology of romantic beauty, one whose fragility exposes and indicts the barbarism of the political world. If the narrative of politics provides the necessary nightmare, then the fiction of romance offers the possibility of occasional harmony. In *Nightspawn*, both the conspiracy and the love-affair end in tragedy, but Ben's supposed love for Helena creates a lyrical tension in his story which accounts for the nostalgic tone of much of the narrative. In keeping with the conventions of the romance-thriller, personal freedom and desire are usually overwhelmed by political intrigue and corruption. Ben is afraid of romanticising his affair with Helena, and so we have a romance plot as confusing and unpredictable as that of the thriller. Love is not exempt from evil and illusion. We are given a version of the past in which no character's true identity or relation with others can be stated with any certainty. From such a conviction, everything and everyone must be reinvented in such a way as to confirm that sceptical faith.

Ben's inclination to romanticise his past with Helena is regularly subverted by his own cynical humour:

> O yes, I knew my part well, the gay pirate with a cutlass in his teeth, laughing heartily in the face of the king and his justice. What a fool, what an incredible fool. I kissed her mouth to silence her, and soon we were making violent and lunging love, causing the bed, the window panes, the very walls to rattle. But afterwards, that sadness returned, and we lay captive in a fearful silence, our wide eyes watching the light grow in the window. (129)

Ben's retrospective image of himself as chivalric hero pitting his love against the world of power is a bitter piece of self-parody. Aside from the rare suggestion of real, achieved intimacy in the above quotation, most of his memories of love are reconstructions of poor theatre, best expressed through pre-scripted stereotypes. All the conventional expressions of romantic love make him wish 'there were better ways of expressing that ancient lie'.

In fact, the plot acknowledges that Ben had been lying to himself about the real object of his desire. He discovers that Helena is Julian's daughter, not his wife. Horrified by this disclosure, or seeming to be so, he does not deny that his true passion was for the boy, Yacinth. Incest, adultery and forbidden love are the secretive forms of lust which lie below appearance and language. We may recall that at the beginning of his tale, Ben confesses, 'My hyacinth is dead, and will never bloom again.' The myth of the beautiful Greek youth Hyacinthus was first used in 'The Possessed', when Wolf told the story to Ben as an allegory of freedom and jealousy. Here it is blended with the legend of Isabella, from Keats's version of Boccaccio's story, in which the distraught mistress seeks to preserve the severed head of her murdered lover by watering it with her tears.[9] The motif of incest was also at the centre of 'The Possessed', in the relationship between Ben and Flora.

Why this preoccupation with myth, legend and forbidden forms of desire? I think it reflects Banville's need to explore emotions and beliefs beyond the reach or taste of social or literary convention. It suggests an eclectic imagination, ready to use any available literary image, from unfamiliar legend to well-worn stereotypes, in order to create a fiction that always acknowledges its own contrivances. This can often result in an extravagant form of expression, melodramatic and grotesque, part of a desire to shock and be shocked.

Although *Nightspawn* suffers from what Ben himself calls his 'self-congratulatory sense of alienation', this confessional novel has a clearly recognisable form of modern protest at its core. It is a cry against the corruption of the human spirit by time and circumstance. In one of the few passages in the novel where the serious expression of belief is not immediately mocked and deflated by a narrator uncomfortable with all expressions of faith, Ben defines the the story's sense of alienated loneliness:

> 'Isn't it strange how all these things work together', I mused. 'The wind lifts the waves, and the waves pound the shore. These strange cycles. People too, with their cycles and reversals that cause so much anguish. It's amazing.'
>
> I looked at Erik. Erik looked at the sea. I went on, 'Imitating the seasons, I suppose. The rages and storms, the silences. If only the world would imitate us once in a while. That would be something, wouldn't it? But the world maintains a contemptuous silence, and what the heart desires, the world is incapable of giving.' (102)

Romantic yearning like this comes as a bit of a surprise in a story narrated by such a gloomy sceptic as Ben. But this note of infinitely fragile hope is what distinguishes so much of Banville's fiction. It is one of those 'pearls' which prevent despair from turning into absolute silence. In the above quotation, alienated man envies the mysterious order and beauty of the natural world, always reminded of his own poverty by such a pattern. This note of saddened envy when contemplating Nature's composure, one which contrasts tragically with the confusion of human affairs, will be heard and felt in the concluding pages of all of Banville's subsequent fiction.

Only briefly in *Nightspawn* does Banville create and hold a compelling fiction of this sense of human sadness in the face of Nature's remote beauty. Such estrangement is occasionally consoled by an invented and imaginative order of beauty and harmony, parallel, but inferior, to the external world. After the violent experimentation of *Nightspawn*, Banville's next novel would find a way of maintaining its fictional purity while conveying a moving and passionate tale without fictional embarrassment.

3

Birchwood

The Past, then, is a constant accumulation of images. It can be easily contemplated and listened to, tested and tasted at random, so that it ceases to mean the orderly alteration of linked events that it does in the large theoretical sense. It is now a generous chaos out of which the genius of total recall ... can pick anything he pleases.

Vladimir Nabokov, *Ada*

AFTER *Long Lankin* and *Nightspawn*, the most striking features of Banville's next novel, *Birchwood* (1973), are its formal discipline, its adventurous design and its refinement of a poetic style. The imaginative setting changes from the modern or contemporary world to a surreal version of nineteenth-century Ireland, and uses the 'Big House' genre in subversive fashion to tell a story about the mysterious nature of identity and knowledge. The historical or social accuracy of the period is not the primary issue here. Banville seems to have chosen this well-known genre and its conventions for their imaginative, metaphorical possibilities, their instant associations with decay, political crisis and, significantly, the image of a class of people increasingly out of touch with reality:

> Obviously I was thinking of Carleton, Somerville and Ross, but no book in particular. I took stock characters, you know, the overbearing father, long-suffering mother, sensitive son, and then also other strands, the quest, the lost child, the doppelgänger.[1]

The Big House genre provides a fictional setting and familiar types, but within this scheme Banville has contrived a plot which draws on the conventions of the romance and its literary cousin, the thriller.[2] The self-conscious artificiality of the form has, as I hope to show, a purpose that is central to the meaning of *Birchwood*. The novel has a fictional rather than a realistic logic of its own, because its narrator can only comprehend and order reality through a subjective imagination.

Like *Nightspawn*, *Birchwood* is a fiction about invention. Its narrator, Gabriel Godkin, is trying to write the story of his childhood in an attempt to understand how the past has led him to his present isolation and confusion. Although he acknowledges the difficulty, sometimes the impossibility, of recalling the past honestly, he tries to give his childhood some retrospective significance. Above all, he wants and needs to understand his mysterious relationship with his family. Godkin's entire account is characterised by a self-conscious tension between a need to relate the facts of a complex past, and the awareness that writing transforms that past into a fiction: 'We imagine that we remember things as they were, while in fact all we carry into the future are fragments which reconstruct a wholly illusory past'.[3] But such a conviction about the limitations, even the futility, of setting memory against Time does not prevent Godkin from continuing his memoirs. Past experience may be beyond understanding, but may also, as a solution and a consolation, be reinvented. His story is an imaginative version of the facts, measured and arranged according to the dictates of perception and desire.

Gabriel begins with the history of his family. This opening section of the novel is entitled 'The Book of the Dead', an allusion to the mortuary verses left with the bodies of the Egyptian dead to help them through the afterlife, and to ensure their salvation through a triumph over Time.[4] Only by the end of Gabriel's story will we see the significance of this mythical gesture. The family tree, as he says himself, 'is a curious one'. Sometime in the distant past, his great-great-grandfather, also called Gabriel Godkin, managed to take over the house and estate which had belonged to the Lawless family for generations. The Lawlesses fought, unsuccessfully, to regain possession, but eventually Gabriel's father, Joseph, married Beatrice Lawless, and Birchwood seemed secured for the Godkins. Because of the family's 'congenital craziness', mismanagement of the estate, 'bled white by agents and gombeen men', and rising peasant rebellion, the estate falls into decay.

In the dilapidated mansion, inhabited by a neurotic father, a disappointed mother and eccentric grandparents, the young Gabriel withdraws into the silent world of 'attics and cellars', what he calls his 'favourite haunts'. One day, Aunt Martha, his father's sister, arrives with her son, Michael, 'this virago and her cretin', and the two boys develop a strange, reluctant intimacy. Gabriel suddenly decides that he has a lost sister, Rose, whom he is determined to find. With both grandparents dead, with the spread of grotesque and farcical incidents, and the estate besieged by an increasingly daring peasantry, the boy leaves home. Soon after leaving, he encounters and then joins a travelling circus, composed of an exotic group of people including two sets of twins. Silas, the head of these colourful nomads, gives Gabriel the 'outlandish alias' of 'Johann Livelb', the first sign of Banville inscribing himself into his own fiction.[5] With a new identity, travelling around Ireland with his adoptive family, he enjoys an unprecedented sense of imaginative freedom. Then famine strikes. The troupe is pursued by hunger and the authorities, and the adventure ends in death and disaster. Once more, Gabriel escapes, only to return to Birchwood. In his absence, the Lawlesses have been slaughtered by the Molly Maguires, 'bands of savage-fanged hermaphrodites', and the estate is now desolate. The sole survivor, Gabriel encounters Michael, now one of this murderous gang, and suddenly realises they are twin brothers, the incestuous sons of Joseph Godkin and his sister, Martha. After this recognition, Michael vanishes. Gabriel takes up a solitary, beleaguered residence in the old house, and starts to write his account of 'the fall and rise of Birchwood'.

Through the complex plot of pursuit, mystery and revelation, Gabriel recreates and invents his past. It is a story that exploits all the stereotypes and conventions of the Big House genre as well as more anachronistic forms and motifs, a tale of terrible, irrational destruction and slaughter, told in such a way as to expurgate the horror of memory, but also to insist on the occasional moments of happiness and beauty during that ordeal. It is also a narrative in which symbolic image, rather than empirical fact, is to be cherished and valued. In the end, such an account manages to explain nearly everything, and yet the original sense of mystery is as strong as ever:

> All that blood! That slaughter! And for what? For the same reason that Papa released his father into the birch wood to die, that Granny Godkin tormented poor mad Beatrice, that Beatrice made Martha believe that Michael was in the burning shed, the same reason that brought about all their absurd tragedies, the reason which does not have a name. So here then is an ending, of a kind, to my story. It may not have been like that, any of it. I invent, necessarily. (174)

The story's strangeness, its self-conscious manner, its superficial resolution which concludes the search for a meaning, one that does not and cannot comprehend its significance – all these formal elements are stylistic devices to dramatise Gabriel's unique kind of perception, his troubled sense of language's unreliability, and his desperate need for an imaginative order to set against the chaos of experience.

In *Birchwood*, for the first time, Banville has found a form and style that convey the 'necessity' of fiction in a dramatically convincing manner: this is a human drama, not a fictional display. Godkin reinvents the past in such a way as to satisfy his need for emotional and imaginative consolation without denying the horrors of existence. He recreates a nightmare but still believes in the value of what he calls 'those extraordinary moments when the pig finds the truffle embedded in the muck'. This striking metaphor of unexpected magic expresses the kind of tension behind Gabriel's degrading but sometimes rewarding quest for beauty and harmony; it also emphasises the paradoxical relation between the physical and the spiritual, the ghastly and the godly. In *Birchwood*, the beautiful is almost overwhelmed by the grotesque, but remains the only image of hope which eases the pain of recollection.

Gabriel's memory of his childhood is measured by occasional moments of imaginative insight into the nature of a beauty constantly menaced by violence and cruelty. One of the novel's most haunting symbols, an image that holds a morbid fascination for the young boy, is the eponymous birchwood itself:

> Our wood was one of nature's cripples. It covered, I suppose, three or four acres of the worst land on the farm, a hillside sloping down crookedly to the untended nether edge of the stagnant pond we called a lake. Under a couple of feet of soil there was a bed of solid rock, that intractable granite for which the area is notorious. On this unfriendly host the trees grew wicked and deformed, some of them so terribly twisted that they crawled horizontally across the hill, their warped branches warring with the undergrowth, while behind them, at some distance, the roots they had struggled to put down were thrust up again by the rock, queer lymphatic mushrooms flourishing in sodden moss, and other things, reddish glandular blobs which I called dwarfs' ears. It was a hideous, secretive and exciting place. I liked it there, and when, surfeited on the fetid air of the lower wood, I sought the sunlight above the hill, there on a high ridge, to lift my spirit, was the eponymous patch of birches, restless gay little trees which sang in summer, and in winter winds rattled together their bare branches as delicate as lace. (31)

This animistic image, elaborately Gothic in its fascination with subterranean presences, is a curious blend of the lyrical and the horrific. For the boy, this distortion of nature has a contradictory appeal because it pleases his perverse sense of fantasy and mystery. Every detail is a sensuous part of a vision of nature fighting against conventional beauty and arrangement, a primitive rhapsody of defiance and struggle. The climax of the description, however, is an image of transcendent beauty, in lyrical opposition to the nightmarish underworld. The 'gay little trees', 'as delicate as lace', afford a kind of visual and emotional relief to the demented forms of nature which threaten but do not reach the summit. The boy's imagination turns instinctively towards the darker forms, as if they held some vital inexpressible secret unavailable to reason.

The image of the wood may be read as a reflected image of the subconscious, dream-like mind, seeking comfort in the unreal. Just as Gabriel recalls his love of attics and cellars as his favourite haunts in the house, so too does the silent sinister world of the wood allow him to relive some primitive, almost forbidden desire. At the beginning of his story, Gabriel wonders, 'what, for instance, did I do in the womb, swimming in those dim red waters with my past time still all before me?' The principal images of *Birchwood* point towards birth and childhood, as the profoundest source of later mystery and confusion, dramas around which Banville creates a narrative about ambiguous identities.

Twins are the central motif in this drama of origin and development. Gabriel's story is a re-enactment of his discovery, based on intuition rather than knowledge, that his cousin Michael is his incestuous twin brother. Looking back, he realises that he invented a fictional sister, and undertook a search for her, in order to deny the existence of this forbidden relationship. As far as the facts are concerned, there was a material purpose, however perverse, to the incestuous union between Martha and Joseph: their children would be Godkins, and the Lawless threat to reclaim the property would be legally overcome. Beatrice was barren, and Aunt Martha supplied a future for inheritance through what Gabriel now sees as her 'two-card trick'. The presence of twins intensifies the conflict within the Godkin family, one already suffering from 'congenital craziness'. Which one would inherit the estate? Joseph and Martha had agreed that Gabriel would be the resident, temporary heir, but that Michael would eventually be the real one. Martha sensed, rightly, that her brother would secretly alter the will, and so her dispossessed son began his merciless revenge.

The point of this narrative scheme is to show how nature and the unforeseen play havoc with human intention. Gabriel now realises that his parents 'made the wrong choices, and thereby came their ruin'. The oppressive sense of determined fates in *Birchwood* has its psychological roots in forbidden desires which yield a permanent feeling of ambiguity and distortion.

The twin-relationship between Gabriel and Michael also allows Banville to suggest a delicate and intuitive intimacy of opposites, a relationship in which Gabriel can watch himself outside himself. Only now does Gabriel suggest that Michael's arrival at Birchwood threatened him in some way – 'only hindsight has endowed me with such a keen nose for nuance'. Their relationship is based on silence and a shared indifference to adults. (In Banville's fiction, silence often seems more expressive of feeling than does speech.) But Gabriel always senses that Michael, that 'homunculus', is older because wiser. Gabriel has yet to discover evil. Like a pair of malevolent imps, they share a 'congenital coldness'. While Michael is left to run wild, Gabriel is forced to take lessons from Aunt Martha. She proves an utterly eccentric instructress, which pleases Gabriel immensely, especially since in subjects like geography he learnt 'not its facts but its poetry'. She introduces him to a book, vaguely recalled as *The Something Twins*, and this fiction inspires Gabriel's misguided search for a long-lost sister called Rose. Now that he understands how and why this fantastic quest was plotted, he is quite frank about the value of what he refers to as 'necessary fantasy': 'There is no girl. There never was. I suppose I always knew that, in my heart. I believed in a sister in order not to believe in *him*, my cold mad brother.' Michael may have tricked him, but Gabriel is glad to have pursued the non-existent. Why? Because Michael, like the present, 'is unthinkable': it was a way of avoiding his darker self. Only fictions and idealisations offer protection and consolation. The psychological justification is transparent here, as when Gabriel remarks, 'I was not a cruel child, only a cold one, and I feared boredom above all else.'

Gabriel sought escape from this boredom within his family by finding an alternative companionship based on a dream. This desire is temporarily satisfied in an encounter with the travelling circus, 'Prospero's Magic Circus', which becomes his new and even stranger family. The circus is a collection of outlandish characters – the paternal figure of Silas and his 'companions', Angel and Sybil; the two men, Mario and Magnus; Rainbird, the scout and magician (who first appeared in *Long Lankin*); and, ominously, two sets of twins, Ada and Ida, Justin and Juliette. This part of the novel, entitled 'Air and Angels', deals with the mystery of harmony between the physical and the spiritual, a theme echoed in the allusion to Donne's love-poem of the same name.[6] A whole range of literary and mythical allusions suggests a dramatic shift towards the exotic, and promises a fantastical and idealistic counterpoint to the oppressive atmosphere of 'The Book of the Dead'. The mythical names of the troupe, combined with the allusions to Donne, Shakespeare, Le Fanu and Nabokov,[7] serve to emphasise the blatancy of the intertextual fiction being pursued.

Gabriel's first problem with his new-found company is, predictably, consanguinity:

> I was confused. The names all slipped away from the faces, into a jumble. The tall slender woman with flame-red hair and agate eyes, Sybil it was, turned her face from the window and looked at me briefly, coldly. Still no one spoke, but some smiled. I felt excitement and unease. It seemed to me that I was being made to undergo a test, or play in a game the rules of which I did not know. Silas put his hands in his pockets and chuckled again, and all at once I recognized the nature of the bond between them. Laughter! O wicked, mind you, and vicious perhaps, but laughter for all that. (107)

Everything about the circus family is deliberately unreal – the theatrical names, the exotic costumes and, above all, the suggestion of some diabolical 'bond' between them. Gabriel, of course, interprets the relationship wrongly, as the subtle allegiances within the group are obscured by appearances. Although Angel seems to be Silas's wife, Sybil is the mother of his twin children, Justin and Juliette, the 'beautiful two-headed monster'. They are doubles in body and spirit, whom Marcus refers to as 'a single entity … called Justinette'. Silas's real lust, however, is reserved for the girl-twins, Ada and Ida, 'androgynous, identical, exquisite'.As if to complete this incestuous puzzle, the solitary child, Sophie, is the unintended result of a passing fancy between Mario and Ada, a couple alike in their 'incoherent rages, dark laughter' and 'careless cruelty'. The calculated mystery within this Gothic line-up is both sacred and profane, a riddle of harmony in which like and unlike seek out each other. The confusion of gender with the 'androgynous' twins, as with the hermaphroditic Molly Maguires, is Gabriel's most lasting fascination.[8] Like the search for the fictional sister, it is a metaphor for the completion of the inadequate self, one which will assume increasing significance in Banville's subsequent fictions.

With the circus, Gabriel enjoys the exhilaration of imaginative release:

> Like our audiences, I also wanted to dream. I knew too that my quest, mocked and laughed at, was fantasy, but I clung to it fiercely, unwilling to betray myself, for if I could not be a knight errant I would not be anything. (118)

His romantic quest seems fulfilled in the character of Ida. Unlike her twin, Ada, whose personality is savage and sadistic, Ida preserves a sense of childlike wonder, 'not innocence, but, on the contrary, a refusal to call ordinary the complex and exquisite ciphers among which her life so tenuously hovered'. Previous flirtations with girls had ended in physical farce, but Ida seems to embody the kind of spiritual beauty which makes the real world a scene of recurrent possibility. Looking back, Gabriel's image of Ida represents the kind of harmony forever threatened by a brute existence. His love for her, or rather his memory of that love, is the lyrical high point of *Birchwood*.

It is also, given the story's cruel logic, the signal for disaster. While picking blackberries with Gabriel, Ida is abducted and then beaten to death by English soldiers who inexplicably appear on the scene. Recalling the tragedy, Gabriel expresses an acquired understanding of the power of evil – 'Disaster waits for moments like this, biding its time.' It suggests an existence controlled by some diabolical sadist, sending the innocent on foolish journeys only to destroy them at the very moment of fulfilment.

Dreams turn, violently, into nightmares. The metaphor of twins represents a kind of existential schizophrenia, by which one aspect of self is confronted or pursued by another: Rose turns into Michael. The final confrontation between Gabriel and Michael suggests an acceptance of a terrible and fateful truth about the contradictions of the individual personality:

> Yes, he was my brother, my twin, I had always known it, but would not admit it, until now, when the admitting made me want to murder him. But the nine long months we had spent together in Martha's womb counted for something in the end … His grin widened. He had not changed. His red hair was as violent as ever, his teeth as terrible. I might have been looking at my own reflection. (168–9)

Knowledge of this kind may solve the riddle of origin and identity, but it is little consolation after so much horror and death. Dramatically, this is a moment of terrifying self-recognition in which Gabriel must submit to his darker irrational self. This burdensome duality runs throughout the whole of Gabriel's recollection and it creates the novel's alternating rhythm of hope destroyed by disaster, beauty by time, and self by anti-self. *Birchwood* is a romance which confronts everything that makes that ideal seem at once precious and impossible, vital and elusive.

As with so many romances, *Birchwood* depends on a version of childhood innocence. Gabriel writes, 'My childhood is gone for ever', and creates an elaborate fantasy which will console as well as explain. Although the pattern of the tale is one of inevitable, irrational violence, it also celebrates moments of wonder and ecstasy once felt and enjoyed. These moments alone justify the recreation of a nightmare and account for the novel's lyrical nostalgia. Gabriel pores over the past 'like an impotent casanova his old love letters, sniffing the dusty scent of violets'. His love for Ida was one of those rare moments of faith; but even earlier ones are recalled which confirm his belief in the precarious survival of beauty, no matter how evil the world:

> Listen, listen, if I know my world, which is doubtful, but if I do, I know it is chaotic, mean and vicious, with laws cast in the wrong moulds, a fair conception gone awry, in short an awful place, and yet, and yet a place capable of glory in those rare moments when a little light breaks forth, and something is not explained, not forgiven, but merely illuminated. (33)

The nervous, hesitant and desperate tone of this conviction captures well the contradictory feel of *Birchwood*. Those 'rare moments' are usually unexpected intervals of imaginative and sensuous pleasure in which some small, redemptive sense of order and harmony is discovered. They are barely translatable moments of poetic inspiration, revealed in the most unpromising circumstances.

This is why the romance element in the novel is not just about Ida or Rose. The two girls represent an important kind of spiritual and sensuous pleasure, but other moments are occasions of knowledge, of harmony perceived through the senses. A memorable example is when Gabriel and Michael first meet and try to find something to share. Gabriel shows Michael his favourite jigsaw 'of over two thousand tiny wafer-thin pieces', a representation of a Renaissance madonna. In snatching this elaborate work from Gabriel, Michael lets it fall, and a horrified Gabriel is pained, not by 'the wasted work', but by 'the unavoidable recognition of the fragility of all that beauty'. (Such a calamity, in which an image of wondrous female beauty is accidentally destroyed, foreshadows the frightful fate of Ida; it also marks the introduction into Banville's fiction of a pictorial metaphor which comes to dominate his imagination in later novels.) To counter this disaster, and to show his power over Gabriel, Michael displays the art of juggling, using 'a chipped blue building block, a marble and a rubber ball'. Once in motion, the rhythm of this performance enthralls Gabriel:

> I found myself thinking of air and angels, of silence, of translucent planes of pale blue glass in space gliding through illusory, gleaming and perfect combinations. My puzzle seemed a paltry thing compared to this beauty, this, this *harmony*. (43)

Moments like this, when Gabriel achieves some sense of supernatural possibility through what at first seemed ordinary and dull, are the truly significant images of recollection. An almost abstract kind of knowledge is revealed through the seemingly insignificant, as if by magic. These epiphanies, as Geert Lernout calls them, 'really structure Gabriel's account'.[9]

1 Johannes Vermeer, *Girl with a Pearl Earring* (c. 1665)

The experience of the circus is, of course, a sustained sense of freedom of this kind, but usually these intimations of the divine or spiritual dimension of an otherwise diabolical existence are quickly overtaken by farce. We can see this in the episode when Granda Godkin teaches the young Gabriel to ride a bicycle (an episode almost identical to one in 'The Visit', from *Long Lankin,* where the young girl is taken for a bicycle ride by Rainbird). The scene is hardly propitious. The boy is perched on a wreck of a bicycle, Granda puffing and wheezing alongside him, and a vicious dog attacking his heels. This scene of rude chaos is swiftly, inexplicably, elevated into something heavenly:

> and then I felt a kind of *click*, I cannot describe it, and the bike was suddenly transformed into a fine delicate instrument as light as air. The taut spokes sang. I flew! That gentle rising against the evening air, that smooth flow onwards into the blue, it is as near as earthbound creatures ever come to flying. It did not last long. I jumped down awkwardly, landed on my crotch on the crossbar, and the back wheel ran over my foot. (58)

As Gabriel's family name suggests, there is always a possibility of the divine in human affairs, but it is tragically rare and quickly dissipated by vulgar comedy. These epiphanies are always moments of silent intuition, beyond linguistic or intellectual account. The magical is revealed in the banal: the commonplace achieves a new significance. Perception always has this teasing, oxymoronic quality to it, as when Gabriel remarks, 'Violets and cowshit, my life has ever been thus.' This is why the quest for beauty and harmony is set during the Irish Famine, where the exquisite may be properly esteemed because of its proximity to the grotesque.

This sense of wonder, which appreciates the elusive beauty of the ordinary world, and which is forever threatened by madness and violence, is what Gabriel tries to recreate in his writing. Only the 'gentle Ida' seemed to personify such beauty and perception. *Birchwood* is a lament for the loss of such poetry at the hands of time and circumstance. As Seamus Deane puts it, Gabriel's story recreates 'a war of attrition between imagination and time'.[10]

Time, 'that word which gives me so much trouble', as Gabriel puts it, is central to his sense of mystery and confusion. The purpose of his fictional version of the past is to defy, or at least conciliate, time. This partly explains why his chronology is often so confused. What matters to him, intensely, is to retrieve something of value from a past which resists accurate recollection, and so he invents, 'necessarily'. He writes

in a form that will try to suggest an entirely subjective sense of understanding and knowledge. What he discovers only confirms his feeling of
essential and preordained loneliness in the world. This sense of home-
lessness is expressed through an insight into the enviable order and pattern of time, especially the seasonal rhythm of nature. Like Stephen
Dedalus in the opening chapters of *Ulysses*, Gabriel conducts his own
physical experiments of vision and perception in order to understand
the principles of reality and knowledge. Drinking with his circus family
in a country pub, he plays a game of closing his eyes, then blinking
rapidly, and suddenly, he remarks, 'it came to me with the clarity and
beauty of a mathematical statement that all movement is composed of
an infinity of minute stillnesses'. He calls this discovery an understanding of 'fixity within continuity'. Moving outside into the night air, the
boy-astronomer contemplates the darkness and the stars, and senses yet
again the paradoxical truth of the celestial order. In a typically self-conscious conclusion to this dream-like observation, he writes:

> And I saw something else, namely that this was how I lived, glancing
> every now and then out of darkness and catching sly time in the act, but
> such glimpses were rare and brief and of hardly any consequence, for
> time, time would go on anyway, without *my* vigilance. (128)

Such fine perception of subtle and delicate balance only deepens his
sense of insignificance. For all his moments of relevatory joy, the world
remains a mystery, its inhabitants strange, more like lost aliens from
some other planet. Gabriel's narrative ends on this note of alienation
– 'Spring has come again, St Brigid's day, right on time. The harmony
of the seasons mocks me.' Even seasonal punctuality, however
uncanny, contrasts with the chaotic mistiming of human activity,
with its shocking catalogue of unexpected, inexplicable deaths and
disasters.

Birchwood is a novel which thrives on its own contradictions:
Gabriel insists that 'the past is incommunicable', yet he communicates
a version of it which tallies with that conviction. The novel's opening
line, 'I am, therefore I think', by reversing the Cartesian principle of
knowledge as intelligent command over experience, announces the
futility of the enterprise in advance; the novel's concluding thought,
'whereof I cannot speak, thereof I must be silent', a direct quotation
from Wittgenstein, completes Gabriel's sense of resignation, by con-
ceding the linguistic limitations of his narrative.[11] Language, unfortunately, chases an experience which cannot be captured.

With its patterns of twins, pairs, opposites and contradictions, *Birchwood* is a fiction about the divided personality of existence and perception. Confused but fascinated by these tantalising patterns, Gabriel laments the fragility of beauty in a world 'capable of glory' but doomed to madness. His mother, Beatrice, 'with her pathetic faith in reason', is a victim of such madness. The 'Lawless' nature of human existence can be apprehended only through a dream-like imagery which captures its feel and quality. Gabriel offers nothing more than images which try to represent an experience too subtle for language. His father, Joseph, already knew the meaninglessness of his own life, which was why he tortured Beatrice and told his son that the whole domestic melodrama was about 'Nothing'.

Gabriel, in the third and final section of the novel, entitled 'Mercury', is supposed to be a messenger from the gods, a mediator between human and divine wisdom. The starving peasantry look upon him as a 'celestial messenger of hope'. However, they are mistaken, since Gabriel has precious little to offer: the god of eloquence is struck dumb. Language seems too artificial a medium to evoke an experience so necessary but so difficult to recall. What he now remembers is meeting their suffering cries with contemptuous silence. Alone in the refuge of the ruined Big House, he writes that he does not even speak 'the language of this wild country'. He started writing about his childhood, so he believes, in order to give it a form and significance which, at the time, it seemed not to possess. At the end of his memoir, he finds that it has little or no referential value. His fiction is no more than a suggestive but misleading duplicate of an experience that will always retain its own secrets – 'Intimations abound, but they are felt only, and words fail to transfix them.'

So we are left with a fiction without pretensions to knowledge, an imaginative pattern of events complete in itself, but no match for the ineffable nature of experience. However, some representations, like Gabriel's jigsaw, sometimes improve on the original they are trying to duplicate. This is a most formal conclusion, elegiac and lyrical, caught between a real sense of imaginative relief and insight, and a contradictory sense of inevitable failure and loss. It is also a conclusion which reveals Banville's postmodern awareness of the arbitrariness of the sign, its disjunction from the reality it hopes to represent and recapture.

Birchwood is a major advance on Banville's earlier fictions. Above all, it achieves an imaginative form perfectly suited to its theme. Less self-indulgent, more confident, more stylish, it is a highly disciplined, yet playful, fable of the nature and meaning of memory and imagination. A novel that stresses the deceptive, illusory nature of its own story has a special kind of credibility to sustain. In *Nightspawn*, this self-consciousness about the uselessness of writing became either a medium for playing intellectual games with a version of the superstitious reader, or an excuse for exercises in narrative obscurity. In *Birchwood*, by giving the story to Gabriel Godkin, a survivor of the events described, a more effective continuity based on a sympathetic character helps to unify the novel. Rather than use Gabriel as a fictional stuntman, Banville uses him to convey a sense of personal and *felt* tragedy, one of genuine grief and lasting pain.

In other words, the fiction about fiction is retained, but is now part of a convincing story about tragic illusion. The elaborate plot, and the central images of war and famine, give the story a dramatic setting crucial to the fictional intention of the novel. The mystery and confusion between identity, childhood, time and recollection are well served by the metaphoric intensity and inventiveness of the language, an effect which finally accounts for so many of the original enigmas while simultaneously reinforcing the narrator's sense of wonder. Banville has commented on this paradoxical effect, saying, 'I like the end of Birchwood, where everything is wrapped up, and nothing is wrapped up.'[12] Whereas in *Nightspawn* this paradox is merely asserted, here it is achieved persuasively.

4

Doctor Copernicus

What hath not man sought out and found,
But his deare God? who yet his glorious law
Embosomes in us, mellowing the ground
With showres and frosts, with love & aw,
So that we need not say, Where's this command?
Poore man, thou searchest round
To find out death, but missest life at hand.

George Herbert, 'Vanitie'

IN A brief preface to *Doctor Copernicus* (1976), Banville acknowledges the help and inspiration of what he calls 'two beautiful, lucid and engaging books' in the composition of his novel, those by Arthur Koestler and Thomas Kuhn on the history of astronomy.[1] Both these studies offer eloquent accounts of scientific theory and speculation, accounts which provide a factual and historical structure for the novel. They also emphasise the importance of imaginative perception, and the political context in which that perception struggles to emerge. Readers familiar with Banville's work up to this point will recognise the significance of these themes in his previous fictions. They will also recall Banville's fascination with the attraction between opposed forms of personality and perception. By turning towards the scientific career of Nicolas Copernicus, Banville's artistic imagination seeks out what modern humanity often takes to be the opposite of creative fiction. In this sense, *Doctor Copernicus* attempts a reconciliation between scientific and literary perception, just as classical astronomy sought to harmonise the earth and the heavens. A truly ambitious novel, it extends our appreciation of the role and power of fiction in humanity's attempt to understand its place in the order of nature. It is not just a literary version of a scientific career: it is also an assertion of the primacy of imagination in all forms of thought and narrative.

Perhaps we should start by trying to understand the attraction of the astronomer's personality and work. The historical evidence is not encouraging. Koestler says that 'Copernicus is perhaps the most colourless figure among those who, by merit or circumstance, shaped mankind's destiny.'[2] His chapter on Copernicus's only publication, *De revolutionibus orbium coelestium*, is entitled 'The book that nobody read'.[3] As for the intrinsic value of *De revolutionibus*, Kuhn remarks that its significance 'lies less in what it says itself than in what it caused others to say'.[4] Both historians agree that the Copernican revolution in astronomy is based on a strange paradox – that it took place despite its author.

Like most of Banville's central characters, Copernicus is a writer. But this famous astronomer's relation to his solitary publication is based on a pattern of intrigue and betrayal which begins to suggest some of the dramatic and artistic possibilities that attract Banville. According to Koestler, Copernicus was terrified of publishing his work, largely because such a theory might not be verified, or verifiable, by observation.[5] It might, he feared, turn out to be a complete fantasy. Furthermore, in a time of political and religious upheaval, the appearance of a revolutionary theory might exacerbate social disorder and weaken respect for traditional authority. Yet the book was finally published, and nobody was scandalised. *De revolutionibus* also seemed to reflect its author's ambiguous personality: as Kuhn points out, the treatise 'has a dual nature. It is at once ancient and modern, conservative and radical.'[6] Copernicus was a failure who, through the intervention of others, became a legend: with the help of friends and enemies, he achieved the legendary status he had worked so carefully to avoid. His vision of the universe succeeded, not because his facts were consistent with observed reality, but because of their suggestive power. The sums were hopelessly wrong, but the idea was vital: words and signs may have failed him, yet the perception behind the failure was truly inspired.

These are some of the historical aspects and motifs of Copernicus's career and theory which reappear in Banville's fictional biography of the astronomer. Taken together, they offer an image of a paradoxical quest, a dream finally overtaken by the unpredictable and cruel forces of political reality.

The ambitiousness of *Doctor Copernicus* is partly fuelled by the Faustian myth that it employs.[7] Banville's story is about a specific form of intellectual pride and ambition which tries to defy and deny time and circumstance. Copernicus's early naivety and enthusiasm are soon replaced by a dehumanising obsession with a vision which disdains the significance and value of the circumstantial, physical world. Banville's version of the Faustian myth gives special place to a form of innocent perception, a recognition of concrete, earthly beauty which Copernicus ignores and, too late, regrets. It is a story about the terrible loneliness of such intellectual obsession and frigidity, but one which also strives for consolatory redemptive knowledge.

The story of Copernicus's life and career, from childhood to death, is structured in four parts. The opening part, 'Orbitas lumenque', deals with childhood and education in Prussia and Italy; the second part, 'Magister ludi' (a nod to Hermann Hesse's novel?), is largely concerned with the traumatic relationship between Copernicus and his brother, Andreas; the third part, 'Cantus mundi', is the only subjective narrative in the novel, and gives us a version of Copernicus by his student and disciple Rheticus, who finally secures publication of *De revolutionibus*; the final part, 'Magnum miraculum', returns to the novel's omniscient narrator, and follows the astronomer's mental and physical decline. This is the first time that Banville uses such a detached form of narrative, removed yet sympathetic, in order to dramatise the thoughts and feelings of his central character. Given the secretive and passive personality of Copernicus, it seems quite appropriate. The exceptional narrative by Rheticus, full of enthusiasm, bitterness and deception, is a familiar strategy in Banville's work. The relation between these narrative viewpoints has a dramatic significance to which I will return.

The opening passages of *Doctor Copernicus* evoke the young boy's innocent fascination with the relation between words and things:

> At first it had no name. It was the thing itself, the vivid thing. It was his friend –
>
> Tree. That was its name. And also: the linden. They were nice words. He had known them a long time before he knew what they meant. They did not mean themselves, they were nothing in themselves, they meant the dancing singing thing outside. In wind, in silence, at night, in the changing air, it changed and yet was changelessly the tree, the linden tree. That was strange.[8]

Sensuous experience of the natural world comes before a language impatient to describe it. The passage, with its echoes of the Kantian

Ding an sich, and of the opening lines of Joyce's *A Portrait of the Artist as a Young Man*, also makes concrete Gabriel Godkin's inverted dictum, 'I am, therefore I think.'[9] The most curious aspect of this primitive contemplation is the supposed correspondence between words and what they represent: 'Everything had a name, but although every name was nothing without the thing named, the thing cared nothing for its name, had no need of a name, and was itself only.' Language seems to have a dependent relation to what it signifies, feeding off something which exists separately and independently from it. Like Gabriel Godkin's jigsaw, it is a complex and ambiguous form of duplication. Banville begins with these innocent distinctions and definitions because he wants to dramatise a pure, untarnished perception in which words are substituted for, but not confused with, things they symbolise. In the course of the novel, this distinction becomes tragically lost, until Copernicus mistakes a theory for the reality it was supposed to uncover and explain. Just as the writer works with a language which fondly imitates, but never matches, experience, so too does the astronomer devise a system of signs and symbols which he may foolishly substitute for a mystery beyond the grasp of such systematic reduction. Young Copernicus's sense of wonder is soon lost, and the narrator tells us that he 'learned to talk as others talked, full of conviction, unquestioningly'. In Banville's story, he spends the rest of his life in search of what he once knew.

Copernicus's quest for such obvious truths is not as simple or as preordained as I have perhaps suggested. Placed between innocent and mature forms of knowledge, he is not just the passive medium for a romantic parable about lost innocence or the primal simplicity of genius. The novel is never so sentimental or naive in its treatment of the process of knowledge, or of the relation between different modes of understanding. Copernicus's wisdom is acquired through coming to terms with everything he tries to deny. Before he attains such self-knowledge and acceptance, he must risk himself in the pursuit of absolute truth. One of the most convincing aspects of the novel is the way Banville dramatises the nature of this process of learning, a process that takes place as much in the daily world of family and nation as in the lonely realm of the astronomer's dreams. The drama of *Doctor Copernicus* lies in the attempt to reconcile these opposites.

As a young, enthusiastic and ambitious student of astronomy, Copernicus sees in science a possible order and harmony which will release him from the suffering and confusion of his present life:

The firmament sang to him like a siren. Out there was unlike here, utterly. Nothing that he knew on earth could match the pristine purity he imagined in the heavens, and when he looked up into the limitless blue he saw beyond the uncertainty and the terror an intoxicating, marvellous grave gaiety. (32)

An important part of Banville's method of characterisation is to suggest this fateful compatibility between personality and pursuit. Astronomy, with its promise of order and harmony, is first an escape, an alternative to a wretched personal existence, and then a superior, Platonic version of reality. It is a form of ambition which accommodates the young man's cold, anxious personality. A certain kind of arrogance, however, the natural result of talent and enthusiasm, makes the young disciple dream of helping his masters to see the folly of inherited orthodoxies, based on Ptolemy, about the static nature of a fictional universe.[10] In a tense and embarrassing interview with Professor Brudzewski, an astronomer of the old school, the young Copernicus insists that science is so obsessed with schemes 'to save the phenomena' that all its work is redundant, merely a sophisticated language which fails to describe the actual nature of planetary motion:

I believe not in names, but in things. I believe that the physical world is amenable to physical investigation, and if astronomers will do no more than sit in their cells counting upon their fingers then they are shirking their responsibility! (46)

In scenes such as these, personality provides an ironic counterpoint to theory. Copernicus's brave words, epitomised in his maxim that 'Knowledge – must become perception', are intellectually sound and impressive, but his tact is abysmal. The interview ends with Copernicus exhausted and humiliated, warned by his professor that celestial mysteries may be named but never explained. Without knowing it, the young student has rejected the advice of his good angel, and will have to find out the truth in his own purgatory of confusion and suffering.

If Ptolemaic astronomy is no more than a fiction about the universe, an elaborate mathematical design with no interest in verification through observation, then Copernicus decides that his work must force or contrive a missing connection between the imaginary and the actual. Astronomy would no longer be an end in itself, but what he calls 'the knife' with which he would cut his way through the labyrinth of useless fictions about the universe: it would become an instrument 'for verifying the real rather than merely postulating the possible'. The tragedy, both personal and intellectual, is that such a neat separation between means and ends proves impossible. The reason for Copernicus's failure and confusion lies with his denial of the inexpressible nature of mysteries beyond systems.

One of the great achievements of the novel is the way Banville traces this painful irony, as much in terms of the scientist's personal decline as in the growing realisation that the whole enterprise is doomed. Copernicus soon senses that the language of astronomy, whether words or mathematical symbols, indeed any language, cannot do justice to his perception. This humiliating discovery is the turning-point of the novel. To his horror, Copernicus sees that his research takes on a life of its own, one like his own personality, increasingly remote from the world he was supposed to explain. What he writes now seems to him like 'gross ungainly travesties of the inexpressibly elegant concepts blazing in his brain'. The pitiful tragedy begins when he realises that he is trapped in the very dilemma he sought to banish:

> It was barbarism on a grand scale. Mathematical edifices of heart-rending frailty and delicacy were shattered at a stroke. He had thought that the working out of his theory would be nothing, mere hackwork: well, that was somewhat true, for there was hacking indeed, bloody butchery. He crouched at his desk by the light of a guttering candle, and suffered: it was a kind of slow internal bleeding. Only vaguely did he understand the nature of his plight. It was not that the theory itself was faulty, but somehow it was being contaminated in the working out. (105)

From the child who instinctively sensed the inadequacy of words in relation to the things they were intended to represent, we are shown the intellectual adult come to a shocked realisation of the same truth. But the enormity of the later perception makes it tragic. Copernicus is mastered by a system he once believed was his willing servant.

Each of Banville's fictions up to this has contained some similar sense of the inadequacy of language, but here this unease becomes fully articulated in a mythical form which makes that sense of despair much more authoritative. In *Birchwood*, when Aunt Martha tries to teach young Gabriel the Latin for 'to love', the boy looks at his primer where 'the words lay dead in ranks, file beside file of slaughtered music'. But Copernicus's perception of this discrepancy amounts to a philosophical nightmare about the nature of knowledge, and his ability to account for reality. Long before the end of the novel, he realises that his work, directly contrary to ambition, is a self-contained, self-regarding fiction: 'He had believed it possible to say the truth; now he saw that all that could be said was the saying. His book was not about the world, but about itself.' Copernicus is forced to accept that his theory is no more than what he calls 'an exalted naming'. Like all those ancient authorities he despised, his own work now joins a tradition of symbolic writing. As a humanist, he had sought to integrate the imaginary and the actual, the old and the new, but the connection did not take place. The heliocentric universe remains a revolutionary *idea*, the result of his creative inspiration and daring imagination. That, of course, is the basis of the Copernican 'revolution'. Banville always retains this fact, but wants to suggest the paradoxical character of the achievement. Copernicus is not just a Faustian puppet: Banville's version of this tragedy adds the vital dimension of language as both a means and an obstacle to knowledge and perception.[11] The novel exposes the illusion of a kind of intellectual ambition which prides itself on the certainty and purity of its method; but it is also a sympathetic dramatisation of great imaginative need and yearning. The failure is not entirely due to the theory itself or to the language in which it is expressed. Alongside the monastic figure of the lonely canon, Banville has recreated a human society and a political world that are central to our interpretation of the story. The rhythm of this novel plays between Copernicus's celestial ambition and the gravitational pull of reality.

A major irony of *Doctor Copernicus* is that its hero, who devises a theory which suggests a limitless universe based on new planetary motions, tries desperately to deny the existence of comparable change in his own society. In this sense, he is both a prophet and a product of his age, engaged in work inspired by the humanist movement in Europe. Yet he is characterised throughout the novel as a man who will neither accept nor acknowledge the ordinary world he seeks to interpret:

> He believed in action, in the absolute necessity for action. Yet action horrified him, tending as it did inevitably to become violence. Nothing was stable: politics became war, law became slavery, life itself became death, sooner or later. Always the ritual collapsed in the face of the hideousness. The real world would not be gainsaid, being the true realm of action, but he must gainsay it, or despair. That was his problem. (38)

In his version of scientific hubris, Banville surrounds the astronomer with a pattern of friends, colleagues and disciples, all of whom, in different ways and with different motives, threaten to recall him to the everyday world of change and disorder.

The most important of these antagonists is his brother, Andreas, whose personality and fate are in direct opposition to those of the cold, secretive canon. Koestler refers to Andreas in terms that at once suggest why Banville adapted him to his narrative: he describes him as a 'rake', a 'mortally infected, contagious leper', who eventually died of syphilis.[12] Andreas is everything that his brother is not, and in the novel he plays the role of Copernicus's haunted and guilty conscience. One of Banville's many grotesques, Andreas is always there to confront his brother with the image of the world as a physical hell. The astronomer's obsession with the heavens is parodied by his sibling's bodily disintegration. As in *Birchwood*, Banville establishes a personal drama based on duality and opposition: Copernicus and Andreas represent a primitive duel between the angelical and the diabolical, the intellectual and the physical, as do Gabriel and Michael. The canon's philosophical sense of discrepancy between the ideal and the actual is reinforced by the tormented relationship with his ghastly brother. One finds consolation in the sky, the other in the brothel: 'There were for him two selves, separate and irreconcilable, the one a mind among the stars, the other a worthless fork of flesh planted firmly in earthly excrement.' Copernicus's distinguishing feature is his frigidity, his fear and loathing of the body.[13] Italy, with its reek of sexual decadence and political intrigue, appals him. His Prussian reserve is a mask worn by the intellectual to protect him from all human contacts which threaten his choice of a solitary existence. Andreas's role is to show his brother a few home truths about the world.

The opposition between the two brothers is not just fictionalised at a realistic level, since each of them, but especially Andreas, has a symbolic dimension to his character in keeping with the novel's mythical structure. Copernicus watches in fear and helplessness his brother's disintegration and thinks of 'the terrible slow fall into the depths of a once glorious marvellously shining angel'. Andreas plays the role of a mocking Lucifer who enjoys tormenting his priestly brother. On one of his several visits to the canon's austere residence, the ghoulish Andreas taunts him:

> 'But tell me what you think of the world, brother', he mumbled. 'Do you think it is a worthy place? Are we incandescent angels inhabiting a heaven? Come now, say, what do you think of it?' (115)

Andreas's part is to voice an alternative vision of the world, fiercely sceptical in its honesty and despair, but never sentimental in its grief. Much of Banville's fiction is based on this kind of dramatic, personalised struggle between the forces of light and darkness. Put that way, however, the opposition is too abstract to do justice to the importance of sensuous detail in the author's creation of those extremes. This is particularly true of the grotesque element in his work. *Doctor Copernicus* documents physical suffering in all its horrific detail, so that the star-gazer's idealism is mocked by the reality he would prefer to ignore. He must witness what it is like to endure physical decay. In the presence of Andreas he can hardly ignore it:

> Now in the candlelight his face was horrible and horribly fascinating, worse even than it had seemed at first sight in the ill-lit porch, a ghastly ultimate thing, a mud mask set with eyes and emitting a frightful familiar voice. He was almost entirely bald above a knotted suppurating forehead. His upper lip was all eaten away on one side, so that his mouth was set lopsidedly in what was not a grin and yet not a snarl either. One of his ears was a mess of crumbled white meat, while the other was untouched, a pinkish shell that in its startling perfection appeared far more hideous than its ruined twin. The nose was pallid and swollen, unreal, dead already, as if there, at the ravaged nostrils, Death the Jester had marked the place where when his time came he would force an entry. (112)

This painstaking catalogue of horror is a powerful version of medieval corruption. With its reference to 'Death the Jester', it also conveys the grim spectacle of the *Totentanz*. Copernicus may represent the brave new world of the humanist adventurer, but Andreas is always there to remind him of an undeniable underworld beneath such exalted ambition. This shocking contrast in imagery and personality is even suggested by the detail of Andreas's ears, the uncannily perfect one alongside 'its ruined twin', a residue of beauty within putrefaction. Flaunting his ugliness is Andreas's way of forcing his brother to accept mortality and the flesh, and thereby that part of human affairs which no messianic idealism should discount.

For Andreas, suffering has become a means of knowledge which his brother is looking for, but in the wrong places.[14] The last chapter of the novel is a hallucinatory dialogue in the mind of the dying astronomer, between himself and the ghost of Andreas, who announces himself as 'the angel of redemption'. In an elaborately surreal episode, Andreas reveals the kind of corrective wisdom which eluded his ambitious brother:

With great courage and great effort you might have succeeded, in the only way it is possible to succeed, by disposing the commonplace, the names, in a beautiful and orderly pattern that would show, by its very beauty and order, the action in our poor world of the other-wordly truths. But you tried to discard the commonplace truths for the transcendent ideas, and so failed.

I do not understand.

But you do. We say only those things that we have the words to express: it is enough.(252)

Andreas's 'wisdom' would be mere sentimental naivety if his suffering were not such a convincing part of the narrative. His own idealism has been earned through pain and an understanding of the difference between language and knowledge, a respect for the limitations of language which, in turn, leads to an acceptance of inadequacy and failure. (This is the same note of acceptance and resignation with which Gabriel Godkin concludes his own narrative in *Birchwood*, where he says 'whereof I cannot speak, thereof I must be silent'.) Andreas expresses a passionate contempt for an ambition mediated through a language which confuses itself with what it tries to reveal. His is a kind of intellectual humility gained through a knowledge of evil and irrationality.

This resolution of the relationship between the two brothers lies beyond the drama of the astronomer's career, and is wholly invented by Banville in order to complete the intellectual and philosophical possibilities of the novel. The kind of redemptive insight offered by Andreas, which is based on an intense awareness of the significance of the actual, is quite a mystical conclusion to a story about the folly of abstraction and system. It recommends a reversion, through imagination, to a childlike perception of reality. Stylistically, it is a very polished coda to the relationship between the brothers, yet it is not the only, or the most satisfying, version of Copernicus's ambition. His relation to other characters offers us different narratives within the novel which tell us a different story, one without the mythical or mystical design of this particular relationship.

The third part of *Doctor Copernicus*, 'Cantus mundi', is a dramatic and subjective narrative by Rheticus, the young and enthusiastic disciple of the great astronomer, professor of mathematics and astronomy at Wittenberg.[15] Rheticus served Copernicus for years, published his own preliminary treatise on the theory in 1540, the *Narratio prima*, and then arranged for the first printed edition of *De revolutionibus* in

1542. When the great work was finally published, it never once mentioned Rheticus. The devoted student got into trouble with the university authorities over his alleged homosexuality and was transferred to Hungary, where, in the last years of his life, he found his own disciple, Valentine Otho, who published Rheticus's mathematical researches. For Koestler, the story of Copernicus is markedly unsensational. The only drama in his otherwise dull life involves Rheticus, and it is documented as a tale of political intrigue and personal betrayal, themes in Banville's fiction which reach back to *Nightspawn* and forward to *The Untouchable*.

The novelist's interest in this disillusioned victim of his master's personality and ecclesiastical politics lies in the way his career mirrors that of his hero. Rheticus arrives in Copernicus's northern province of Ermland full of the same kind of babbling enthusiasm which we have already noticed in his master's first interview. Written many years later about his former self, Rheticus's account is a piece of revenge and self-vindication. Like that of Beckett's Malone, the voice is weary but defiant:

> I am at peace at last, after all the furious years. An old man now, yes, a forlorn and weary wanderer come to the end of the journey, I am past caring. But I don't forgive them! No! *The devil shit on the lot of you.* (171)

What follows is Banville's fictional version of an unacknowledged hero of astronomy. Rheticus's account is characterised by a splenetic fury that his good faith could be treated with such contumely.

His vigorous, direct and often hysterical tale of working with Copernicus tries to lay bare the plot that exploited his labour and then dispatched him to the footnotes of history. His contribution to the novel dramatises the role of manipulative forces in what he mistakenly took to be an alliance devoted to pure knowledge. It is, we might say, a political as much as a personal version of lost innocence. He now believes that his greatest mistake was to think that science was free of the political influence of the Reformation. As a Protestant scholar from the heart of Reformation Germany, he did not realise that his relationship with Copernicus in Catholic Ermland was viewed by many, on both sides, as an unacceptable link.The humanist ideal did not reckon with the political designs and ambitions of a Machiavellian order of strategic interests. His narrative, like so many others in Banville's work, is the record of a betrayal.

His recollected evidence of betrayal is haunted by one consoling image of tenderness and love – that of Raphaël, a beautiful young boy who kept house for him. Rheticus is finally removed from his post because his superiors believe that he has corrupted an innocent. In this version of events, Raphaël becomes a function of the narrator's claim to innocence, and is recalled as the only source of joy in an otherwise degrading and corrupt past:

> I see it still, the scene, the sunlight, and the rippling of the horse's glossy blue-black flanks, the groom's hand upon the bridle, and the slim, capped and crimson-caped, booted, beautiful boy, that scene, I see it, and wonder that such a frail tender thing survived so long, to bring me comfort now, and make me young again, here in this horrid place. Raphaël. I write down the name, slowly, say it softly aloud and hear aetherial echoes of seraphs singing. (212)

We see a familiar motif here: just as Gabriel Godkin found, or invented, comfort through the romantic image of 'gentle Ida' in *Birchwood* so too does Rheticus defy his experience of evil and betrayal by preserving a dream of innocence. In both fictions, the nostalgic grief is made all the more poignant, all the more delusory, because of the dramatic and personal immediacy of the narrative form. Like Gabriel, Rheticus is making it up as he goes along. It is something of a predictable surprise, therefore, that we are told by Rheticus, near the end of his account, that Raphaël never existed, and needed simply to be imagined. The fiction is a necessary deceit. The reason he gives for this fiction – 'I had to find something, you see, some terrible tangible thing, to represent the great wrongs done me by Copernicus' – is understandable if pathetic. As with *Birchwood*, the tricks and illusions of memory are an important theme in this purposeful narrative. The empirical past must always be viewed, as Rheticus puts it, through the 'membrane of melancholy'. Personality and temperament seem to determine the tone and the shape of his story, what we might call, in medieval terms, the 'humour' of melancholy. Rheticus, like Ben White and Gabriel Godkin, is afflicted by depression, but 'worst of all is the heartache, the accidie'. A kind of dementia, born out of failure and isolation, informs Rheticus's obsessive narrative.

The historical reasons for Rheticus's outrage over the public presentation of *De revolutionibus*, and his subsequent bitterness, seem uncannily appropriate to the fictional design of such a formalist writer as Banville. The historical structure of events concerning the long-awaited publication are retained by the novelist but he adds a dramatic picture of personal despair.

If *De revolutionibus* decentred the universe, then the history of its publication became a textual drama of instability. Although Rheticus originally supervised the early printing of the book, he was soon removed because of the charges of misconduct, and Andreas Osiander, a Lutheran theologian, saw the printing through to final publication.[16] When the book finally appeared, a horrified Rheticus and a bewildered Copernicus saw that Osiander had written a preface in which the entire theory was explained to be a fiction, an account never intended as an explanation of actual planetary motion. The apologetic preface concluded:

> So far as hypotheses are concerned, let no one expect anything certain from astronomy, which cannot furnish it, lest he accept as the truth ideas conceived for another purpose – and depart from this study a greater fool than when he entered it.[17]

A lifetime's work was now excused as a splendid, but inaccurate, fantasy, what we might now call a 'postmodernist' fiction. Even the title of the work suffered a significant alteration, from *De revolutionibus orbium mundi* to *De revolutionibus orbium coelestium*, thereby severing any lingering impression or hope that the book was about the 'real' world.

Banville reinforces this humiliating irony by having Copernicus predict his own failure. The ageing astronomer, haunted by his brother's despair, confesses to a confused Rheticus the secret that has eluded him for so long, and that accounts for the colossal misunderstanding:

> You imagine that my book is a kind of mirror in which the real world is reflected; but you are mistaken, you must realize that. In order to build such a mirror, I should need to be able to perceive the world whole, in its entirety and in its essence. But our lives are lived in such a tiny, confined space, and in such disorder, that this perception is not possible. There is no contact, none worth mentioning, between the universe and the place in which we live. (219)

This intellectual submission, contracted partly from Andreas, is the beginning of Rheticus's madness. In Banville's postmodernist version of this complex history, one which relishes all forms of deception, Rheticus now confides that he was aware of the absurdity of the theory all the time, and had kept his secret in the hope of climbing to fame on the back of Copernicus's achievement. For Rheticus, the cruel farce is now complete: the revolutionary theory, though transparently absurd, is publicly accepted, while his own vital role in the work results in the punishment and humiliation of oblivion. The anonymous canon is now famous, while the man who forced him into history is dismissed.

Rheticus is one of Banville's many victims of deception and manipulation, not just of his own superstitious veneration and academic cunning, but of a powerful and ruthless political order which is defined in terms of religious alliances.[18] One of the great dramas of the novel is the constant pressure of European politics upon the private careers of both men. The outcome of their research, as well as their shared despair, is deeply conditioned by their experience of the machinations of political and religious power. At one stage, Rheticus had thought of himself and his master as 'angels, playing an endless, celestial game', but that fond belief was brutally overwhelmed by ideological expediency. Whatever the Church thought of *De revolutionibus*, it would hardly have been diplomatic to have its preface signed by a Protestant homosexual. Copernicus tried, unsuccessfully, to keep the world of political and ecclesiastical intrigue at bay. In his own words, he 'wanted no part in that raucous public world', yet it is forced upon him. Both men ignore or deny any connection between the private and the public spheres; ultimately, power insists upon its supremacy over idealism.

The precarious existence of private ambition is always at the centre of the novel, and is mirrored in the political fate of Ermland, the vulnerable statelet surrounded by threatening empires. When his small country is the unexpected arena for major political ambitions, Copernicus is shocked by this barbaric intrusion into his academic hideaway. Once again Banville creates a character – Albrecht, Grand Master of the Teutonic Knights – who challenges belief in the separability of the actual and the imaginary, the private and the public. In conversation with the saturnine astronomer, Albrecht tutors the scientist on their common interest:

> The common people. But they have suffered always, and always will. It is in a way what they are for. You flinch. Herr Doctor, I am disappointed in you. The common people? – pah. What are they to us? You and I, *mein Freund*, we are lords of the earth, the great ones, the major men, the makers of supreme fictions. (149)

This is an ominous, and a fearful, moment for Copernicus, as Albrecht points out the similarity of their ambitions. For the cynical soldier, ordinary human suffering can be simply dismissed in the pursuit of a dream of conquest. Albrecht, like Andreas, is used by Banville to present a darker, sinister reflection of the astronomer's ego. Like a pub drunk, Albrecht assumes a familiarity that the scientist finds quite embarrassing and distressing, but which also seems quite irrefutable: his overpowering physicality is an affront to Copernicus's 'congenital coldness', his incurable aversion to intimacy and the flesh. In this novel, Banville arranges a network of characters who warn Copernicus of the price of such a denial. As in *Birchwood*, the political background is there to show the fragility, sometimes the immorality, of escapism. Like Faustus, he acquires and regrets this knowledge after it is too late for redemption.

It is characteristic of Banville that such a personal tragedy should provoke an oppositional claim to an alternative faith that Andreas calls 'redemptive despair'. Both Andreas and Rheticus, for different reasons, reject Copernicus's nihilism. For Andreas, an understanding of reality comes from an acceptance of its madness and cruelty. Only by sub-mitting to the limits of knowledge, paradoxically, can any under-standing of the world be attained. Andreas offers a faith based upon humility, compassion and patience, a disposition towards ordinary experience that will open up a sense of the absolute. This is a form of mystical animism which strains to achieve a humane alternative to the sterile vanities of intellect. The absolute is found in the concrete, and joy is reached through an acceptance of mortality: in terms which recall William Blake, there is no advance without contradiction.

Rheticus, more convincingly integrated into the resolution of the novel than Andreas, enjoys an unexpected consolation for his loss of faith. His rage is so personal that he insists that the Copernican theory which removes the earth from the centre of the universe is the direct result of its author's barren and perverse character. He believes that the heliocentric theory deliberately sets out to prove, in his words, that 'the world turns upon chaos'. For Rheticus, Copernicus's book is the product and the reflection of a benighted and spiteful personality:

> It destroyed my faith, in God and Man – but not in the Devil. Lucifer sits at the centre of that book, smiling a familiar cold grey smile. You were evil, Koppernigk, and you filled the world with despair. (231)

From this depth of anger and regret, Rheticus suddenly achieves, through a circumstance which gives him a final illusion of the prestige denied to him by his master, a miraculous sense of transcendent hope. An enthusiastic student, Otho, arrives to serve him in his own research: as Rheticus says, noting a familar pattern, 'The past comes back transfigured.'

This familiar, although unexpected, relationship is the third and final version of the student–master bond in the novel, one through which Banville explores the relation between age and youth, hope and cynicism, future and past, experience and imagination. The balance in that relation usually favours the power of doubt over faith. However, in a story which seems to reject the possibility of absolute forms of knowledge, hope now assumes a reinvigorated character. The master is reborn:

> I am Doctor Rheticus! I am a believer. Lift your head, then, strange new glorious creature, incandescent angel, and gaze upon the world. It is not diminished! Even in that he failed. The sky is blue, and shall be forever blue, and the earth shall blossom forever in spring, and this planet shall forever be the centre of all we know. I believe it, I think. *Vale.* (232)

Even the final, hesitant afterthought does not undermine the significance and force of this sudden revelation. It is left to Rheticus to express a new form of earthly wonder, inspired, ironically, by Copernican despair. Earth, dismissed from the heart of the universe, is suddenly brought into new dramatic perspective and focus.

The heliocentric theory is the beginning of modern man's sense of loneliness in the world. Like a second Fall, this new scientific fiction banishes humanity from the security of a static central presence in the universe, to the reduced status of a small dependent sphere revolving in the cold wastes of the firmament. Banville's understanding of the modern significance of the Copernican revolution, notably the way such a discovery undermined an earlier sense of security and centrality, is very similar to that offered by Sigmund Freud at the turn of the twentieth century, when he saw it as one of a series of scientific blows to what he called 'man's craving for grandiosity':

> Humanity has in the course of time had to endure from the hands of science two great outrages upon the naive self-love. The first was when it realized that our earth was not the centre of the universe, but only a tiny speck in a world-system of a magnitude hardly conceivable; this is associated in our minds with the name of Copernicus, although Alexandrian doctrines taught something very similar. The second was when biological research robbed man of his peculiar privilege of having been specially created, and relegated him to a descent from the animal world, implying an ineradicable animal nature in him: this transvalua-

tion has been accomplished in our own time upon the instigation of Charles Darwin, Wallace and their predecessors, and not without the most violent opposition from their contemporaries.[19]

A large part of the force of Banville's tetralogy comes from its engagement with these ideas, especially with a modern version of the Fall, a loss of grace and innocence. Seen in these terms, and from such a perspective, the tetralogy, and much else in Banville, is an Edenic parable.

The Copernican revolution is the start of a modern sense of an impassable gulf between the spiritual and the material worlds. This sense of separation is often expressed in a passionate nostalgia for some original unity of being. If restored, such harmony might offer a clue to a new kind of redemption, the kind Copernicus imagined when dreaming of Greece and Rome, 'when the world had known an almost divine unity of spirit and matter, of purpose and consequence'. Both Andreas and Rheticus articulate this alternative perception of man's desolation and disappointment, and assert a new spiritual advantage in the loss of false certainties. Humanity, stripped of its original security, falls back on its own imaginative resources, and must cling to the beautiful and the concrete as the new forms of knowledge.

A lyrical envy of Nature in its most enduring and concrete forms concludes *Doctor Copernicus*. It is a poetic part of the myth of exile and alienation that informs Banville's fiction. *Nightspawn* and *Birchwood* end with a similar sense of diminishment in the face of Nature's sublime indifference and remote beauty, and now Copernicus's final moments of consciousness recall a similar regret:

> Nicolas, straining to catch that melody, heard the voices of evening rising to meet him from without: the herdsman's call, the cries of children at play, the rumbling of the carts returning from market; and there were other voices too, of churchbells gravely tolling the hour, of dogs that barked afar, of the sea, of the earth itself, turning in its course, and of the wind, out of huge blue air, sighing in the leaves of the linden. All called and called to him, and called, calling him away. (254)

The gentle hypnotic rhythm of this concluding passage, its pastoral images of daily routine, capture a kind of emotional exhaustion after the distracted and obsessive pattern of his career. In a manner reminiscent of Gabriel Conroy's last sensations in Joyce's 'The Dead', it suggests a surrender to the rhythm of ordinary life. The final image of the novel recalls the opening one – the linden tree of childhood – as if to suggest, not just the endurance of this kind of concrete mystery, but a return to a perception denied and rejected for so long.[20]

Like much contemporary fiction, Banville's work is based on a contradictory self-consciousness about the relation between language and reality. The writer is forced to deal with a reality which cannot, or will not, be described. Writing about the futility of writing is, or may become, a tricky business. *Doctor Copernicus* is an adventurous version of that dilemma, all the more effective because its central character deals with mathematical symbols, not just the language of words. This version of the fiction-maker gives a unique and powerful generalising force to the myth of the inexpressible. The astronomer's greatness lies in his passionate determination and ability to construct a symbolic order; his tragedy lies in his inability to recognise the fictionality of that order.

Banville's novel discovers an alternative security in the knowledge that language should not be confused with the mystery that it may evoke. In his acknowledgement of the poverty of words, a renewed sense of their proper value is achieved. The poetic inspiration for this paradox is suggested in the epigraph to the novel, lines from Wallace Stevens's *Notes toward a Supreme Fiction:*

> You must become an ignorant man again
> And see the sun again with an ignorant eye
> And see it clearly in the idea of it.[21]

The opening section of the poem, from which the epigraph is taken, is about the need to trust imagination to do the work of naming the world, and not to allow perception to be deadened by the language of habit. The world comes first, as does the linden tree; what it is called remains of secondary and ambivalent value. Only by respecting and remembering this distinction will the burden of language become a revitalised means of knowledge.[22]

A great new sense of fictional possibility has been opened up, and the balance between ideas and imagination, annnounced in *Doctor Copernicus*, will find its most satisfying harmony in the next part of the tetralogy – *Kepler*.

5

Kepler

To see a World in a Grain of Sand
And a Heaven in a Wild Flower,
Hold Infinity in the palm of your hand
And Eternity in an hour.
William Blake, 'Auguries of Innocence'

KEPLER (1981) continues the historical theme of *Doctor Copernicus*, the pioneering struggle of Renaissance science to open up a new vision of celestial and earthly order. Johannes Kepler, born in Swabia in south-west Germany in 1571, inherited the Copernican theory of a sun-centred universe. He was the first successor of Copernicus to give the heliocentric theory a precise mathematical foundation based on painstaking observation, research that owed a great deal to Tycho Brahe, the Danish astronomer. Besides inventing the new science of dioptrics, the study of the laws of refraction, Kepler also formulated three important laws of modern physical astronomy.[1] Unlike Copernicus, Kepler was a prodigious writer and publisher, producing a series of major scientific studies – *Mysterium cosmographicum* (1597), *Astronomia nova* (1610), *Dioptrice* (1612), *Harmonice mundi* (1619) and a science-fiction fantasy, *Somnium*, published posthumously. The five chapters of Banville's novel are honorifically named after these works.

Kepler, like *Doctor Copernicus*, is a story about extraordinary ambition, but the contrast in personality between the eponymous heroes is a significant difference. A perfect contrast in spirit, but children of the same imaginative impulse, they are the adventurous twins of the new science. Whereas Copernicus, that 'mournful angel', was presented as a man who shunned any physical contact with family or the unpleasant side of earthly reality, Banville's Kepler is his most sympathetic character to date. Absolutely dedicated to his science and, like Copernicus, often seeing it as a defence against the disorder of religious and political realities, Kepler retains a compassion and innocence missing from his famous predecessor. If Copernicus succeeded despite himself, then the exact opposite applies to Kepler. The austere canon tried to keep reality at bay in order to contemplate the harmony of the spheres; Banville's *Kepler* celebrates a character whose acceptance of ordinary reality yields the clue to his astronomical discovery and knowledge. *Doctor Copernicus* is about the tragedy of personality; *Kepler* is about the triumph of character.

As we would expect from Banville, *Kepler* is structured around a drama of anticlimax and revelation, rather than any strict chronology of a scientific career. The narrative pattern of the novel, like the pattern of planetary motion famously discovered by Kepler, is elliptical.[2] It begins, not with childhood, as in *Doctor Copernicus*, but with Kepler's first job as apprentice to the outlandish and eccentric figure of Tycho Brahe. This master–apprentice relationship, with its deceptive promise of inspiration and instruction, is a version of the contest between arrogance and enthusiasm, experience and innocence, which by now is a familiar motif in Banville's fiction. In the opening scenes of the novel, Banville arranges a pattern of ironic contrast which characterises the rest of his protagonist's life. Arriving at Brahe's castle of Benatek, outside Prague, the young Kepler's expectations are quickly and absurdly deflated. As usual, things are not what they seem or promise to be; worse still, they are too often a total travesty of fond imaginings. Greeted by a court dwarf instead of the host, surrounded by chaotic building-in-progress and painfully aware of his outraged scolding wife, Kepler faces yet another farcical version of the unexpected:

> Despite misgivings he had in his heart expected something large and lavish of Benatek, gold rooms and spontaneous applause, the attention of magnificent serious people, light and space and ease: not this grey, these deformities, the clamour and confusion of other lives, this familiar – O familiar! – disorder.[3]

Revelation is the happier version of surprise, but irony is the surer. Several of Kepler's flashes of momentous inspiration occur in the most outlandish and improbable circumstances, moments of exquisite joy and insight intensified by the chaotic and banal conditions of their birth. Yet Kepler's weary familiarity with the trickery of hope remains a basic feature of his character and, most importantly, becomes the key to his stoicism.

The outstanding feature of that character is his refusal to submit to the temptation of despair. In theology he rejects absolutely the Calvinist doctrine of predestination; in science he retains faith in an imaginative order. Kepler's struggle is always with the unforeseeable. The most convincing part of Banville's story is when the dual nature of that mysterious intervention in human affairs is acknowledged: to equate the unexpected with the tragic is simply to define fate as a cruel machine, rather than the instructive mystery that Kepler believes it to be.

Much of our sympathy for the character of Kepler, especially for his endurance, comes from his personal innocence and social vulnerability. While waiting for the great Brahe to appear, Kepler, who comes from a poor background, is left watching the ordinary routine of the castle, a servant watching servants.[4] He is, as the narrator remarks, 'hopelessly of that class which notices the state of servants' feet'. As a picaresque hero, wandering all over Europe in search of peace and security in which to work and to raise his family, Kepler always remains outside the ranks of power and influence. Although working with Brahe and corresponding with the great Italian astronomer Galileo, his physical existence is that of a scholarly tramp. This is another significant contrast with Copernicus, who thrived on monastic privacy and loathed everything adventurous or exotic. Felix, an Italian mercenary in Brahe's entourage, arouses only sympathy and envy in Kepler. Having nursed the soldier out of a fever caused by a terrible wound, Kepler is fascinated by this new bond between soldier and scholar, man of action and dreamer:

> Perhaps, then, a kind of awful comradeship, by which he might gain entry to that world of action and intensity, that Italy of the spirit, of which this renegade was an envoy. Life, life, that was it! In the Italian he seemed to know at last, however vicariously, the splendid and exhilarating sordidness of real life. (69)

The childlike nature of this brilliant astronomer and mathematician, with his sense of wonder and adventure, makes Kepler such a sympathetic yet complex character. It is a quality which Koestler describes as a 'mystic's mature innocence'.[5]

Although Kepler as astronomer is the subject of the novel, his personal and domestic life is important for a full appreciation of his character. This relationship between the private and the public worlds is what provides the real drama in the novel. Copernicus's tragedy is the result of his determination to keep these two worlds utterly separate, being convinced that the everyday can teach him nothing. His brother Andreas tries to explain the personal and intellectual price to be paid for denying 'the splendid and exhilarating sordidness of real life'. As a counter-figure to Copernicus, Kepler is forever entangled with his family. The point of dramatising so fully this side of the scientist's career is not simply to romanticise Kepler as an 'ordinary' man: on the contrary, it shows his special kind of imaginative empathy and perception, his sympathetic and symbolic way of reading the commonplace.

Portrayed as a shy husband, henpecked by a shrewish wife, the great astronomer is a sorry spectacle. The domesticated scientist is an amusing, often farcical, element in the novel, but one with a serious purpose. Kepler works in the back room on his theory of celestial harmony, while his wife is screaming in the kitchen about his lack of social ambition. Several children are born, most of them dying shortly after birth. Because of the religious and political wars in Germany and Austria, the family is forever on the move. This great astronomer, imperial mathematician to Rudolph II, is entertained at court but never paid. His father-in-law worries about his daughter's financial situation, since she married someone without a steady or a proper job. In the midst of all these domestic and public trials, Kepler has to deal with the legal authorities who have charged his mother with witchcraft. Even if he wanted to, Kepler cannot ignore the circumstantial world.

Banville pays detailed attention to the chaos and lunacy of Kepler's private life. At one level, it shows the impossibility of rising above the pressure of the mundane and the subjective, and recalls individual ambition to personal responsibility. But Banville's intention is not as moral as that might suggest. Kepler has indeed a lot to put up with, but so do those around him. Banville wants to represent a personalised version of chaos which is as instructive as the larger chaos in Kepler's struggle with the heavenly order. The domestic is an ironic counterpoint to the intellectual. At another level, its apparent irrelevance to ambition is entirely deceptive. Copernicus denied any significance to such details; Kepler never forgets them.

Kepler's appreciation of celestial harmony begins at home. The purpose of this irony is to intensify the contradictory and wondrous nature of a revelation that suddenly accepts the mysteriousness of the obvious and the obviousness of the mysterious. A central theme of the novel is the ultimate simplicity of a kind of knowledge only achieved through labour of extraordinary complication and exhausting dedication. Ironically, it often seems to Kepler that he had already known what it took a lifetime to see. This ludicrous but uplifting insight is what connects the personal to the scientific in the story. Such a perception is finally revealed as innate – but it takes an eternity of labour to recall. During that time, however, Kepler senses, on many occasions and through several personal relationships, the nature of the simple secret that his intellectual pursuit obscures. Before looking at the scientific forms of revelation, we may note the pattern of personalised images of beauty in Kepler's turbulent domestic life which foreshadows his final vision of celestial harmony.

Women play a crucial role in Kepler's evolving sense of the mystery of beauty. When we first meet Kepler arriving at Benatek, he is accompanied by his wife, Barbara, and stepdaughter, Regina. Inherited from his wife's previous marriage, Regina is his only consolation for this misalliance. As a figure of silent hypnotic beauty, she is a familiar image in Banville's fictional design, someone whose grace of character symbolises the kind of harmony usually absent from the world. Like Gabriel's Rose and Rheticus's Raphaël, she embodies an exquisite dream-like quality which corresponds to the astronomer's intellectual goal. In the middle of one of many domestic arguments, Regina's magical presence is observed by Kepler:

> Regina came in, effecting a small but palpable adjustment in the atmosphere. She shut the big oak door behind her with elaborate care, as if she were assembling part of the wall. The world was built on too large a scale for her. Johannes could sympathize. (20)

This silent observation, based on imaginative empathy for such delicacy of motion, all the more precious for its contrast with the drudgery of the domestic dispute, is a characteristic effect of the whole novel. Regina is one of those symbolic female characters who represent a mute form of innocent and natural harmony which Kepler will eventually discover in the divine universe. She is evidence, in earthly form, of the magical in human affairs.

Kepler's love for, and fascination with, his stepdaughter endures for most of his life. At the height of his fame, but still struggling with the laws of planetary motion, optics and physical astronomy, Kepler continues to be fascinated by her oracular presence:

Why was it, he wondered, that her candid gaze so pleased him always; how did she manage to make it seem a signal of support and understanding? She was like a marvellous and enigmatic work of art, which he was content to stand and contemplate with a dreamy smile, careless of the artist's intentions. To try to tell her what he felt would be as superfluous as talking to a picture. (99)

As an aesthetic figure, Regina represents an imaginative ideal, a non-intellectual, lyrical image of innate, cryptic beauty. She has read her father's work, but offers no opinion on it. Her role, of course, is quite different from that of colleague or commentator: she is a premonitory presence who offers a clue to what her scholarly father seeks through intellect. This opposition between male knowledge and female wisdom, one which elevates feminine mystery above manly comprehension, occurs in a variety of forms throughout Banville's entire fiction.

Having seen this kind of Platonic ideal before, in *Birchwood* and *Doctor Copernicus*, it is not surprising, however disappointing, that such love turns sour. Regina marries, and Kepler feels abandoned by the only figure of spiritual beauty in his life. To make his disappointment all the more bitter, her new husband supervises letters to Kepler, hounding him for settlement of dowry and inheritance money, completing the sense of degradation. There is, of course, an important fictional difference between Regina and the corresponding figures of Rose and Raphaël: she is not, as they are, figments of the imagination. She is, for a short while, a living consolation whose exquisite beauty amidst chaos makes her seem all the more unreal.

Other members of Kepler's family reveal a similar kind of primitive innocence. This is especially true of Heinrich, Kepler's younger brother, a hulking epileptic and, a former soldier, now living like an overgrown child with his sorceress mother. Kepler's fascination with Heinrich is based on the same sense of contrast that he felt between himself and Felix, the mercenary. One of life's inarticulate victims, but full of awe and curiosity for his famous brother, Heinrich's ignorance and experience intrigue Kepler:

> But he had been to the wars. What unimaginable spectacles of plunder and rape had those bland brown eyes witnessed in their time? From such wonderings Kepler's mind delicately averted itself. He had peculiar need of *this* Heinrich, a forty-year-old child, eager and unlovely, and always hugely amused by a world he had never quite learned how to manage. (93–4)

Like Regina, Heinrich *feels* the world rather than knows it. Kepler has yet to experience this sensation, although he can empathise with it. Images of innocence, mute and intuitive, play an important part in the development of his perception and knowledge. These images are reminders of a different imaginative outlook which Kepler always respects, but which comes to him at the end of his life by a most circuitous route.

Banville's attraction to Kepler lies in the relation between character and achievement. Now that we have looked at the nature of that character and its private dimension, we might turn to the science which transformed character into genius. The novel accepts the outline of Kepler's scientific career, especially the arduous discovery of new laws of planetary motion. Banville's fictional interest in the historical Kepler lies more with the actual process of discovery than with the scientific facts discovered by that process.

Kepler's first 'discovery' – that the universe is based on five perfect geometric forms – was quite false, as fictional as anything by Copernicus. Kepler announced this principle of symmetry in his first book, *Mysterium cosmographicum*, which is also the title of the novel's first chapter.[6] It is not difficult to see Banville's fascination with the fictional character of this scientific proposition. Kepler, while teaching at a school in Graz, is wondering why there are only six planets, and why the distances between them seem so fixed:

> On that ordinary morning in July came the answering angel. He was in class. The day was warm and bright. A fly buzzed in the tall window, a rhomb of sunlight lay at his feet. His students, stunned with boredom, gazed over his head out of glazed eyes. He was demonstrating a theorem out of Euclid – afterwards, try as he might, he could not remember which – and had prepared on the blackboard an equilateral triangle. He took up the big wooden compass, and immediately, as it always contrived to do, the monstrous thing bit him. With his wounded thumb in his mouth he turned to the easel and began to trace two circles, one within the triangle touching it on three sides, the second circumscribed and intersecting the vertices. He stepped back, into that box of dusty sunlight, and blinked, and suddenly something, his heart perhaps, dropped and bounced, like an athlete performing a miraculous feat upon a trampoline, and he thought, with rapturous inconsequence: I shall live forever. (30)

The angel of revelation always arrives unexpectedly and unannounced into the most prosaic of situations. Kepler's discovery here is intuitive, accidental and false, but it is the richest error of his scientific career.[7] Looking at the figure on the blackboard, he believes that geometry is the key to the design of the physical universe. There are only six planets, the logic argues, because there are only five perfect solids known to science, and the solids 'fit' perfectly and harmoniously between those planets, revealing the distances between them. Kepler's mystical faith in geometrical form and the supernatural significance of numbers is part of his Neoplatonic and neo-Pythagorean inheritance.[8]

The idea of geometrical symmetry as the divine plan of a harmonious celestial order is pleasing as a theory, but Kepler cannot prove it mathematically. This *a priori* discovery forces him, through a lifetime's work of observation and calculation, to achieve his famous laws of physical astronomy. For Banville, Kepler's revelations show the crucial role of imaginative faith, even if it is initially no more than fiction. In this instance, the fiction of a geometric universe is especially significant to the novel, as it suggests a simple form of harmony at the heart of things. Fiction, it turns out, may be the surest road to reality. This, on Banville's part, is an artistic compliment from one formalist to another.

The path from fiction to fact is the real imaginative miracle of the novel. It is a dramatisation of insight by one of Koestler's great 'sleepwalkers', a discovery based as much on accident as design, on vision as on intellect. The story of Kepler's career demonstrates, above all, the primary truths of imagination and the intellect's slow return to what imagination originally reveals. Kepler's first law, announced in his second book, *Astronomia nova*, declares that the planets move, not in circles, but in elliptical orbits. Because of his misleading obsession with perfect shapes, he took years to discover what he knew was already there. This intellectual search for mathematical confirmation of the ellipse is the primary motif of the novel's design, an enigma to which the narrative keeps returning. The secret first occurs to Kepler in the opening lines of the novel, while he sleeps and dreams:

> Johannes Kepler, asleep in his ruff, has dreamed the solution to the cosmic mystery. He holds it cupped in his mind as in his hands he would a precious something of unearthly frailty and splendour. O do not wake! But he will. Mistress Barbara, with a grain of grim satisfaction, shook him by his ill-shod foot, and at once the fabulous egg burst, leaving only a bit of glair and a few coordinates of broken shell.
>   And 0.00429. (9)

The theatrical manner of the narrator, with his Prospero-like evocation of mystery, lifts the curtain on a childlike genius. For the reader, the final number, set apart as a significant afterthought, stands alone without explanation. What does it mean? The reader, like Kepler, will have to wait. The mysterious number is given to us at the opening to suggest a knowledge that has yet to be consciously understood.

As an apprentice to Tycho Brahe, Kepler is deliberately assigned to the observation of Mars, a planet with the most eccentric orbit of all. (This piece of spite on Brahe's part eventually leads to Kepler's greatest discoveries.) Kepler immediately lays a wager that he will solve the riddle of Mars in seven days. Seven years later, he makes the final breakthrough. In a letter to a friend, in the 'Harmonice Mundi' chapter of the novel, Kepler details the excruciating process of his discovery that the number 0.00429, a figure in his mind all those years, turned out to be the formula for an ellipse:

> There is a final act to this comedy. Having tried to construct the orbit by using the equation I had just discovered, I made an error in geometry, and failed again. In despair, I threw out the formula, in order to try a new hypothesis, namely, that the orbit might be an ellipse. When I had constructed such a figure, by means of geometry, I saw of course that the two methods produced the same result, and that my equation was, in fact, *the mathematical expression of an ellipse*. Imagine, Doctor, my amazement, joy & embarrassment. I had been staring at the solution, without recognizing it! Now I was able to express the thing as a law, simple, elegant, and true: *The planets move in ellipses with the sun at one focus.* (148)

Not only does Kepler, to his mortified amusement, discover what he already knew, but he wonders at the workings of the human mind and its strange, teasing progress. The moral of such an irony is not, of course, that the scientific labour was a waste of time and effort. On the contrary, however Sisyphean such a labour might seem, Kepler emerges as a heroic, indomitable figure. Intellect is simply a slow affair compared with imagination: sometimes it is the only path back to a kind of understanding obscured by science. When Kepler triumphantly concludes that the law was 'simple, elegant, and true', we are reminded of Regina's character. The imaginative intellect of Kepler has discovered, or rather confirmed, the underlying simplicity of the celestial harmonies. The details of his theory of the five perfect solids were wrong, but the purity and the symbolism of the idea were true. In that same letter to his friend, Kepler writes, 'Thus do we progress, my dear Doctor, blunderingly, in a dream, like wise but undeveloped children!'

Kepler's greatness, in contrast to that of Copernicus, lies in this kind of humility. For him, the greatest discovery of all is his understanding of imaginative perception as the link between human and heavenly order.

All this is to characterise Kepler as a Neoplatonist, an astronomer who insists on the symbolic relation between the actual and the ideal, the material and the spiritual. The clearest and most eloquent expression of his philosophy comes in the fourth chapter of the novel, '*Harmonice mundi*'. Based on a circular pattern of twenty letters from Kepler to ten recipients composed of family and colleagues, it is the only chapter in which Kepler speaks directly, free from the ironic sympathy of the narrator. The letters begin in 1605, progress up to 1612, and then return to their original starting-point. This 'elliptical' pattern is a playful device by Banville both to imitate the key geometric image of the novel and to illustrate the pattern of original enlightenment. Just to heighten the symbolism of this pattern, the letters begin and end with the season of suffering and transfiguration, sacrifice and redemption – Ash Wednesday and Easter. It is a chapter whose rhythm, form and structure are worthy of the great astronomer himself, who declares in one of the letters, 'It is ever thus with me: in the beginning is the shape!' Progress, according to this pattern, is an inexorable form of recollection.

Throughout these letters, Kepler explains his belief that the universe is based on geometric forms placed there by God, hence the perfection of the spheres. To understand God's creation requires an understanding of these forms. This knowledge, Kepler insists, is latent in every person, but revealed only through imaginative perception. His work has discovered a divine harmony which was already inscribed in the mind and soul:

> In this I take issue seriously with Aristotle, who holds that the mind is a *tabula rasa* upon which sense perceptions write. This is wrong, wrong. The mind learns all mathematical ideas & figures out of itself; by empirical signs it only remembers what it knows already. Mathematical ideas are the essence of the soul … the mind determines how the eye must be, and therefore the eye is so, because the mind is so, and not vice versa. Geometry was not received through the eyes: it was already there inside. (146)

The tribute to God is also a tribute to a human perception capable of seeing His reflection. Man, in this special sense, is the centre of Kepler's universe, the real *magnum miraculum*. Kepler's joy is the result of this *human* discovery, his recognition of the divine within the earthly. All his work has led him back to a sense of simple, intuitive and original harmony. The Copernican, heliocentric theory of the universe may have displaced the earth from the centre of all we know and see, but Kepler's work reinstates the human imagination at the centre of all we understand. Kepler is a romantic of the sciences, a believer in the innate gift of an all-seeing imagination.

Banville's stylistic expression of these discoveries is not always in such an exalted tone. Kepler's belief in the miracle of perception, as well as the beauty of that which is perceived, is eventually conveyed in the rather formal mode of scholarly correspondence. But the actual moments of revelation which are afterwards formulated as laws are a typical mixture of the sublime and the ridiculous. We may recall Kepler's amazement at the significance of the forms he casually chalked on the classroom blackboard, all the while nursing his injured thumb. Later, he hits upon the principle of uniform velocity for these elliptical orbits while retching into a street-drain after carousing with whores in a tavern (an incident similar in kind and spirit to that in *Birchwood* where Gabriel, after tumbling out of a country pub, suddenly has a celestial visionof the principle of 'fixity within continuity'). Only once, in his sudden insight into a third law concerning the mathematical relation between a planet's period and its distance, does Banville omit any ironic form of deflation. This time, inspiration comes in unalloyed majesty:

> When the solution came, it came, as always, through a back door of the mind, hesitating shyly, an announcing angel dazed by the immensity of its journey. One morning in the middle of May, while Europe was buckling on its sword, he felt the wing-tip touch him, and heard the mild voice say *I am here.* (176)

The imagery of angelic inspiration is a common feature of Banville's fiction, as we saw in *Birchwood* and *Doctor Copernicus*. The difference in *Kepler* is that its beatific character has no diabolical counterpart or *doppelgänger*. Kepler, unlike Copernicus, is the great synthesiser. The aptly named *Harmonice mundi*, Kepler's final vision of world harmony, is the work which brings together the human and the divine, the imaginative and the rational.

The story of Kepler's achievement is one of exalted serendipity. So much is discovered that was not looked for, especially this new appreciation of the shaping power of the imagination. In his early days,

Kepler, like Copernicus, had thought of science as a realm of abstraction and order that would defend him against the encroaches of violence and sectarianism in European politics and a chaotic personal life. But, like the pattern of the 'Harmonice mundi' chapter itself, his achievement brings him back to an original innocence which illuminates the ordinary world he would rather have denied.

Celebration of the ordinary and visible reality of God's design is a recurrent and organising motif in the novel, at first only an impression, but finally a spiritual revelation. Throughout Kepler's story, there are intimations of this secret harmony and beauty, always alternating with scientific struggle and political danger. This pattern of renewed vision based on recollected images is seen, for example, in the episode where Kepler and his wife, at the height of the row over payment from Brahe, leave the castle and appeal to Baron Hoffmann for help. They are met with the same kind of patrician arrogance as before. Distracted by these humiliations, Kepler suddenly hears music through the window and walks over to look into the garden:

> The rain shower had passed, and the garden brimmed with light. Clasping his hands behind him and swaying gently on heel and toe he gazed out at the poplars and the dazzled pond, the drenched clouds of flowers, that jigsaw of lawn trying to reassemble itself between the stone balusters of a balcony. How innocent, how inanely lovely, the surface of the world! The mystery of simple things assailed him. (62)

This lyrical image, in its careful arrangement of sensuous and orderly detail, suggests a delicacy and sensitivity in the perceiver as well as in what is being perceived. Banville's way of animating certain scenes, especially here with the image of the lawn 'trying to reassemble itself' like a jigsaw, always emphasises the vitality and animism of Kepler's way of looking at the world. That world is also watching Kepler, arranging itself stealthily into shapes and forms pleasing to the onlooker. Much later on in his researches, while labouring with an astronomical chart for the Emperor Rudolph, and hating his bondage to this kind of power, Kepler recalls the image of that garden scene:

> The demented dreamer in him rebelled. He remembered that vision he had glimpsed in Baron Hoffmann's garden, and was again assailed by the mysteriousness of the commonplace. *Give this world's praise to the angel!* He had only the vaguest notion of what he meant. (84–5)

It may still be no more than an intimation for Kepler, but for the reader, perhaps, the significance is clearer. The celestial voice which

Kepler hears, a quotation from the visionary poet Rainer Maria Rilke, urges him to celebrate the sensuous world, to see it anew in the light of his heavenly experience.[9] Banville is trying to capture a visionary experience of the ordinary, whereby the tangible world assumes a new, or renewed, significance. With this revived sense of the beauty and magic of the natural world comes an appreciation of man's proper human scale. Kepler realises that harmony is not so much an objective set of facts about an uninhabited realm of the universe, but a projected faculty of ecstatic perception, a faculty made possible by the existence of an innate appreciation of harmony. He now recalls a scene from his childhood, long forgotten, which confirms this new sense of wonder. He remembers his innocent fascination at watching a snail crawl up a window-pane:

> Pressed in a lavish embrace upon the pane, the creature gave up its frilled grey-green underparts to his gaze, while the head strained away from the glass, moving blindly from side to side, the horns weaving as if feeling out enormous forms in air. But what had held Johannes was its method of crawling. He would have expected some sort of awful convulsions, but instead there was a series of uniform small smooth waves flowing endlessly upward along its length, like a visible heart-beat. The economy, the heedless beauty of it, baffled him. (98)

As so often in Banville's style, an elaborate metaphor from the parallel world of Nature captures something of humankind's poignant struggle for knowledge. This mesmeric image of delicate, patient ascent suggests Kepler's own somnambulant career. Such a miniature form of struggle and effort, in a place which shows the beauty and the absurdity of such determination, gives the onlooker an insight into humanity's humble place in the vastness of creation. At the end of the novel, sick and delirious, Kepler dreams of the same image of small but wondrous survival – 'Turn up a flat stone and there it is, myriad and profligate! Such a dream I had ... *Es war doch so schön*'.[10] The star-gazer, whose story begins and ends with a dream, has rediscovered his earthly sphere.

Kepler is one of Banville's most romantic figures, someone Koestler describes as 'the most reckless and erratic spiritual adventurer of the scientific revolution'.[11] His appeal lies in a childlike sense of fascination which he never loses, which is paradoxically restored by science. He is also a man of courage and determination. However much preoccupied by the stars, Kepler has to fight to survive in a Europe dominated by political and religious intrigue. Without this background of persecution and cruelty, which does not spare Kepler and his family, the novel could only assert intellectual achievement. 'Pure' science does not exist in the novel: it emerges only after doing battle with time and circumstance. Like Godkin, Kepler is a miraculous survivor.

Kepler's story is marked by constant exile. As a Lutheran, but a famed astronomer, he is only just tolerated in Catholic Austria; in Lutheran Germany, he is suspected of Calvinism. The looming Thirty Years War manipulates his fate as surely as the astrologer's stars. Like Copernicus, he never takes sides: 'In the matter of faith he was stubborn. He could not fully agree with any party, Catholic, Lutheran or Calvinist, and so was taken for an enemy by all three.'

Banished finally from Austria, then excommunicated by the Lutheran Church, Kepler's only consolation is his work and what remains of his family. Religious politics repeatedly intrude on his life, setting up a constant tension between the private and the public spheres. While working for the Emperor on the Rudolphine Tables, he is summoned home for the arraignment of his mother as a witch. In an

2 Albrecht Dürer, *Knight with Death and the Devil* (1513)

extraordinary scene in which the inquisitors display the instruments of torture to encourage a confession from the old woman, Kepler notices his mother's proud but dangerous indifference to the drama around her. After such a hard life, the old woman's stubborness evokes Kepler's 'rueful admiration'. Later, his wife contracts typhus, a disease which the Austrian troops had brought with them into Prague. For the first time, Kepler appreciates what she has had to endure, and then pays tribute to her in a letter to Regina. His favourite son, Friedrich, aged 6, 'a fair child, a hyacinth of the morning in the first days of spring, our hope, our joy', dies of smallpox. One of his few trusted friends, Wincklemann, a Jewish lens-grinder, goes missing, another victim of inquisitorial enthusiasm. Kepler's personal life is a series of cruel disasters, yet his dream of harmony and beauty becomes all the more necessary in the face of such barbarism.

Kepler's heroic quality comes from his refusal to despair. Overwhelmed by personal grief, cheated and betrayed by political and religious authorities, he finds consolation in a picture of artistic stoicism based on faith:

> The vision of the harmony of the world is always before me, calling me on. God will not abandon me. I shall survive. I keep with me a copy of that engraving by the great Dürer of Nuremberg, which is called Knight with Death & the Devil, an image of stoic grandeur & fortitude from which I derive much solace: for this is how one must live, facing into the future, indifferent to terrors and yet undeceived by foolish hopes. (128)

This is very much like the image of his mother before the inquisition.[12] Kepler's faith in himself is calm yet eloquent, humanistic yet deeply religious. Like all romantics, he defies the world to beat him down. His idealism seems authenticated by the horrors that it has to endure and overcome.

The important role of imagination in Kepler's character is formally underlined, as we have seen, by the dreams which introduce and conclude the novel. A pleasing historical coincidence between Banville's characterisation and his hero's private writings is found in the title of the novel's final chapter, '*Somnium*', after a science-fiction fantasy which Kepler composes at intervals in his career.[13] *Somnium* is a story about a future visit to the moon in which Kepler tries to fictionalise some of his theories about force and gravity. In the final episode of Banville's novel, Kepler looks back on his writings:

None of his books had given him such peculiar pleasure as this one. It was as if some old strain of longing and love were at last being freed. The story of the boy Duracotus, and his mother Fiolxhilda the witch, and the strange sad stunted creatures of the moon, filled him with quiet inner laughter, at himself, at his science, at the mild foolishness of everything. (183)

The astronomer is secretly a novelist. His fabulous fiction, in which the man is transformed into a boy, and accompanied by his sorceress mother, is Kepler's most satisfying book because it harmonises the dream of childhood with the knowledge of adulthood. By 'childhood', Banville seems to suggest not so much the actual state itself, but a mode of vital perception. Kepler smiles at 'the mild foolishness of everything' because he realises the ultimate absurdity of trying to explain mystery. His imaginative side laughs at his rational side to see how long it took to recognise what was simply there. He also smiles because now he remembers that so many examples of this truth were already revealed to him in different forms. His old friend Wincklemann, for example, possessed this mystical knowledge:

> What was it the Jew said? Everything is told us, but nothing explained. Yes. We must take it all on trust. That's the secret. How simple! He smiled. It was not a mere book that was thus thrown away, but the foundation of a life's work. It seemed not to matter. (185)

Kepler has found a strange paradoxical consolation: loss is transformed into a new certainty, and ignorance suddenly seems full of renewed significance.

Put abstractly, *Kepler* is about an epistemological tug-of-war between two kinds of knowledge, the imaginative and the intellectual, the poetic and the scientific. Kepler harmonises old and new forms of understanding, opening up original modes of perception based on ancient faith in a harmonious universe. Though he dismisses the use of astrology for political ends, Kepler believes in the heavenly influence of the stars upon humanity; he also believes passionately in the new science of physical astronomy which promises knowledge based upon reason and observation. Ultimately, his knowledge is part of the emergent Enlightenment, as much a contribution to humankind's expanded perception as a triumph of self-understanding.

Although Kepler is attracted towards two very different kinds of knowledge, he is never stranded between them. Whereas Copernicus is represented as a scientist without faith or love, Kepler is a most sociable hero. This quality gives the second novel in the tetralogy a very different effect. In *Doctor Copernicus,* Banville had to represent a largely negative character and outlook; in *Kepler,* he can celebrate a human as well as a scientific achievement, and relate both to a poetic form of seeing the world. Because of its central character, *Kepler* is a simpler, less tortured, more lyrical novel, whose playful sense of harmony and design is directly inspired by its subject. Copernicus and Kepler, we might say, represent the most dynamic version of opposites in Banville's fiction so far. Like Michael and Gabriel in *Birchwood,* these twin-figures of imagination complement each other's vision: together, they complete this stage of Banville's epic story about the creative struggle between science and poetry.

6

The Newton Letter

History is nothing more than the belief in the senses, the belief in falsehood.

Friedrich Nietzsche, Twilight of the Idols

AFTER THE epic scale of *Doctor Copernicus* and *Kepler*, the next part of Banville's tetralogy has a very different, but not entirely unfamiliar, character. *The Newton Letter* (1982), subtitled An Interlude, is a novella which attempts a contemporary version of the astronomical theme, and which includes one of Banville's most intriguing intertextual dramas. In several ways, it represents a relaxation of the historical structure of the original design, and a return to certain features of Banville's earlier fiction, notably the Irish landscape of the Big House genre.[1] Historically and chronologically, however, it develops the story of the intellectual revolution begun by Copernicus and Kepler, now culminating in the work of Isaac Newton (1642–1727), whose discoveries in the fields of gravity and optics were strongly based on Kepler's achievement. With Newton, the great humanistic alliance between imagination and reason is concluded.

The 'Letter' in the novella's title is based on a biographical incident which Banville uses and reinterprets in order to complete his gallery of 'those high cold heroes who renounced the world and human happiness to pursue the big game of the intellect'. In September 1693, after months of silence, Newton had sent a paranoid letter to his former friend, the philosopher John Locke, containing wild accusations of betrayal and conspiracy.[2] A reconciliation followed, but Newton thereafter abandoned science. The reasons for this nervous collapse and loss of faith are scripted by Banville's second 'Letter', a borrowing from

Hugo von Hofmannsthal's classic fiction 'Ein Brief', in which Lord Chandos explains to Francis Bacon the reasons for his inability to continue writing.[3] This second letter is used to explain the first, and suggests that the imaginative and intellectual crisis has been caused by a dramatic and critical change of vision, a revelation which recalls the earlier crises of faith expressed by Copernicus and Kepler. As with the first two astronomers, Banville has reshaped the historical character of his protagonist in order to create a subjective conflict between scientific knowledge and artistic perception. Many of the facts are already there, awaiting selection: the novelist replaces them in a new fictional context which intensifies the personal drama behind speculative accounts of experience.

The novella takes the form of an autobiographical memoir addressed to Clio, the Muse of History. Told by an anonymous biographer of Newton, it relates the short and painful events of his stay in County Wexford, while trying to write his book. A personal crisis forces him to abandon his research. Everything is transformed by this personal trauma: biography becomes autobiography; detached scholarship becomes an anguished confession. By another trick of time and imagination, the biographer's fate mirrors that of his seventeenth-century subject. The title of the novella becomes an ambiguous message about the powerful influence of the imagined past on the present.

Looking back on more innocent times, the narrator-scholar recalls his arrival in Ferns, County Wexford, where he sought peace and privacy in order to write his study of Newton. He rents accommodation from the Lawless family, Charlotte, Ottilie and Edward, owners of a run-down Big House. Delighted by the calm and grace of these apparently typical Protestant landowners, who have style if not money, he looks forward to a rural idyll while researching his *magnum opus*. This plan is soon confused by his growing intimacy with the family. A child, Michael, also appears in the house. The narrator remembers being baffled by the precise relationship between the four residents. Despite a lustful affair with Ottilie, he secretly yearns for Charlotte. Edward turns out to be a former nurseryman on the estate, not a brother, while Michael belongs to none of them, having been adopted. Other mortifying discoveries follow: the Lawlesses are, in fact, Catholic not Protestant, and Edward's strangeness is the result of a terminal disease, not of shyness. No longer trusting his assumptions, frustrated in love, bewildered and saddened by the mysteries of this strange household where appearances always trick him out of confidence and belief, the biographer decides to abandon both his research and the country. Instead of returning to Cambridge, he finds a new post in Finland, a place more congenial to his chastened heart. The novella, one in which the ambiguous relationship between historical and fictional letters creates the narrator's sense of textual crisis, ends with the recollection of a final letter, this time from Ottilie to the failed biographer, telling him of her unexpected pregnancy. Reading this news, the narrator ends his tale with a mixture of hope and dread for the future, drawing to a close this confession of intellectual breakdown and imaginative hope.

In form and style, *The Newton Letter* breaks with the narrative pattern of the tetralogy and recalls the more personalised, subjective account by Gabriel Godkin in *Birchwood*. In quite a daring synthesis, Banville has produced a Big House version of the scientific mind. The Lawless family signals this adaptation of an Irish setting and genre to the scientific theme. The plot reveals other familiar correspondences between the two fictions: the enigma of actual family relations as opposed to the narrator's original assumptions about them; the presence of Michael, 'unbending, silent, inviolably private'; and a final sense of the inadequacy of the text itself. On a thematic level, as Geert Lernout suggests, *The Newton Letter* 'answers the questions formulated in *Birchwood*'.[4]

Despite these correspondences with *Birchwood*, the novella has a narrator who is an unprecedented type – the academic. As a disillusioned scholar, he tries to recall the reasons for a loss of faith in what he calls 'the primacy of text'. This gives his recollections an ironic tension and self-conscious unease, a manner which mocks his earlier personality:

> I'm confused. I feel ridiculous and melodramatic, and comically exposed. I have shinned up to this high perch and can't see how to get down, and of the spectators below, some are embarrassed and the rest are about to start laughing.[5]

After seven years of writing his biography of Newton, the narrator no longer believes in the value or the meaning of his interpretation. In an uncanny way, he is re-enacting the story of his own book and turning into his subject. This is why there are two alternating tales in the novella: the one set in contemporary Ireland, the other a biographical recreation of Newton's crisis of belief. Wiser now, the narrator realises that the original separation of thought and experience which led to

Newton's mental breakdown is precisely his own problem. Like the great scientist, Banville's narrator experiences the revolt of language against his ego, and is left with a childlike sense of wonder at the mystery of ordinary experience and everyday phenomena. Before reaching that state, however, he singles out his own profession for its deadening use of language. Receiving a copy of another biography of Newton, by an enthusiastic colleague named Popov, the narrator contemplates the stereotype:

> I met him once, an awful little man with ferret eyes and a greasy suit. Reminded me of an embalmer. Which, come to think of it, is apt. I like his disclaimer: *Before the phenomenon of Isaac Newton, the historian, like Freud when he came to contemplate Leonardo, can only shake his head and retire with as much good grace as he can muster.* That is what I was doing too, embalming old N.'s big corpse, only I *did* have the grace to pop off before the deathshead grin was properly fixed. (29)

This derisive caricature of the scholar, contemptuous and witty, captures the narrator's sense of guilt and relief. Glad to be deceived no longer (or so he likes to believe) by the foolishness of a certain kind of intellectualism, he is now writing a very different sort of story which will try to recover the personal experience that was responsible for his disillusionment. This time, he will have the advantage of a sceptical self-knowledge. A similar kind of narrative strategy and hope characterises Gabriel Godkin's efforts in *Birchwood*.

Apart from the digressions on Newton and the biographical study, most of the story is about tragic and confusing flirtations with Ottilie and Charlotte. The experience of that summer in Ferns is described as a series of shocks and revelations which were always unpredictable and usually shameful. The academic's early confidence of thought and action is repeatedly undermined by people and relationships whose appearance is totally misleading. Nothing, it seems, was every entirely innocent. Formerly, the scholar thought of himself as the hero of a romantic drama; now he realises that he was only the dunce in a farce. Writing about that experience of confusion, his retrospective story tries to suggest the strangeness of that past, an unreal quality best described through literary analogies of a contrived and pre-scripted art:

> Then I would see Charlotte herself, in wellingtons and an old cardigan, hauling out a bucket of feed to the henhouse. Next comes Ottilie, in a sleepy trance, with the child by the hand. He is off to school. He carries his satchel like a hunchback's hump. Edward is last, I am at work before

I spy him about his mysterious business. It all has the air of a pastoral mime, with the shepherd's wife and the shepherd, and Cupid and the maid, and, scribbling within a crystal cave, myself, a haggard-eyed Damon. (20)

Recollection becomes a literary fiction filled with familiar conventional types acting out prescribed parts. At one point, the narrator recalls rushing along the lawn with Ottilie after the child has had an accident – 'We must have looked like an illustration from a Victorian novelette, marching forward across the swallow-swept lawn.' Ottilie's parents, killed in a car accident, are described as 'a kind of Scott and Zelda, beautiful and doomed'. All these fictive analogies create a dream-like quality in the narrator's account of the past, and suggest the crucial and melodramatic role of fancy in shaping and defining experience. He now realises that he invented a version of the Lawlesses which was merely a second-rate fiction. All the time thinking he knew what was going on, he now knows that his patronising image of the family deluded him into a series of interpretations which only served to expose his vanity and ignorance. Pastoral fictions were part of a secret design in which he unwittingly played a prescribed role. He now suspects that even 'the unbroken fine summer weather was a part of the plot'. Ordinary experience has taught him the lesson of his life, and humbled his conceit.

The narrator recalls being assailed by unanswerable questions about the exact relationship between the Lawlesses, especially the question of the child who, like a malevolent Cupid in this demented romance, never says a word. At first he thought Michael was Ottilie's child, then Charlotte's. Did Edward seduce the young Ottilie? Why, then, is he sleeping with Charlotte? Only now does the narrator appreciate Edward's loneliness, his 'sense of oneness with all poor dumb things'. It turns out that most of his suspicions about this incestuous family are sensational and groundless. He also discovers that Edward used to write poetry, but that, like the scholar and the scientist, he has abandoned the work . The three men no longer believe in the value of narrative (even though the narrator of the novella goes to the trouble of writing a story about the pointlessness of having written a story).

Loneliness is also the source of Ottilie's affair with the biographer. Initially very passionate, the relationship starts to cool when the narrator realises that he has confused the two women (an entity he calls 'Charlottilie') and that he secretly lusts after Charlotte.[6] No longer working on his book, he becomes fascinated by 'this spawning of multiple selves' and hypnotised by the 'daily minutiae' of the little drama in the enclosed world of Ferns. One part of him continues the physical affair with Ottilie, while the other fantasises about Charlotte. The sexual flirtation soon palls, and his treatment of Ottilie becomes cruel and cold. His longing for Charlotte is really a form of vanity, since he sees himself as a gallant intruder, rescuing her from an alcoholic Edward. After a while, strongly assisted by a lurid imagination, he begins to sense a latent madness in the family:

> They were altered, the way someone you have known all your life will be altered after appearing, all menace and maniacal laughter, in a half-remembered dream. Up to now they had been each a separate entity. I hadn't thought of them as husband and wife, mother, son, niece, aunt – aunt! – but now suddenly they were a family, a closed, mysterious organism. (67)

As in previous fictions, Banville tries to convey a primitive and sinister sense of mystery behind conventional facades. Following a crisis, the everyday and the familiar, when contemplated so intensely, seem frighteningly significant. It is as if Nature had been spying on the biographer all the time. This is the eerie feeling expressed at the opening of the narrative when he recalls the trip past Killiney on the train down to Wexford. Details and images of the landscape then seemed unremarkable, but now he believes that they colluded in a well-orchestrated deception. 'Such remembered scraps', he writes, 'seem to me abounding in significance. They are at once commonplace and unique, like clues at the scene of a crime.' This analogy captures perfectly the bizarre quality of his experience and later revelation: the observer becomes the observed. His world is alive with signs and meanings, an animate significance undreamt of by intellect.

The fictional conceit played out in *The Newton Letter* is one whereby the biographer's mental crisis one summer in Wexford has already been scripted by Newton's similar breakdown in the summer of 1693 at Cambridge. Without realising it, the historian was looking at a prefiguration of his own fate. This strange coincidence of roles, by which a historical fiction reappears in a new and most unlikely setting, chills the biographer's heart because it suggests a subtlety of design and purpose he had never imagined. This is the point at which the alternating narratives of the story coincide, and the scholar sees himself reflected in Newton's plight. Earlier detachment from his research is now replaced by a feeling that the history book he has been writing is undergoing a metamorphosis into a strange kind of disguised auto-biography.

This is the revelation of Newton's second, wholly fictional letter to which the biographer keeps returning. His own commentary, alive with a growing sense of something familiar, reflects on the details of Newton's crisis:

> But then suddenly he is talking about the excursions he makes nowa-days along the banks of the Cam, and of his encounters, not with the great men of the college, but with tradesmen, the sellers and the mak-ers of things. (59)

Newton tries to explain to Locke that the ordinary sensuous world seems to be addressing him, but in a language without words. After the scientific exploration of absolutes of time, space and motion, he suddenly feels that relative human truths are much more mysterious. Once he senses that the common world of experience contains this alternative, cryptic significance, Newton writes:

3 Diego Velázquez, *The Toilet of Venus* (c. 1648)

> *My dear Doctor, expect no more philosophy from my pen. The language in which I might be able not only to write but to think is neither Latin nor English, but a language none of whose words is known to me; a language in which commonplace things speak to me; and wherein I may one day have to justify myself before an unknown judge.* Then comes that cold, that brave, that almost carven signature: *Newton.* (59)

This literary echo of Hofmannsthal,[7] grafted onto his historical fiction about Newton's crisis, completes Banville's tale about the scientist, while suggesting an epistemological reason for the biographer's change of heart. Through these lines from Hofmannsthal, themselves a twentieth-century postmodernist fiction about seventeenth-century philosophy, the novella suddenly assumes a self-reflexive character, a rhetorical hesitancy, which is at the heart of contemporary fiction. The crisis, not surprisingly, is about language. Once it suffers from such profound suspicion, expression is never quite the same again. This is, of course, Banville's favourite territory, one in which that sense of dislocation and separation between words and experience struggles for fictional harmony. Artistically, if this mystery is to remain mysterious, then the nature of the revelation that follows the disillusionment with language must remain rhetorical and assertive. A new faith, even if it concedes the inadequacy of words, or the superiority of silence, must be proclaimed through language.

The biographer, finally exiled in the cold North, and now corresponding with Ottilie, comes to enjoy some kind of compensatory hope after the débâcle in Wexford. Simply to fail and despair is never the pattern of resolution in Banville's fiction. Disillusionment, especially with language, always reveals an alternative, usually richer, way of seeing and writing. When the biographer hears from Ottilie that she is pregnant with his child, he experiences a unique sense of elation mixed with fear. The idea of a child gives him a feeling of inexpressible wonder at human accident and design. Like Kepler, he feels creative and almost certain of immortality, summing up this novel sensation through Rilke's line 'Supernumerous existence wells up in my heart'.[8] He even imagines himself as a woman, as someone who carries a new prospect for the future – 'I am pregnant myself, in a way.' Such lyrical joy, we are made to feel, has been earned out of confusion and deception. It is all the more authentic in a context where such desperate hope is always mindful of the probability of destruction:

Yet I'm wary. Shall I have to go off again, leaving my research, my book
and everything else unfinished? Shall I awake in a few months, in a few
years, broken and deceived, in the midst of new ruins? (92)

Hope, qualified by fearful experience, and terror, softened by memories of joy, hold between them the ambivalent experience typical of
Banville's characters. Like Kepler, the persona in *The Newton Letter* is
too maimed by experience to be naive, but is also too imaginative to
despair.

In Newton, Banville found and exploited a pattern of experience,
from intellectual achievement to a chastened innocence, which is a
major theme of the tetralogy so far. That pattern is proclaimed in the
novella's famous epigraph about playing as a boy on the seashore,
'whilst the great ocean of truth lay all undiscovered before me'.[9] The
story of Copernicus ended with the linden tree of his childhood;
Kepler's last work was a fantasy about a boy and his mother travelling
to the moon. Newton's anecdote reinforces this motif of innocence
after experience. Even the biographer, in his foolishness, 'felt briefly
like a child, pressing his face against the cold unyielding pane of adult
knowingness'. This is a pattern of experience and perception based on
a paradoxical version of rational development. Even though most of
Banville's writers question the value of their intellectual sanity or
achievement, the stories should not be construed as anti-intellectual or
in any way scornful of scientific ambition and curiosity. Only such
adventurous minds, allied to imaginative character, can fully appreciate the limits of intellect so intensely.

In a wider context, *The Newton Letter* has a special significance in the
self-conscious way it reflects upon, and engages with, one of the major
theoretical and philosophical issues of late – twentieth-century literary
criticism – the deconstruction of rationalist metanarratives, the decen-
tring of totalising systems of knowledge and enquiry. This is a small fiction about grandiose theory. Both Geert Lernout and Brian McIlroy
have pointed out that the tetralogy in general, and *The Newton Letter*
in particular, may be read as artistic versions of Thomas Kuhn's theory
of 'paradigm change'.[10] Kuhn (whose studies of the scientific revolution
are acknowledged by Banville as key sources for *Doctor Copernicus*)
sees the history of modern science in terms of conceptual frameworks,
or 'paradigms', which characterise momentous changes in perspective
and understanding. When a conceptual crisis occurs, the inherited paradigm may be reworked, or dismissed, or replaced by a revolutionary
paradigm which radically upsets a traditional world-view. This dialec-

tical account of the world of scientific knowledge and progress, which is essentially concerned with challenges to the rationalist world-view of the Enlightenment, provides Banville with an artistic paradigm of his own, one which addresses a contemporary sense of loss and dis-illusion as the result of these challenges to all-embracing systems of knowledge. Most of Banville's characters are orphans of a post-Enlightenment world which, in Georg Lukács's phrase, 'has been aban-doned by God'.[11] The loss of old certainties and securities in the scientific world finds a contemporary and sympathetic echo in Banville's tetralogy, where, in McIlroy's apt phrase, 'the humbling of the intellectual' is the principal motif. This challenge to the vanity of the male intellect is not a purely academic one, or at least not one which is presented or felt in purely intellectual terms. The sense of loss and disappointment which marks the stories in the tetralogy reflects the subject's sense of a divided self, one which devoted an excess of reason to a project which deprives that self of some essential sense of humanity. In *The Newton Letter*, the academic historian loses all faith in 'the primacy of text', and does so in a narrative which emphasises his emotional and sexual illiteracy as much as his intellectual confusion.

As an 'Interlude', *The Newton Letter* is a leisurely, stylish episode in the demanding scale of the tetralogy. Although certain forms and themes will be familiar, the novelty lies in its economy, its sustained mood of hypnotised fascination with images of the past and – an often unacknowledged element in Banville's fiction – its sly humour.

7

Mefisto

Writing may not really be able to give voice to utter desolation, to the nullity of life, to those moments when it is simply a void, privation and horror. The mere fact of writing in some way fills that void, gives it form, makes the horror of it communicable and therefore, even if minimally, triumphs over it.

Claudio Magris, *Danube*

MEFISTO (1986) presents us with a strange resolution to Banvilles tetralogy. A reader who has followed this extended narrative of the scientific imagination, which began a decade beforehand with *Doctor Copernicus*, will inevitably have developed expectations of style and theme. This is especially true of the historical dimension of the series, including *The Newton Letter*, despite the novella's disarming subtitle of *An Interlude*. So far, much of the authority and fascination of these fictions lies with the recreation of famed, historical genius. However, as Banville himself has remarked, such a framework was invented to serve his own themes, and not simply to give us a historical fiction obedient to fact.[1]

As a coda to the tetralogy, *Mefisto* retains many familiar motifs and dramatises them, not in the world of Renaissance humanism but, as in *The Newton Letter*, in modern Ireland. This time, Banville has chosen not to centre his fiction on a name associated with creative genius: rather, *Mefisto* is a demonic and mythological conclusion to a series dominated by the Faustian legend.[2] Finally, after three tales of frustrated ambition and paradoxical achievement, it is the turn of that malevolent character behind the pitiful hero to assert his power over human enterprise.

The novel takes the form of a Proustian recollection by a single narrator, Gabriel Swan. In many ways his story recalls *Birchwood* rather than the series which it is supposed to conclude.[3] Swan's story, a phantasmagoric blend of memory and fantasy, is about his survival. It tells of his strange childhood as a mathematical prodigy who escapes from home and rural boredom into a world of bizarre and freakish companions, then experiences appalling suffering and isolation, clings desperately to a dream of love and order, and is finally reduced to writing what he calls this 'black book', in order to reach some understanding of his wreckage. The only obvious features of the novel which confirm its place in the tetralogy are the boy's mathematical prowess (a gift which is never fully explored) and the legendary title-character who eventually appears under the perverse soubriquet of Felix. Whatever Banville's intentions, *Mefisto* retains a symbolic rather than a substantial connection with its 'scientific' predecessors. As a tortured memoir of childhood, it echoes the form of *Birchwood*; as a bizarre adventure, it resembles the fictional contrivances of *Nightspawn*. No matter how we classify or categorise it (always a tempting exercise with such a parodic and intertextual writer as Banville), *Mefisto* is an eclectic blend of the familiar and the original.

The motif of twins or a twinned identity reappears as the central image of the novel, just as it did in *Birchwood*.[4] Whether as contrast or opposition, this idea of a split or dualistic personality, forever at war with itself, is also at the heart of the Faustian legend. Banville uses this traditional drama of the sundered personality to develop a distinctively modern sense of isolation and alienation. In *Mefisto* he develops the motif to suggest a fateful, inherited and deterministic pattern of chance and design. Swan's memoir begins, as did Godkin's, with his foetal existence:

> I don't know when it was that I first heard of the existence, if that's the word, of my dead brother. From the start I knew I was the survivor of some small catastrophe, the shock-waves were still reverberating faintly inside me ... The perils we missed were many. We might have been siamese. One of us might have exsanguinated into the other's circulation. Or we might simply have strangled one another. All this we escaped, and surfaced at last, gasping. I came first. My brother was a poor second. Spent swimmer, he drowned in air.[5]

This gestation and birth, a contradiction between design and chance, cleverly provides Swan's tale with an opening myth of original and fundamental mystery based on hazard. Existence then becomes an extension of that opening trauma, a life characterised by inexplicable and precarious survival. Swan's entire narrative preserves this distinctive sense of shock and fascination. His quest is not, like that of Godkin, for a lost half, but for the significance of the numerical order behind such a random and schizoid existence: his interest is impersonal, one in search of a Newtonian order behind seeming arbitrariness.

The motif of twins also accounts for the story's obsession with 'freaks of nature', a phrase which captures both the original marvel and Banville's method of characterisation. At school, the young Swan is mesmerised by another pair of twins, especially by 'the thought of being able to escape effortlessly, as if by magic, into another name, another self'. Feeling part of this exotic brotherhood explains his preoccupation with, and subsequent gift for, numbers:

> I remember a toy abacus that I treasured for years, with multi coloured wooden beads, and a wooden frame, and little carved feet for it to stand on. My party piece was to add up large numbers instantly in my head, frowning, a hand to my brow, my eyes downcast. It was not the manipulation of things that pleased me, the mere facility, but the sense of order I felt, of harmony, of symmetry and completeness.(19)

How or why the phenomenon of twins should lead to such an interest is a less convincing part of Gabriel's character than his extraordinary receptivity towards the grotesque and the odd. This attraction is a predetermined curiosity towards wondrous creatures who allow him to forget his ordinary existence and to indulge his rare imagination.

Gabriel's narrative is in two complementary parts, 'Marionettes' and 'Angels', the first based on innocence and wonder, the second on pain and horror. In a fashion similar to but less stereotyped than that of *Birchwood*, it recalls a familiar kind of anguished family surrounding a stubbornly silent child. Mathematical fantasies are the child's only escape from an embittered mother and an indifferent father. Bored by school and home, Gabriel accidentally encounters the weird new inhabitants of the local Big House in Ashburn, an exotic trio whose influence on him proves to be fatal. The first of these is Mr Kasperl, a large, sinister, ruminative Faust, who surveys the local countryside for some shady mining company. Like so many of Banville's characters, he is strikingly bisexual in appearance, with an 'odd womanly walk, at once ponderous and mincing'. With Kasperl is a young woman called Sophie, a deaf and dumb beauty whose silent grace and playfulness contrast pointedly with her restless, unnerving companion. The third member of this outlandish group is Felix, the actual 'Mefisto' of the novel, and one of its most convincing characters. When first recalled, Felix resembles something between a cartoon villain and a tramp:

> He was thin, with a narrow foxy face and high cheek-bones and a long tapering jaw. His skin was pale as paper, his hair a vivid red. He wore a shabby pinstriped suit, that had been tailored for someone more robust than he, and a grimy white shirt without a collar. (35–6)

Felix is the diabolical medium of the story, a mocking and sadistic tempter who persuades young Gabriel to join the bizarre company in the cavernous interior of Ashburn House. In contrast to his fictional cousin, Godkin, this Gabriel escapes *into* the decaying world of the Big House, an omen of the disaster which awaits him.

For the rest of 'Marionettes', the narrative is more concerned with recollected perceptions and impressions of these characters than with events and episodes which develop the story. Kasperl, who never says a word, spends all of his time writing out elaborate mathematical equations which are, or seem to be, part of his mining project. Gabriel is enthralled by this fellow sorcerer – 'But his was a grandmaster game, and I was a novice. Such intricacy, such elegance!' Sophie seems to him as mysterious as the hieroglyphics in Kasperl's book: 'She communicated in an airy, insubstantial language consisting not of words but moving forms, transparent, yet precise and sharp, like glass shapes in air.' Her silence seems a gift rather than a defect, a choice which intensifies her awareness and responsiveness. Felix is always a malicious but witty presence around this childlike couple, ever ready with ironic literary captions for their silent, hypnotic alliance. He dubs them 'Hansel and Gretel', refers to Sophie as Keats's 'still unravished bride of quietness', and to Gabriel, ominously, as 'bird-boy'. Like a fiendish jester, he is forever playing some contrived role, speaking mostly through literary quotation and pun. His names for Gabriel include Malvolio, Icarus, Caliban, Castor, Philomen and Melmoth, names which both define and anticipate Gabriel's search for a new identity. Names in *Mefisto*, as in all of Banville's previous novels, have a deliberately contrived, mythical or allusive significance in order to emphasise a character's frank sense of unreality and artificiality.[6] Gabriel's recognition of this sense of fictive manipulation occurs in a scene when Sophie arranges a game of toy-marionettes for the boy, giving each of the figurines a familiar face in miniature. Gabriel contemplates the lifelike puppets:

I thought of the marionettes, twitching on their strings, striving to be human, their glazed grins, the way they held out their arms, stiffly, imploringly. Such eagerness, such longing. I understood them, I, poor Pinocchio, counting and capering, trying to be real. (118)

Only uncanny metaphors like these speechless toys correspond to Gabriel's sense of unreality. This same sense of fictional recognition is expressed in his love of fairy-tales in which 'there was something dismayingly familiar ... the mad logic, the discontinuities, the random cruelty of fate'. This observation captures well the design and ambition of *Mefisto* itself.

4 After Nicolas Poussin, *Sleeping Nymphs Surprised by Satyrs* (c. 1640)

Gabriel comes to realise that Felix has pimped Sophie and himself for Kasperl's sensual and intellectual requirements. The mining project, however, meets with disaster when the pits explode without warning. The townspeople turn against the strange outsiders and Felix announces his abrupt departure, while assuring Gabriel that they will meet again. The boy, now abandoned by his new family, wanders back to Ashburn House to contemplate the marionettes once more. Suddenly, an inferno overwhelms the house and Gabriel remembers falling through the flames. Whether the fire was accidental or the result of local revenge is ambiguous.

The second section of the novel, 'Angels', recalls Gabriel's horrific return from immolation to a barely human existence. In the opening pages of this nightmarish episode, he details the pain of his new life as a physical freak:

> Scorched hands, scorched back, shins charred to the bone. Bald, of course. And my face. My face. A wad of living dough, blotched and bubbled, with clown's nose, no chin, two watery little eyes peering out in disbelief. (125)

Gabriel has become a monstrous marionette himself, at the mercy of the 'ministering angels' in the hospital, human and medical. He survives through pain-killers, which he calls collectively *Lamia*, the deceptive serpent-woman of Keats's mythological poem. If 'Marionettes' represents an innocent, vulnerable way of seeing the world, then 'Angels' reveals that same world in permanent darkness and pain. Gabriel, like Andreas in *Doctor Copernicus*, is now reborn as a grotesque. In his first existence, he was a freak of biological chance; now he is a deformed casualty of human circumstance. There is a nightmarish pattern to his lonely existence, sadistic and unpredictable. One day he wanders into the maternity ward and studies the new-born babes, 'prune-faced mites in their plastic coats', and recognises himself. Once he has recovered enough mobility to walk, he is turned out into the unknown and unexperienced world of the metropolis. Like the babes, he has just been released into reality but, unlike them, he has already suffered its madness.

The pattern of events and the nature of characters in 'Angels' are very similar to those in 'Marionettes'. The only significant difference is that now the city becomes a surrealistic underworld in which Gabriel finds new, and some old, friends.

He first meets the ubiquitous Felix, who recognises Gabriel

instantly, remarking breezily, 'I never forget a face.' Felix then introduces the boy into a company almost identical to that of Ashburn
House. A wizened old professor, Kosok, yet another reincarnation of
Faust, is in charge of a scheme which illegally uses a fabulous computer to investigate a project whose objective is never really explained.
Felix, as before, 'procures' Gabriel to assist Kosok in this mathematical
labyrinth. They are then joined by Adele, a sorrowful junkie (who, we
are told much later, is Kosok's daughter), and a motley assortment of
types drawn from the seedy, outrageous world of drug-trafficking and
industrial espionage. Gabriel offers two valuable gifts to this underworld – his unlimited supply of drugs from the hospital and his passion
for mathematical enigma.

The plot of this section, like those of Gabriel's fairy-tales, is random
in the extreme. As in a fun-fair ghost-tunnel, freakish and lurid figures
simply pop up and, disappear, never to be seen again. The most coherent part of the narrative concerns Gabriel's painful new sensitivity to
the world about him, where 'everything was new and yet unaccount-
ably familiar'. He has a farcical affair with Adele, who offers him physical intimacy in exchange for drugs. The search for mathematical
harmonies turns out to be as frustrating as the search for love. Kosok's
computer fails to yield up any of its abstract secrets, notwithstanding
Gabriel's ingenuity. Months go by with Gabriel silently drifting
between the unobtainable and the inexplicable. The climax of this
fruitless activity occurs one evening when, in a bar full of addicts to
whom he ministers, Gabriel decides to step outside the claustrophobic
frenzy in order to reflect on his situation:

> Then suddenly I was outside in the cold black glossy night, under an
> amazement of stars. I could smell the pines, and hear the wind rushing
> in their branches. My head swam. Something surged within me, yearn-
> ing outwards into the darkness. And all at once I saw again clearly the
> secret I had lost sight of for so long, that chaos is nothing but an infinite
> number of ordered things. Wind, those stars, that water falling on
> stones, all the shifting, ramshackle world could be solved. (183)

This apparent revelation, identical in spirit and situation to that experienced by Godkin in the 'Air and Angels' section of *Birchwood*, is the
clearest link between *Mefisto* and the predominant theme of the tetralogy. Like Copernicus, Kepler and Newton, Swan realises that a certain
kind of abstraction has prevented him from seeing something simple
and obvious. Such a realisation must admit to itself, in hindsight, that
this perception is based on a deceptive paradox – 'the more I knew, the

less I seemed to understand'. Even Kosok, driven to his wits' end by the inscrutable machine, screams at his superiors in exasperation, 'You want certainty, order, all that? Then invent it!' Like his illustrious fictional predecessors, Gabriel can finally see the crucial and humiliating difference between system and purpose, methodology and ambition. Numbers, he realises, are a method, and not the end, of knowledge and understanding. In a familiar expression of resignation, he now sees that 'It was here, in the big world, that I would meet what I was waiting for.'

Other literary allusions and references echo the earlier novels on this theme, as when Gabriel half-quotes Kepler's ideal: 'I was after simplicity now, the pure, uncluttered thing.' Although Gabriel's relation to the astronomers is signalled by lines such as these, neither his character nor the narrative which expresses the development of that character is as convincing as the earlier versions of this ambitious fictional adventure.

The most effective and most original element of this part of the novel comes from Banville's precise poetic evocation of a disembodied malevolence which, like Felix, pursues and haunts Gabriel:

> The feeling was so strong I began to think I was being followed, as if really some flickering presence had materialized behind me. I would stop in the street and turn quickly, and at once everything would assume a studied air of innocence, the shopfronts and facades of houses looking suspiciously flat and insubstantial, like a hastily errected stage-set. (186)

Gabriel's imagination, released from fact and abstraction, now animates everything he sees. This paranoid sensitivity to the malevolent personality of the city is the price of that release, as if the spirit, if not the person, of Felix, were alive in the very brickwork of the seemingly inert metropolis. Personal tragedy and pain revolutionise the familiar world, making it at once exquisitely precious and remote. *Mefisto* is a radical example of Banville's way of mythologising the ordinary through a perception heightened by suffering.

Swan's narrative concludes by recalling a pattern of failure and tragedy which leaves him alone, like so many of Banville's narrators, with a haunted memory and a book to write. Kosok's computer scheme is abandoned, Adele dies from an overdose and Felix plans to move on from the debris he helped to invent. The macabre events in the city seem like a sadistic replay of Swan's earlier days at Ashburn. Writing about his suffering is not so much a consolation as an exorcism. Like Godkin, Swan is a refugee trying to recreate a life without meaning or compensation, and in a form doomed to misunderstanding. His fiction is just that, an imposition of fancy upon experience, inadequate but irresistible. Sensitive to the form of his narrative right up to the end, Gabriel acknowledges the control of his fiction over his experience: 'Have I tied up all the ends? Even an invented world has its rules, tedious, absurd perhaps, but not to be gainsaid.' Despite the grim pessimism of Gabriel's 'black book', a hesitant pledge is made in its final lines which recalls the novel's opening: 'In future, I will leave things, I will try to leave things, to chance.' Like *Birchwood, Mefisto* is a back-to-front account: its cryptic opening is a conclusion waiting to be demonstrated. The enclosed circular pattern of the memoir has a symmetry inspired by terrified doubt or, to put it in Gabriel's own terms, by a conviction that the seeming pattern of order is, on closer inspection, a conspiracy of chance and calamity. The meaning of Swan's story is foreshadowed by the phenomenon of twins, which, like his subsequent experience of the world, is a mysterious complicity of design and accident.

Mefisto, as I have tried to indicate, is a difficult and not wholly satisfying conclusion to Banvilles own imaginative design. Much of this problem lies with the character of Gabriel Swan. His precocious talent for mathematical speculation gives him an initial token association with the classic astronomers; but once the novel becomes a kind of intellectual horror story, this gift never develops, as it did in the previous fictions, into a consuming passion. Given the form of *Mefisto*, such latent genius has no place in which to develop. The encounters with Kasperl and Kosok show a fascinated child observer, but one who never actually works at his obsession. The painstaking drama of the astronomers' work never finds a corresponding force in *Mefisto*, whose 'scientific' theme is asserted but never fully realised. Looking back on the novel, Banville himself has expressed similar reservations about its form:

> A lot of things got into it that I didn't understand, but I let them stay. The book caused me terrible problems because I finished it with the technical problems unsolved. I didn't get the tone, but I was very proud of having finished it in spite of not solving the problems.[7]

It might be argued that Banville tried to write a very different kind of novel from the one which the tetralogy might have led us to expect, that he tried to retain the major themes of the scientific drama in a form which could not contain them. This is perhaps true, as *Mefisto* seems to have more in common with the introverted consciousness of *Nightspawn* than with any other work by Banville, especially in its gallery of human oddities, its reckless episodic plot, and a heavy, sometimes intrusive, framework of literary allusion. Both novels suffer from carefully planned obscurity. *Mefisto* has some wonderful moments, and Banville's descriptive style is as poetically precise and daring as ever, but overall the novel does not successfully blend the design of *Nightspawn* with the purpose of the tetralogy. It is, in some ways, too clever, perhaps a fictional victim of that mental complication which sometimes prevents Banville's characters themselves from expressing 'the pure, uncluttered thing'.

8

The Book of Evidence

But now crime has degraded me beneath the meanest animal. No guilt, no mischief, no malignity, no misery, can be found comparable to mine. When I run over the frightful catalogue of my sins, I cannot believe that I am the same creature whose thoughts were once filled with sublime and transcendent visions of the beauty and the majesty of goodness. But it is even so; the fallen angel becomes a malignant devil.

Mary Shelley, *Frankenstein*

FOR MANY who have followed the progress of Banville's literary career, The *Book of Evidence* still seems like the novelist's definitive, and most accomplished, fiction. After the formal and technical problems of *Mefisto*, here was a *tour de force* of the confessional imagination, a tale of a brutal murder told by the murderer, Freddie Montgomery, whose literary submission is held together by the intensity of his manic eloquence. In many ways, *The Book of Evidence* is the least complicated, the most concentrated, fiction yet created by Banville, depending for its effect and power upon a sustained dramatic monologue, a form already evident in the earlier fictions, but here achieving a quite unprecedented, and aesthetically satisfying, narrative coherence. The novel also achieved greater public recognition than anything Banville had written previously, winning what was, at the time, Europe's most lucrative literary prize, the Guinness Peat Aviation Award, and being shortlisted for Britain's most prestigious literary honour, the Booker Prize.

While *The Book of Evidence* certainly ranks high amongst Banville's 'supreme fictions', its plot was inspired by some brutal realities in contemporary Dublin involving a sensational murder case which had dramatic political consequences in Ireland. In July 1982, Malcolm

Macarthur, the son of a well-to-do family, murdered a young nurse, Bridie Gargan, in Dublin's Phoenix Park. Macarthur had wandered into the park, chanced to meet the young woman, and had then forced her into her own car, where he beat her senseless with a hammer. For several weeks, the police were completely baffled by what seemed like an unpremeditated crime against an innocent woman. Macarthur was eventually discovered staying at the home of the Irish Attorney-General. The government of the day, led by Charles J. Haughey, was scandalised by this unlikely, and inexplicable, link between a murderer and the highest law officer in the land. Haughey, in a phrase which came to haunt his government (and which might apply with equal force to the behaviour of Freddie Montgomery), described the whole affair as 'grotesque, unbelievable, bizarre and unprecedented'. Macarthur was arrested, charged, convicted of the murder, and then sentenced to life with penal servitude; at the trial, he pleaded guilty to the charge.[1]

Banville's attraction towards these events lies almost exclusively with the mind and motivation of the murderer. Macarthur, it was revealed at the trial, had deceived many people in Dublin society through a series of fictions about his past and pedigree. Acting the part of a cultured man-about-town, a gentleman of leisure, he had relied, successfully, on appearances to ingratiate himself with Dublin's upper middle classes. In Banville's translation of Macarthur, Freddie Montgomery recalls his theatrical talent as one of his defining characteristics – 'What an actor the world has lost in me!' – a talent which enabled him to survive for so long, and which eventually destroyed his slender understanding of the real world.

The entire narrative in *The Book of Evidence* is controlled by Freddie and his eloquent, often hallucinatory, imagination. This is Freddie's (and Banville's) best performance so far, one in which he reveals, not only his split personality, but a remarkable ability to hold and sustain the attention of his fictive audience through an intense, menacing and poetical appeal. In certain respects, Freddie is the refined issue of several of Banville's earlier narrators who possess the same compulsive need to share their disturbing tale, a postmodern version of the Ancient Mariner. Seamus Deane has noted the typicality, as well as the originality, of Freddie's character:

> He has many of the characteristics of a Banville 'hero' – morally delinquent, neurasthenically sensitive, astray in the hall of mirrors he calls his consciousness, a connoisseur of his own emotions and a despoiler of those of others.[2]

The challenge behind Freddie's rhetorical performance is to acknowledge his depravity in a style which forces us to consider an aesthetic
rather than a moral assessment of that depravity. This is a murderer
with style. Always the charmer, this killer hopes to persuade us that
conventional morality cannot begin to imagine the refinement of his
wickedness, that the law cannot find a language that would do justice
to the bestiality of his imagination. Freddie's script promises to be the
ultimate self-indictment, wherein we may observe, from an intrigued
but safe distance, the aesthetic dimension of the criminal mind.

The Book of Evidence, like Camus's The Outsider, explores an evil personality and the personality of Evil. Both novels are based on the
casual murder of an innocent, and both allow the murderer to confess
much more than his guilt: in Banville's novel, the murderer openly
attributes the horrific deed to a failure of his imagination. Freddie's
passionate script, written to illustrate, not explain, is similar to that by
Gabriel Godkin in Birchwood, a memoir to banish ghosts and to console him in his refuge. Above all, Freddie's disillusionment with
scientific knowledge (he had earlier embarked upon, then abandoned,
a career in science), and his belated wonder at the beauty and mystery
of the phenomenal world, draw on the thematic legacy of the astronomical tetralogy. However, these similarities to earlier and other fictions do not explain the novel's most distinctive and original
embellishment – painting as a metaphor for Nature's speechless and
deceptive familiarity.

Freddie's imagination is obsessively pictorial, and his crime, he
would have us believe, is the result of his preference for Art over Life,
for a woman in a painting whose aesthetic fascination blinded him to
the life of the woman he murdered. Banville's earlier narrators were
always enraptured by images of women, actual or fantastical; in The
Book of Evidence the male imagination once again reveals its fixation
with dream-like women, but this time it places them firmly in the aesthetic realm of pictorial art. Freddie's elaborate narrative turns out to
be an interpretation of a painting.[3]

The narrative takes the form of a prison-memoir written to account
for his identity and crime, a tale to be placed alongside what he calls
the 'official fictions' about his deed. Throughout the novel, Banville
tries to give the illusion of spontaneous composition to his narrator's
fictional script, with Freddie ever sensitive to the misinterpretation of
his story by judge, jury and what he sneeringly refers to as 'amateur
psychologists'. He repeatedly expresses weariness with his own inven-

tion, even disgust, but is determined to see what his past might offer. The nostalgic structure of his evidence involves much more than simple motivation or culpability: now imprisoned like some 'exotic animal', he offers an imaginative autobiography of a man who foolishly believed in freedom.

The style of his story intensifies the artificial character of the imagined past, as if he could now see that he had always been an unwitting actor in a version of his life scripted by someone else. In ways which recall *Nightspawn*, the novel's memory reaches back to a holiday which Freddie and his wife, Daphne, spent on a Mediterranean island, enjoying a way of life which encouraged illusions. In a witty and amusing scenario full of cinematic stereotypes, Freddie recalls his casual and fatal involvement with the drug underworld. Blackmailed by a local baron, he returns home to find the money he owes to a syndicate. A dream-like voyage takes him back to Ireland, where he immediately sets off to his ancestral home, the Big House estate at Coolgrange, a family ruin inhabited by his distracted mother. In a series of drunken, operatic confrontations, he discovers that she cannot help him financially, having sold all the valuable paintings that formerly graced the walls of the house. Rejected by his mother and haunted by the memory of his perversely eccentric father, he feels that his dilemma resembles that 'same old squabble: money and betrayal'. But he quickly finds out that the paintings have passed through the hands of a wealthy neighbouring family, the Behrens, and he makes a frantic visit to retrieve his fancied inheritance. While wandering around the house, he is fascinated by one particular painting, a Dutch portrait of a woman. He returns the next day and, in the act of stealing the painting, is interrupted by a young maid, Josie Bell, whom he abducts. Soon after, he beats the young woman to death with a hammer. The painting is abandoned and he goes to Dublin, where he renews an acquaintance with Charlie French, an old family friend, who offers him shelter without any questions. Freddie's last few days of refuge are spent in reckless and tormented self-indulgence, until the police arrive and arrest him. Only when he is finally manacled does he feel free of the burdensome mask he has worn for so long.

This is the plot of Freddie's story, summarised with a continuity which does not yet take into account the many imaginative digressions and interruptions which weave themselves across such a frenzied sequence, and which give the narrative its yearning quality. Easily and willingly captivated by the images and faces conjured up by his inquisitive memory, he builds up a series of 'sub-texts', which seem to signify more than the facts of the plot. For example, we learn that he was once a lecturer in science at an American university, determined to become 'one of those great, cold technicians, the secret masters of the world'. In California he had met two women from Ireland, Daphne and Anna, and had married the former, later realising he was secretly in love with the latter (a similar regretful 'troilism' is seen in *The Newton Letter*). The next time he meets Anna is when he comes looking for the paintings. By a studied coincidence, she is a neighbour, daughter of the Behrens family. There is a strong sense that the lady in the portrait awakens his memory of Anna, hence attracting his hypnotised attention, while triggering a fatal confusion between real and fictional women.

These 'sub-texts' within the main narrative seem to provide Freddie with the real evidence for his guilt. Memory suddenly perceives patterns, coincidences and designs which he was blind to at the time, but which now reveal a sinister, predetermined order to his fateful existence. The logic of these subconscious designs, now laid bare, confirms his feeling that the murder was premeditated but not intentional.

A fiction about the criminal mind is also one about the system of order being challenged. 'Law and Order' in this novel may be seen as an earthly, and political, version of the scientific system of absolutes by which the human, everyday order is interpreted. Banville's aesthetic always interrogates these abstract codes of belief through the counter-evidence of a poetic sensibility. It may be shocking, therefore, but hardly surprising, that Freddie Montgomery finally claims that 'failure of imagination is my real crime, the one that made the others possible'.

In a fiction dominated by images of art, Freddie's guilt is rendered aesthetic, a more profoundly human charge than the legal one he has always accepted. The law's understanding of motive never comes near the final imaginative understanding of his own animalism. The legal system and process of inquisition are a great source of entertainment to Freddie, because they will only state the obvious, and do so in a language that could never describe the ghastly irrational personality of most human behaviour. The law's version of innocence and guilt produces only a snickering parody from Freddie:

> I realised that I had done the things I did because I could do no other. Please, do not imagine, my lord, I hasten to say it, do not imagine that you detect here the insinuation of an apologia, or even of a defence. I

wish to claim full responsibility for my actions – after all, they are the only things I can call my own – and I declare in advance that I shall accept without demur the verdict of the court. I am merely asking, with all respect, whether it is feasible to hold on to the principle of moral culpability once the notion of free will has been abandoned. It is, I grant you, a tricky one, the sort of thing we love to discuss in here of an evening, over our cocoa and our fags, when time hangs heavy.[4]

This is precisely the kind of philosophical conundrum that Nietzsche, in examining the innocent element in supposedly evil actions, held up to bourgeois morality:

> The evil acts at which we are now most indignant rest on the error that he who perpetrates them against us possessed free-will, that is to say, that he could have *chosen* not to cause us this harm. It is this belief in choice that engenders hatred, revengefulness, deceitfulness, complete degradation of the imagination, while we are far less censorious towards an animal because we regard it as unaccountable.[5]

Rationalism, argues Nietzsche, wrongly assumes a free subject behind violent acts of this kind. Reduced to his 'natural' state, Freddie now scrutinises the language of 'evil', and finds that it never quite matches his understanding. It usually implies a freedom that never existed; or it judges, without imagination, a hopelessly inadequate version of events. The morality of the law is as mystifying as its language. Like Camus's Meursault, Freddie never expresses regret or sorrow, and is thus confirmed as an inhuman monster; both characters also look forward to the spectacle of public retribution. But Freddie realises that his crime is greater than anyone imagines, and he refuses to act out emotions expected or required by the court, precisely because such a display may only encourage clemency. No system is necessary to prove what he already knows:

> The deed was done, and would not be cancelled by cries of anguish and repentance. Done, yes, finished, as nothing ever before in my life had been finished and done – and yet there would be no end to it, I saw that straight away. I was, I told myself, responsible, with all the weight that word implied. In killing Josie Bell I had destroyed a part of the world. Those hammer-blows had shattered a complex of memories and sensations and possibilities – a life, in short – which was irreplaceable, but which, somehow, must be replaced. (151–2)

He declares that his own 'symbolic death' at the hands of the law may be necessary, even desirable, but Josie Bell must be 'brought back to life' in his own mind. His careless murder can be atoned for only by facing what was previously unimaginable.

Freddie's crime is explained, not excused, by an inherited schizophrenia which determined actions he had mistaken for choices. He was always a marionette, he confesses, and never a free man. Prison, in this sense, is a homecoming. Through his narrator's experience, Banville tries to dramatise an existential sense of the theatricality of rational behaviour, a life spent denying the reality of chance and the power of the demonic self. To avoid substituting the abstractions of psychology for those of philosophy, Banville creates a pattern of biographical detail which 'explains' Freddie's confusion in terms of familiar, often farcical, fictions. Stereotypes and clichés are indispensable to this kind of absurdism. Outrageous and exotic names are a favoured contrivance in suggesting the unreal, staged quality of Freddie's altered perspective of the world and its odd inhabitants, such as the lavish Gaelic of his barrister, Maolseachlinn Mac Giolla Gunna, or the allegorical nastiness of his interrogators, Kickham and Barker. Nothing seems funnier, or more touching, than the seriousness with which the law takes Freddie. Its comic pretensions never fail to tickle him.

Equally playful, but more profound, is the fatal imprint of genetic inheritance, a recurrent motif in Banville. Family, parents and childhood suddenly seem crucial. Son of a father who prided himself on being a 'Castle Catholic' (who insisted on the colonial name 'Kingstown' instead of the post-colonial 'Dun Laoghaire') and a mother descended from 'King Billy's henchmen', even his immediate family seems like a violation or betrayal of nature and convention. Looking back on his solitary childhood, he now sees the tragic dualism of his personality: outside, the cultured intelligent son of the Big House, but inside, a violent sadistic brute trying to be free, a monster he names 'Bunter'. On the day of his crime, he recalls, 'Bunter was restive, aching to get out.' In a sense only appreciated by Freddie, the wrong self has been arrested. After the murder, the triumph of evil is recalled by Freddie with grim, fascinated acceptance:

> Now I had struck a blow for the inner man, that guffawing, fat foul-mouth who had been telling me all along I was living a lie. And he had burst out at last, it was he, the ogre, who was pounding along in this lemon-coloured light, with blood on his pelt, and me slung helpless over his back. Everything was gone, the past, Coolgrange, Daphne, all my previous life, gone, abandoned, drained of its essence, its significance. To do the worst thing, the very worst thing, that's the way to be

free. I would never again need to pretend to myself to be what I was not. (124–5)

Such sentiments are an affront to logic as well as to morality. Contrary to superstition, the 'inner man' turns out to be a devil, not an angel. But this is a subjective testimony based on emotion rather than reason, and Freddie's honesty limits itself to a personal sense of being at odds with the civilised world. His 'truth' is tentative, paradoxical and defiant. The only way he can overthrow or resist the pattern of his life and crime is through an imaginative effort. His only consolation is a belated acceptance of the significance of recollected images.

The implied solution to Freddie's crime lies in the relationship between two pictures – the Dutch portrait and a photograph of Josie Bell. How are we meant to understand his obsessive attraction towards the painting? He was, he believes, 'lured' to the painting by the presence of Anna, his fantasy woman. In prison, he recalls his first sighting of the portrait, and offers a lover's detailed anatomy of her seductive image:

> You have seen the picture in the papers, you know what she looks like. A youngish woman in a black dress with a broad white collar, standing with her hands folded in front of her, one gloved, the other hidden except for the fingers, which are flexed, ringless. She is wearing something on her head, a cap or clasp of some sort, which holds her hair drawn tightly back from her brow. Her prominent black eyes have a faintly oriental slant. The nose is large, the lips full. She is not beautiful. In her right hand she holds a folded fan, or it might be a book. She is standing in what I take to be the lighted doorway of a room. Part of a couch can be seen, or maybe a bed, with a brocade cover. The darkness behind her is dense and yet mysteriously weightless. Her gaze is calm, inexpectant, though there is a trace of challenge, of hostility, even, in the set of her mouth. She does not want to be here, and yet cannot be elsewhere. The gold brooch that secures the wings of her wide collar is expensive and ugly. All this you have seen, all this you know. Yet I put it to you, gentle connoisseurs of the jury, that even knowing all this you still know nothing, next to nothing. You do not know the fortitude and pathos of her presence. You have not come upon her suddenly in a golden room on a summer eve, as I have. You have not held her in your arms, you have not seen her asprawl in a ditch. You have not – ah no! – you have not killed for her. (78–9)

Not long after this rhetorical description of the painting and its violent emotional impact on him, Freddie submits a brief, technical account of the work, delivered in his newly acquired manner of a connoisseur of such images:

> The painting is called, as everyone must know by now, *Portrait of a Woman with Gloves*. It measures eighty-two centimetres by sixty-five. From internal evidence – in particular the woman's attire – it has been dated between 1655 and 1660. The black dress and broad white collar and cuffs of the woman are lightened only by a brooch and gold ornamentation on the gloves. The face has a slightly Eastern cast. (I am quoting from the guidebook to Whitewater House.) The picture has been variously attributed to Rembrandt and Frans Hals, even to Vermeer. However, it is safest to regard it as the work of an anonymous master. (104)[6]

All four women in Freddie's imagination – the portrait, Josie Bell, Anna and Daphne – now become confused and, to some extent, interchangeable, as if each were an essential part of his female fantasy. His

5 Johannes Vermeer (?), *Portrait of a Woman* (c. 1658)

last image of Daphne, when leaving America (an image he now wishes he had painted instead of merely observed), was of her standing by a window, framed by the light. Fifteen years later, Anna now appears 'like one of Klimt's gem-encrusted lovers'. Freddie's preference is for the seeming security and distance of 'artistic' women, an ordering or 'framing' of voyeuristic desire.

Contemplating the Dutch portrait (a reproduction of which Anna has brought him as a gift) in the privacy of his cell, Freddie creates an elaborate fantasy about the possible background to the making of the portrait. He imagines an old Dutch merchant commissioning a portrait of his only daughter, who then reluctantly agrees to sit for a picture which the doting father hopes will immortalise his beloved child. In this fantasy upon desire, Freddie is fascinated by the sensuous texture of the artist's chaotic and foul-smelling studio, and with the young woman's nervous and sceptical presence. When the painting is completed, the woman is enthralled – 'She had expected it would be like looking in a mirror, but this is someone she does not recognise, and yet knows.' Numbed with happiness, she 'steps out into a commonplace world'. That world, unfortunately for Freddie, is the one which Josie Bell inhabits.

Freddie is willing and able to summon up the world behind the work of art, but he simply cannot recreate Josie Bell's 'commonplace world'. Shortly after the murder, he buys a newspaper to see if there is any news of the horrific event, and he comes across a photograph of Josie Bell, 'gazing out solemn-eyed from a blurred background ... she was wearing a long ugly dress with an elaborate collar, and was clutching something, flowers, perhaps, in her hands'. The contrast with his reading and interpretative ability in relation to the Dutch portrait is striking. Freddie invented the story of the portrait's origins because, in his own words, 'she was asking me to let her live'. If his crime is indeed, as he claims, 'a failure of imagination', it also reveals his blind contempt for a lower class of woman. A servant has been murdered by a young master; a 'native' has been erased by an Anglo-Irish gentleman, albeit a displaced and confused one. Freddie recalls being led from the courthouse, and noticing the hostile crowd – 'That was when I realised, for the first time, it was *one of theirs* I had killed.' Confessing his shame at having taken so long to beat her to death, he hears his barrister remark, 'Hardy people ... they don't die easily.' Freddie's crime is part of a pattern of calculated cruelty in the novel, but his irrationality is mediated through the imagery of art in a way that suggests a disturbing link between culture, perception and violence. He can see Anna Behrens in terms of the Dutch masters, or his mother as one of 'Lautrec's ruined doxies', but he cannot discover an artistic parallel for the world of Josie Bell. Only after his crime, and especially when he no longer has to pretend, does he see the relation between perception and knowledge. The meaning of his evidence, he insists repeatedly, is to be sensed in its images. Fiction becomes his only hope.

As with so many of Banville's narrators, the shock to Freddie's imaginative system releases a previously unfelt sympathy for the imagery of innocence. Like the astronomers, he comes to feel an exquisite regret and wonder at having forgotten or ignored the obvious. He remembers wandering around Dublin after the murder, 'a quavering Dr Jekyll', as if he was seeing the place for the very first time:

> I felt I had never until now looked at the ordinary world around me, the people, places, things. How innocent it all seemed, innocent, and doomed. How can I express the tangle of emotions that thrashed inside me as I prowled the city streets, letting my monstrous heart feed its fill on the sights and sounds of the commonplace? (172–3)

His crime against this innocent world endears it to him, but also ensures his banishment from it. Every detail of the world's texture suddenly seems precious and tragic when viewed for the first and the last time. Like Gabriel Swan, Freddie is an emblem of deformed and, therefore, 'true' humanity. This is why he pursues the freaks of Dublin's nightlife, the 'maimed and the mad', who now seem to him the very epitome of his own sad race. In scenes which recall the final episodes of *Mefisto*, Freddie discovers a community of tormented souls like himself, and can only feel pity and amazement at their survival.

The greatest artistic and stylistic challenge that faces Banville is to persuade us that Freddie is, somehow, innocent. Such a stylistic illusion is achieved through this myth of a nature damaged at birth, after which only glimpses of harmony are possible. Freddie is a poetic animal, not a fallen angel. Prison is the obvious, even traditional, metaphor for such an intelligent beast who realises that sanity requires an unbearable degree of mimicry. (A similar kind of relief is felt by Beckett's Murphy when he discovers his real 'home' in the mental hospital.) Once he is housed in jail, the artifice can be dispensed with and his true nature released. As he slyly remarks, 'To place all faith in the mask, that seems to me now the true stamp of refined humanity.' Prison reduces existence to a simpler, more meaningful equation of good and evil, guilt and innocence, and provides Freddie with a perfect vantage point from which he can see the world in its authentic innocence. It also liberates the lyricist in him. The cell window provides him with a barred frame through which he watches, and is watched by, the ordinary world of sky and tree. This miniaturist perspective on the world is all he needs: his imagination will do the rest.

Reality, whether that of the prison or the outside world, always comes as a surprise to Freddie. His fanciful notions of what to expect usually prove embarrassing or ludicrously off the mark. Yet it is often these very delusions, once confessed, which bring him a revitalised and self-critical understanding. The story's sense of the absurd comes from his ability to watch himself and others behave like poor actors, all the time thinking they are free and purposeful. This is the art and humour of existential bathos. Now free to watch himself, he recalls his surprise on first entering prison: his 'hopelessly romantic' expectations of jail led him to picture himself as 'Jean-Jacques the cultured killer', but the reality has an unforeseen and unforeseeable elusiveness and originality which subvert the imaginative script. Forever looking for the wrong kind of melodrama in the wrong place, he soon sees that 'in here is like out there, only more so'. Without theatrical roles, the world would come to a silent standstill. Most of the players in his story can be memorised only in terms of an exotic farce which cannot distinguish between the natural and the contrived. Playing comic roles seriously is the greatest source of derisive humour for Freddie. His pursuit and arrest now seem worthy of a Hollywood thriller, with the police smashing their way into the house, only to find the psychopath having a quiet supper. The many lurid versions of his appearance offered by eyewitnesses now seem to him 'like a chorus of brigands in an Italian opera'. Freddie's satirical imagination is overstocked with artistic and literary analogies, leaving him little or no room for direct encounter with the real world.

Not everything, however, is reduced to farce by this obsessively mocking imagination. There are moments in his evidence when Freddie glimpses images of rare, silent beauty which overwhelm him, as if this fallen, demented world still preserved traces of purity and perfection, like fossils of lost harmony. Normally his imagination leaves him floundering, only confirmed in his sense of the unbridgeable discrepancy between hope and reality, order and chaos. Yet, occasionally, as if some authentic script had been prepared for him without his knowledge, he is the enraptured witness to the poetry of revelation. Usually, this revelation occurs in the least poetic of circumstances, as if beauty were the gift of genuine surprise. This mystical, idealistic strain is present in nearly all of Banville's fiction, a necessary part of its dark vision, and is protected from the pitfalls of an easy assertive romanticism by a sense of the pain and absurdity which usually precede and follow it. Freddie's imagistic memory is particularly attracted to those interludes of calm which seem to symbolise some divine artistry in the natural world, as when he remembers sitting on the deck of the mail-boat from Wales to Ireland, on the eve of his downfall:

> I had expected to arrive in rain, and at Holyhead, indeed, a fine, warm drizzle was falling, but when we got out on the channel the sun broke through again. It was evening. The sea was calm, an oiled, taut meniscus, mauve-tinted and curiously high and curved. From the forward lounge where I sat the prow seemed to rise and rise, as if the whole ship were straining to take to the air. The sky before us was a smear of crimson on the palest of pale blue and silvery green. I held my face up to the calm sea-light, entranced, expectant, grinning like a loon. I confess I was not entirely sober, I had already broken into my allowance of duty-free booze, and the skin at my temples and around my eyes was tightening alarmingly. It was not just the drink, though, that was making me happy, but the tenderness of things, the simple goodness of the world. This sunset, for instance, how lavishly it was laid on, the clouds, the light on the sea, that heartbreaking, blue-green distance, laid on, all of it, as if to console some lost, suffering wayfarer. (26)

It is that sense of nature being 'laid on' which captures Freddie's animistic imagination, as if an invisible landscape artist had arranged the scene specially for him. The world becomes an aesthetic and fictional production, all the more beautiful for being carefully rehearsed. What gives moments like this their distinctive poignancy is the inclusion of sad, human detail, some contrasting image of earthly insignificance. It is as if a utopian simplicity of design had suddenly been noticed, a world which retains its purity and form, and which itself silently observes the lunatic antics of the fallen world. These intimations of beauty are always prompted by the commonplace, but especially by silence. Very little is ever spoken in Banville's fiction: when people speak, they usually spoil the silence.

Through the motif of painting, Banville has created a series of metaphors that are perfectly in harmony with his poetic sense of fiction. Deeply intertextual and allusive, scholarly but sceptical, such fiction always returns to the sensuous image for expressive meaning. The silent image pretends to bypass language, appealing directly to the heart and the subconscious mind. As with masks, Freddie comes to trust only externals, since, he concludes, 'that's where there is depth'. Viewed this way, appearances are everything. As Freddie's pictorical imagination understands it, images can retain an honesty which words will only confuse. Of course, the most teasing paradox about all this is that Banville's language, so metaphoric and magnetic, should have the stylistic confidence to convey a story which denies the adequacy of language. Freddie himself finally expresses this ironic achievement:

> I had Daphne bring me big thick books on Dutch painting, not only the history but the techniques, the secrets of the masters. I studied accounts of the methods of grinding colours, of the trade in oils and dyes, of the flax industry in Flanders. I read the lives of the painters and their patrons. I became a minor expert on the Dutch republic in the seventeenth century. But in the end it was no good: all this learning, this information, merely built up and petrified, like coral encrusting a sunken wreck. (214)

Even failure and ignorance, as captured in that final inspired analogy, have precious aesthetic value when acknowledged by the liberated imagination.

Like Newton, but this time through a very different set of metaphors, Freddie sees systematised knowledge as an illusory distraction from an earthly order which was watching him all the time, waiting to be noticed and recognised. Other echoes of the astronomers' experience are heard in this new arrangement, most significantly the ideas of perception and perspective. Freddie, like his fictional relations in the tetralogy, finds a new way of looking at the familiar world, a place whose beauty is evident only to those who accept their own insignificance. This conclusive view of personal insignificance comes as a relief, and with a sense of renewed hope, usually signalled by the promise of spring.

In the old order of things, Man placed himself at the centre of the universe, master of all he surveyed. Now, that order is reversed, and the universe includes Man in its silent gaze. The astronomer in Freddie offers a metaphysical conceit to describe this tragic reversal:

> I have never really got used to being on this earth. Sometimes I think our presence here is due to a cosmic blunder, that we were meant for another planet altogether, with other arrangements, and other laws, and other, grimmer skies. I try to imagine it, our true place, off on the far side of the galaxy, whirling and whirling. And the ones who were

meant for here, are they out there, baffled and homesick, like us? No, they would have become extinct long ago. How could they survive, these gentle earthlings, in a world that was made to contain *us*? (26–7)

An ingenious parable of perception, *The Book of Evidence* completes Banville's vision of a decentred universe in which humanity protects and consoles itself through a fantastical, if fractured, imagination.

9

Ghosts

Votre âme est un paysage choisi
Que vont charmant masques et bergamasques
Jouant du luth et dansant et quasi
Tristes sous leurs déguisements fantasques.
Paul Verlaine, 'Clair de lune'

IF *The Book of Evidence* closes the case for and against Freddie Mont-gomery, *Ghosts* reopens it, and does so in ways which reveal the cyclical design of Banville's imagination. Here is yet another of Fred-die's stories, this time told from an island refuge ten years after being released from prison, a richly intertextual tale which recalls and revis-its the scene of his original crime, as well as a host of characters from Banville's earlier fictions. The 'ghosts' summoned up by Freddie are fellow inmates of Banville's imagination, characters, motifs and types whose fictional lives extend well beyond their earlier textual ones. Thomas Kilroy sees *Ghosts* as a fiction about all the other fictions:

> Yes indeed, this is The Return of Freddie, but *Ghosts* is no prosaic sequel to *The Book of Evidence*. Rather it is yet another elaboration … on the totality of Banville's work, its gallery of icy heroes, its fiercely intelli-gent pursuit of certain ideas about writing and their relationship to what we optimistically call the real world.[1]

One of the many narrative challenges set by *Ghosts* is precisely this close relationship with *The Book of Evidence*. In such an incestuous world of fiction, where characters drift in and out, and back and forth, between stories, no single narrative achieves full resonance and coher-ence alone. We might consider each novel as an episode in an ever-extending, deeply self-absorbed, metanarrative.

To what extent, we may ask, does an understanding of *Ghosts* depend upon a familiarity with *The Book of Evidence*? Banville's fiction seems to develop according to a kind of imaginative and intellectual interplay whereby an idea as much as a character must always reveal, or discover, its opposite, its counter-narrative. Sometimes, as with *The Newton Letter*, for example, the fiction is a form of imaginative digression, or pause, a chance to revisit an earlier theme, not so much a novel, but an elaborate, playful conceit around that theme. In *Ghosts*, Banville has returned to ideas which were adumbrated in *The Book of Evidence* and made them the primary puzzle of a highly 'staged' narrative. These ideas revolve around the contemplation and love of pictures. Freddie's original crime of murder was inseparable from his love of a painting; in *Ghosts*, Freddie now has time and space in which to reflect upon his voyeuristic obsession with the enigma of this speechless art.

Whereas the manic memoir of *The Book of Evidence* was inspired and structured by history, personal and social, *Ghosts* is designed around a series of artful mythologies, all of them based on a fabulous journey to an island. These mythologies, principally that of Shakespeare's *The Tempest* (which provided 'Prospero's Circus' in *Birchwood*), confer a dream-like, wholly imagined, quality to a narrative related by Freddie, a 'little god', as he calls himself, who recreates his own journey from the prison to the island, and then the ghostly appearance of seven shipwrecked visitors to his new home. *Ghosts* also recalls the astronomical mythology of earlier fictions, most crucially Freddie's conviction, expressed in *The Book of Evidence*, that he must have come from some other god-forsaken planet, and that the real, deserving inhabitants of the earth are somewhere beyond in the outer reaches of the universe, 'baffled and homesick, like us'. This sense of alienation and displacement, one which usually anticipates a journey in search of recovery, is signalled in the epigraph to the novel, 'There were ghosts that returned to earth to hear his phrases', taken from a poem by Wallace Stevens in which he imagines the sensuous ecstasy that only the poetic imagination can restore to those who have lost their humanity.[2] Another defining textual allusion in the novel is to Rimbaud's *Le Bateau ivre* (1871), a surreal expedition of the symbolist imagination, in which the poet dramatises what he refers to as elsewhere as a '*dérèglement de tous les sens*'.[3] This structural pattern of fictional allusion is complemented and heightened by the central image of the novel, one which comes to dominate and define Freddie's search for meaning and being, that of a painting, *Le Monde d'or*, here a fictional version of Watteau's representations of mythical voyages to the Greek island of Cythera, home of Aphrodite.

Watteau's voyages, focusing on imminent departure or return rather than on the journey itself, established the genre of the *fête galante* in the history of painting, a genre defined by Marianne Roland Michel:

> The term characterises those gatherings of men and women, usually dressed with studied refinement, who flirt decorously, dance, make music or talk freely, in a landscape or in a sumptuously unreal architectural setting. The shimmering coloured silk of their theatrical clothes – their *'habits modernes'* – raises the initial question – who are these figures, and who are they supposed to represent? For, although mostly drawn from the life, these figures seem to lose all aura of reality when brought together by the chance arrangement of the canvas.[4]

Banville's *Ghosts* tries to achieve a narrative version of a *fête galante*, drawing on the genre's mythical symbolism and its love of theatrical artifice. This is a curiously 'suspended' narrative, like the paintings which inspired it, reflecting back upon its own ghostly provenance, and using a pattern of elaborate metaphor to dwell upon 'the necessary hypocrisy' of art, both literary and pictorial. It is a kind of interregnum in the progress of Banville's fiction, an opportunity to isolate the idea of representation, and to do so in a fictional landscape which is itself isolated from the demands and expectations of conventional narrative.

In the final pages of *The Book of Evidence*, Freddie tells of how he spent years of his prison-life studying the history of painting, becoming what he calls 'a minor expert on the Dutch republic in the seventeenth century'. In *Ghosts*, this criminal-turned-scholar holds a letter of introduction from his old acquaintance Anna Behrens, who urges him to contact a Professor Kreutznaer, a world expert on art who lives with his manservant, Licht, on a small island off the south coast of Ireland. Freddie becomes an amanuensis to the professor, who is trying to write and complete his *magnum opus* on the art and life of the painter Jean Vaublin. In ways which recall the doomed biography in *The Newton Letter*, and Freddie's thespian talents, Kreutznaer abandons the work, leaving his new student to act the part of historian and interpreter. Freddie becomes a 'ghost writer', delighted, as ever, to have a new role, 'the best it has ever been my privilege to play, and I have played many'. The illusion of security and order enjoyed by Freddie is disrupted, in classic Banvillean fashion, by a rude intrusion from the outside world.

The novel opens *in media res*, not with Freddie's arrival on the island, but with the subsequent appearance of the motley crew from a boat which had run aground upon a sandbank off the island, a mishap allegedly caused by the drunken captain. This is where the worlds of *The Tempest* and *Le Bateau ivre* meet the ghosts of Freddie's past. In the ensuing collision and confusion of identities, Freddie becomes a kind of Hibernian Caliban, a brute susceptible to the siren call of beauty, Licht becomes a demented version of Ariel, and the professor reverts to a dumb parody of Prospero.[5] The seven survivors of the shipwreck are led by a character who first appeared in *Mefisto*, Felix, the sinister joker who assisted Kasperl in that novel, and who now reintroduces himself to a terminally withdrawn Kreutznaer. The lengthy opening sequence of *Ghosts* is devoted entirely to Freddie's recollection of this exotic troupe, who hang around the house, wander around the island, disport themselves as if taking part in some bizarre latter-day *fête galante*, unsettling the already strained atmosphere between Freddie and his hosts. Most unsettling of all is the languorous presence of Flora, a girl-like figure who recalls Adele from *Mefisto*. Versions of Flora appear throughout Banville's fiction, damaged, vulnerable types of femininity who come to haunt the story-teller's consciousness, objects of voyeuristic, often lecherous, attention. For Freddie, who has murdered an innocent woman, Flora reminds him of his need to make what he terms '*proper restitution*', to find some way of re-imagining Josie Bell. Towards the end of this opening section of the novel, Freddie believes that somehow the arrival of Flora has helped him see her with an intimacy and immediacy which were previously lacking in him:

> And as she talked I found myself looking at her and seeing her as if for the first time, not as a gathering of details, but all of a piece, solid and singular and amazing. No, not amazing. That is the point. She was simply there, an incarnation of herself, no longer a nexus of adjectives but pure and present noun. I noticed the little fine hairs on her legs, a scarp of dried skin along the edge of her foot, a speck of sleep in the carthus of her eye. No longer Our Lady of the Enigmas, but a girl, just a girl. And somehow by being suddenly herself like this she made the things around her be there too. In her, and in what she spoke, the world, the little world in which we sat, found its grounding and was realised.[6]

This account of how the observing self frees itself from intellectual conditioning, or artistic predisposition, and suddenly, for no clear reason, or perhaps through some kind of imaginative epiphany, sees and embraces the sensuous reality of a woman, emerges as one of the dominant themes of the narrative, one which will later merge with the greater philosophical issue of the mimetic nature of great art.

Freddie believes that his ability to relate to women, real and imagined, is deeply defective, and that his understanding of that defect is perhaps the key to a greater understanding of the relation between reality and representation. The man as well as the scholar needs to solve this mystery. Shortly before the visitors arrive, Freddie enjoys a brief relationship with a Dutch woman, Mrs Vanden, who lives a hermit's life on the island. After her death, Freddie suspects that his attraction towards women, since it clearly has nothing to do with sexual desire, is probably of the deepest, most genetic, kind:

> A sort of lust for knowledge, the passionate desire to delve my way into womanhood and taste the very temper of its being. Dangerous talk, I know. Well, go ahead, misunderstand me, I don't care. Perhaps I have always wanted to be a woman, perhaps that's it. If so, I have reached the halfway stage, unsexed poor androgyne that I am become by now. (69–70)

Gender, rather than sexuality, is what fascinates and disturbs Freddie, especially how the company of women, real or imaginary, affects his already schizoid identity. As we shall see later, this kind of ambiguity also marks his contemplation of great works of art, suggesting the possible secret of their power over the beholder.

This lengthy opening sequence to *Ghosts* (which takes up more than half the novel) drifts back and forth between past and present, and between the various characters in the exotic troupe of survivors. There are many passages of exquisite descriptive writing, beautifully rendered cameos, always capturing Freddie's odd, distracted, intense gaze upon the texture of people and landscape. Yet there is a sense of Banville going through the stylistic motions, content simply to drift, under no narrative pressure to advance the story or reveal any plot.

The second section of *Ghosts* continues with the motif of a fabulous journey, but one which precedes that of the seven stranded voyagers, the journey which first took Freddie to the island. He now recalls that trip south from Dublin in self-consciously mythical terms, 'a sort of epic journey and I an Odysseus, homeless now, setting out once more, a last time, from Ithaca'. What follows in this section is one of the most evocative and coherent narratives in the novel, in which this opening piece of self-dramatisation sets up a mock-epic version of the hero's return, a journey complete with a loyal companion, fears of domestic betrayal, a mute reunion with a long-forgotten son, and the final humiliation of seeing his ancestral home abandoned by his faithless wife. In Freddie's imagination, epic simile invariably prepares the way for travesty. The quality of this outstanding piece of narrative recalls much of *The Book of Evidence*, especially its wicked humour, but also its richly poetic sense of a mind hypnotised by its own strange way of perceiving the world, at once remote and intimate, in a permanent state of imaginative intoxication with the theatricality of reality.

Freddie remembers the day he was released from jail, everything in the city looking like 'an elaborate stage-set, plausible but not real'. He meets up with another ex-convict, Billy (who was introduced in the final pages of *The Book of Evidence*, serving time for 'murder and multiple rape'); and over drinks in a pub by the river, called The Boatman, Freddie persuades his companion to drive him south, where, he explains, he has to catch a boat. On their way, Freddie decides to make a sentimental detour to his former home, where, he tells Billy, his wife still lives. In a landscape and a house which recall the crumbled world of *Birchwood*, Freddie re-enters his past:

> I shut the door behind me and stood and took another deep breath, like a diver poised on the springboard's thrumming tip. The furniture hung about pretending not to look at me. Stillness lay like a dustsheet over everything. There was no one at home, I could sense it. I walked here and there, my footsteps falling without sound. I had a strange sensation in my ears, a sort of fullness, as if I were in a vessel fathoms deep with the weight of the ocean pressing all around me. The objects that I looked at seemed insulated, as if they had been painted with a protective coating of some invisible stuff, cool and thick and smooth as enamel, and when I touched them I could not seem to feel them. I thought of being here, a solemn little boy in a grubby jersey, cropheaded and frowning, with inky fingers and defenceless, translucent pink ears, sitting at this table hunched over my homework on a winter evening and dreaming of the future. Can I really ever have been thus? Can that child be me? (180)

The fact that Freddie has consumed a bottle of gin before braving this return to the past helps explain some of the unreality of the scene and his hypersensitive amaze at its animated texture. His feverish imagination, always reaching for analogies of physical and emotional sensation, is intrigued by the composition of objects, seeing in them a presence, a solidity, which he lacks and envies. This was also the house in which he passed his childhood, a state of seeming innocence almost unthinkable for him now. Suddenly, his son, Van, now a young man but still a handicapped mute, appears in the room. Like Heinrich, the scientist's simpleton sibling in *Kepler*, Van retains his innocence through his damaged mind, and his survival and joy reduce Freddie to pieces: such ghostly delicacy and fragility enthrals and terrifies him. He abandons the house and his son, rejoins the waiting Billy, and they continue their odyssey south. Freddie's parting reflection – 'Dear Jesus, all my ghosts are gathering here' – suggests a man who knows that his past will not simply haunt him, but will be his constant companion, that other, spectral self whose existence seems more real than his own.

The remainder of his journey to the island is recalled with an exhilarated sense of its absurdity as well as its poignancy, with Freddie's manic musings lurching between Enlightenment theories of art and the beckoning beauty of the approaching island. Like a cross between Lazarus and the Prodigal Son, Freddie finally introduces himself to Licht and Kreutznaer, and after the customary chaotic preliminaries, his letter from Anna Behrens secures his admittance into this bizarre retreat. When he first sees Kreutznaer, he suddenly realises they have met before, 'many years ago, in a golden world now gone'. Another ghost from the past, Kreutznaer had lectured at the Behrenses' house on his specialism, the art of Jean Vaublin, twenty years beforehand, a lecture which Freddie remembers having attended. Freddie can scarcely contain his excitement when he learns that the professor is presently researching the art and provenance of Vaublin's *Le Monde d'or*, a work that Freddie suggests is 'the centrepiece' of the artist's life-work. Reflections upon this painting form the imaginative climax of the novel.

This climax seems to present itself, and its attendant promise of revelation, in the third, very brief, section of the novel, in which Freddie describes *Le Monde d'or*. More precisely, he moves between the objective manner of a catalogue entry and that of a subjective fantasy elicited by the work. Gazing upon the imagery of *Le Monde d'or*, Freddie scans every aspect of its form and detail, looking for clues to its overall meaning, only to conclude that this kind of art withholds any desired or necessary revelation. A broad clue to the source, but not the significance, of the painting is heralded in the closing pages of the previous section when, full of expectancy, Freddie declares, 'I had sailed the sea and come to Cythera.'

The painting which offers itself to his loving and troubled gaze conflates three famous paintings by the French artist Watteau (1684–1721), renowned for his representations of *fêtes galantes* and the characters of the Italian *commedia dell'arte*. With significant changes to some of the images' details, Banville has reproduced Watteau's *Gilles*, and superimposed it upon the artist's two versions of the legendary journey to the island of love, *Pilgrimage to Cythera*.[7] Freddie's enthralled account opens with a description of *Gilles*, a painting originally named Pierrot, after the tragic clown introduced by the wandering players of the *commedia dell'arte*. Two details of Freddie's version of *Gilles* (details absent in Watteau) indicate a ghostly link between his narcissistic gaze and his violent past. In his newly acquired manner of art connoisseur, Freddie notes, 'The X-rays show beneath his face another face which may be that of a woman', and further, 'He does not usually carry a club; in this instance, he does.' Freddie poses repeated

6 Antoine Watteau, *Pierrot, dit autrefois Gilles* (c. 1719)

critical questions about the meaning of the image, but concludes, almost with satisfaction, that the artistic object mocks any intellectual enquiry. He is also aware that the figure in the painting watches him with equal intensity, to the point where we are made to feel that Freddie is contemplating a self-portrait. His persistent search for a satisfactory aesthetic leads him to conclude that the painting is 'a masterpiece of pure composition', one in which 'the mystery of things is preserved'.

Reflections upon *Le Monde d'or* in earlier parts of the novel seem to confirm this part's sense that the painting contains an uncanny significance for Freddie himself, that his own journey to the island, his haunted memory of violence, his confused sexuality, are all speaking to him through this composition of legendary and mythical images. A coloured reproduction of the painting hangs on the wall above the bed in which Flora sleeps, an image which baffles and disturbs the young woman, who senses, as does Freddie, a latent violence in the work, masked by outward innocence. Freddie sees the painting as darkest pastoral, a deceptively serene *fête galante*:

> Even in *Le monde d'or*, apparently so chaste, so ethereal, a certain hectic air of expectancy bespeaks excesses remembered or to come. The figure of Pierrot is suggestively androgynous, the blonde woman walking away on the arm of the old man – who himself has the touch of the roué – wears a wearily knowing air, while the two boys, those pallid, slightly ravaged putti, seem to have seen more things than they should. Even the little girl with the braided hair who leads the lady by the hand has the aura of a fledgling Justine or Juliette, a potential victim in whom old men might repose dark dreams of tender abuse. (96)

This is a bucolic scene under threat, an image of innocence waiting for disaster to strike. By combining this version of *Gilles* with the two versions of *Cythera*, Banville juxtaposes the idyllic and the demonic: dominating the landscape of sensuous delight and romantic partnership, that of the *fête galante*, stands the malevolent clown, Pierrot, an artistic cousin of Shakespeare's Caliban and of Frankenstein's monster, who continually threatens to sabotage the world which banishes him.[8] *Le Monde d'or* serves as a kind of visual parable of Freddie's world, a landscape, even an escape, he yearns for, but one which he will never enjoy.

Banville's attraction towards, and use of, Watteau's cryptic and fabulous images is perhaps easier to appreciate if we recall the romantic strain running throughout this, and his earlier, fiction, one which contemplates a fallen world from an exiled perspective. Donald Posner describes the appeal and function of this genre of painting in terms which may help to suggest their special relevance and resonance for Banville:

> The *fête galante* was an escapist activity, as pastoral poetry was an escapist literature. They did not represent real goals in life. They were imaginings, temporary illusions that ease one's cares and charm the soul. Watteau's paintings embody these illusions and are also avenues of escape. They do not show real life veiled in fantasy, but a fantasy in the shape of everyday reality ... In Watteau's work the momentary dream appears as permanent reality: the placid city park is all of nature, and amorous play is the centre of man's universe.[9]

Banville's intertextual games in *Ghosts* show a very specific attraction towards eighteenth-century forms of representation and aesthetic theory, Watteau being one of those figures who seem to combine a wholly 'contrived' art and a deeply impersonal presence in that art. Freddie is repeatedly struck, and impressed, by Nature's indifference to humanity, what he calls its 'universal dispassion', and believes that because of human envy, 'Nature did not exist until we invented it one eighteenth-century morning radiant with Alpine light.' For Freddie, these 'constructions' of Nature are a poignant, and transparent, attempt to satisfy an imaginative desire to 'humanise' the world of Nature, to enable the viewer or spectator to see it as if for the first time, to see it innocently and dramatically.

Freddie's self-conscious theorising about eighteenth-century aesthetics seems to have entered his narrative through Banville's own researches on Diderot, one of the leading figures of the French Enlightenment and principal author of the *Encyclopédie*. Reviewing a new biography of Diderot in the year before *Ghosts* was published, Banville emphasised the 'modernity' of the philosopher's ideas about the 'construction' of Nature, and those forms of art, especially sculpture, which exemplified Diderot's ideal of an impersonal, but richly communicative, presence in the eye of the beholder.[10] Consistent with his belief in the superior reality of artifice, and the need to reinvent his own personality, Freddie cites the instructive beliefs of the French *philosophe*:

> Diderot developed a theory of ethics based on the idea of the statue: if we would be good, he said, we must become sculptures of the self. Virtue is not natural to us; we achieve it, if at all, through a kind of artis-

tic striving, cutting and shaping the material of which we are made, the intransigent stone of selfhood, and erecting an idealised effigy of ourselves in our own minds and in the minds of those around us and living as best we can according to its sublime example. I like this notion. There is something grand and tragic in it, and something of tragic gaiety, too. (196)

Diderot's defence of a special kind of artifice seems to vindicate Freddie's faith in the theatrical roles he adopts. Diderot also held up Watteau as the artist who best exemplified the self-absorption of great art, its indifference to being watched or observed, going so far as to declare, 'I would give ten Watteaus for one Téniers.'[11] Diderot found distasteful that kind of art which was blatantly 'theatrical', in the sense of appealing for attention, or 'playing to the audience'. In its stead, Diderot recommended an art which is 'innocent':

> All that is true is not naive, but all that is naive is true, but with a truth that is alluring, original, and rare. Almost all of Poussin's figures are naive, that is, perfectly and purely what they ought to be. Almost all Raphael's old men, women, children, and angels are naive, that is, they have a certain originality of nature, a grace with which they were born and which is not the product of instruction.[12]

Contemplating *Le Monde d'or*, Freddie echoes this perspective on an art which keeps its distance from the beholder, and for that very reason enraptures the beholder:

> Art imitates nature not by mimesis but by achieving for itself a natural objectivity, I of all people should know that. Yet in this picture there seems to be a kind of valour in operation, a kind of tight-lipped, admirable fortitude, as if the painter knows something that he will not divulge, whether to deprive us or to spare us is uncertain. Such stillness; though the scene moves there is no movement; in this twilight glade the helpless tumbling of things through time has come to a halt: what other painter before or after has managed to illustrate this fundamental paradox of art with such profound yet playful artistry? These creatures will not die, even if they have never lived. (95)

Killer turned aesthete, Freddie declares his faith in art, strongly prompted by Banville's aesthetic preference for a non-realist fiction and a symbolist style of representation and communication. To what extent does this manifesto describe, or even indicate, Banville's own style and strategy in *Ghosts*? Is this the novel describing, revealing, itself? Banville's postmodern fiction has constructed a myth about the enviable ideal of an art form, unlike the novel, that does not depend upon language, but upon 'silent form', the kind that Keats observes in 'Ode on a Grecian Urn', which 'dost tease us out of thought'. This is a fiction which contemplates a kind of silence that is alien to literary narrative, one in which the narrative is endlessly reflecting upon itself, driven by what Freddie calls his 'incurable solipsism'. *Ghosts*, like so many of Banville's fictions, is an exercise in contemplative nostalgia for an art which is exempt from the kind of self-conscious intellectualism upon which so much of the force and appeal of postmodern fiction depends, including that by Banville.

In the short coda to *Ghosts*, Freddie returns to a sensuous narrative which itself returns to the present, and the imminent departure of Felix and his motley crew of visitors, who are now ready to leave the island and sail back to the mainland – all except Flora, who wishes to remain on the island, asking Freddie to intercede with the professor and Licht on her behalf. Once again, Freddie creates a *tableau vivant* of Flora, trying to define and illustrate her mesmeric attraction, struck, above all, by her physical vulnerability, what he calls, by way of synecdoche, her 'popliteal frailty'. This way of gazing upon female innocence, especially where the woman being observed is oblivious to his stare, conjures up the ghost of Josie Bell from *The Book of Evidence*, and Freddie's self-image in that novel of 'Gilles the Terrible', an allusion to the murderous misogynist who served as prototype for the story of Bluebeard.[13]

The departing group, setting off for the boat under an evening sky dominated by the appearance of Venus, restores the novel's guiding motif of a *fête galante*. Felix's parting words to Freddie, delivered with his customary allusive pose, reinforce the latter's memory of his unrequitable violence, linking it with yet another fateful voyage:

> 'I cannot set my foot on board a ship', he said, 'without the memory coming back of sailing to the frozen north pole. I wonder, have you ever been up there? The tundra and the towering bergs, the sun that never sets: such solitude! such cold! And yet how beautiful, this land of ice! We sailed out of Archangel and due north we ploughed our way, all day, and all the night, for weeks. And then one morning when I looked out from the deck I saw the strangest sight: a figure, in the distance, on a sled, a giant man, it seemed, with whip and dogs, at great speed travelling on the floes, due north, like us. And then another' – Then he paused, and said: 'I think you know this story, though? ' (242)

This parallel tale of Frankenstein's monster, driven to the desolate edge of the world, in self-imposed exile from the society of companionship and love, completes and concludes the novel's elaborate pattern of literary and mythical allusion, joining the motif of the voyage with a literary legend of fallen glory and lost innocence. Felix, in his role as Mephistophelean tormentor, cannot resist one final revelation, and tells Freddie that *Le Monde d'or*, the sacred centre of his researches, is a fake, a copy probably made by Kreutznaer. Freddie receives this news with resignation. If he has learned anything from *Le Monde d'or*, or from his own ambiguous sense of self, it is that appearances usually conceal, and occasionally betray, their opposites. Fake and fiction, painting and self, both represent necessary forms of illusion.

10

Athena

That's my last Duchess painted on the wall,
Looking as if she were alive.
           Robert Browning, 'My Last Duchess'

THE 'incurable solipsism' which Freddie Montgomery repeatedly
identifies as his narrative trademark may help to explain why his
story never really ends, but simply enters another fictional landscape,
one in which he is condemned, yet again, like Coleridge's Ancient
Mariner, to relive and retell his ghostly tale. One more foray by
Banville into the mind and imagination of a compulsive monologist,
Athena seems to complete a trilogy of narratives about this character
and his murderous past, This is the old Freddie with a new identity, or
at least a new name, 'Morrow', chosen, he tells us, 'for its faintly hopeful hint of futurity, and, of course, the Wellsian echo'. *Athena* is a fiction about invented lives, not just the one adopted by Morrow, but a
variety of staged performances in which everyone except Morrow
seems to know the difference between fact and fiction, the real and the
fake, the true and the false. The novel confirms the impression that
Banville's fiction is by now wholly self-sustaining and self-generating,
that it feeds upon its own rich store of character, landscape and sensibility, while pausing only to add or invent new analogies, structural
and incidental, through which an unchanging theme may be replayed
and recalled. *Athena* is a new way of imagining an old story. This quest
for an authentic self, for reliable knowledge of the world, predates
Morrow's fictional birth, and can be seen as far back as *Nightspawn*
and *Birchwood*. To use one of Banville's favoured analogies, *Athena* is
both an original and a carefully copied work, an authentic duplication

of other, earlier fictions, here brought together in a wholly invented, new rearrangement.

Like *The Book of Evidence, Athena* draws upon the contemporary underworld of Irish crime for its story-line, which then provides a dramatic plot for further explorations of the imaginative sensibility. In 1986, the world's second-biggest art robbery took place in Ireland, when a criminal gang stole eleven paintings from the collection of Sir Alfred Beit, at his home in Russborough House, near Blessington in County Wicklow. The leader of the gang was Martin Cahill, known as 'The General', a notorious character who never revealed his face in public, and who enjoyed provoking the police with his various exotic disguises. In *Athena*, this character appears as 'The Da', the master-mind behind the robbery of eight priceless paintings which he hopes Morrow will help him authenticate and evaluate, so that he can sell them on the international black market.[1] As far back as *Nightspawn*, Banville has shown his fascination for this kind of encounter between a 'cultured' type and the nether world of criminal intrigue. In the trilogy centred on Freddie/Morrow, the plot is, so to speak, ready-made, a fictionalised version of a contemporary drama involving violent characters with a taste for the theatrical.

Morrow's reinvolvement with the criminal fraternity, we are asked to believe, is an inexorable part of his fictional destiny. He often reflects upon what he calls 'a lamentable weakness for the low life'. The frustrated quest for authenticity, signalled at the conclusion of *Ghosts*, when Vaublin's *Le Monde d'or* is revealed, or claimed, to be a fake, is the driving theme of Morrow's new life in Dublin, and, once again, it involves the same kind of hermeneutic riddles about inter-pretation and authentication of meaning and provenance in art. Mor-row's new life begins with what he first thought of as a chance encounter with two unannounced, but familiar, shady stereotypes, Morden ('less David's Robespierre than Rodin's Balzac') and 'Francie the Fixer', a reincarnation of Felix from *Ghosts*, who persuade him to use his technical expertise to authenticate eight seventeenth-century mythological paintings they have stolen from Whitewater House (from where Freddie had once stolen his own beloved portrait). Behind these two characters stands 'The Da', who lovingly orchestrates the entire deception. At the same time as he is being propositioned by these gangsters, Morrow meets a young woman – very much like those vul-nerable, neurotic and seductive nymphets represented by Flora in *Ghosts* – who he names 'A', who obsesses his romantic and erotic imagination throughout the narrative, and to whom his narrative is addressed. Parallel with this fevered relationship with A is that with his Aunt Corky, one of the best realised, most theatrically convincing eccentrics in the entire novel. The theft of the paintings introduces Inspector Hackett to the plot (Hackett, of course, strongly resembles Inspector Haslet from *The Book of Evidence*), who also seeks to authenticate the paintings. In the background to these encounters, the police are on the trail of a serial killer who has been committing unspeakable violence against women in the city. Surrounded on both sides by parties with an identical interest in his treasured collection, Morrow eventually discovers that he has been a pawn in an elaborate game played out between the criminals and the police. Other humiliations coincide with this discovery, notably, that all of the paintings, except one, are copies and not originals, and that his beloved A was the principal agent of his delusion. Everyone in the novel, except Morrow, knows what kind of charade is being played out, and acts according to a prepared and well-plotted script. Like the anonymous narrator in *The Newton Letter*, Morrow eventually realises that he never understood anything or anyone and, like that narrator, he addresses his memoir to a mythical woman who robbed him of old certainties. *Athena* is Morrow's love-letter to his earlier fictional self.

Writing the letter is Morrow's way of recreating and preserving his fantasy about A, a woman whom he once thought he had met by accident or destiny, but whom he now understands to have been his principal tormentor in a cruel game of carefully prearranged misrepresentation. What Morrow calls 'the props of fate' were assembled in such a way as to make him believe that his own powers of volition had something to do with his passion for A; the letter is a humbled confession of his hopeless susceptibility to the power of images. His recollection of A summons up a kind of adolescent succubus, an outwardly innocent figure, but one with powerful, provocative sexual appeal, 'like that of a spoiled, dissatisfied, far too clever twelve-year-old'. A's sexuality is a disturbing blend of virginal insouciance and sly knowingness, reminding the art historian in Morrow of what he calls the 'jaded lewdness' of a Balthus painting. His descriptions of her are those of a disbelieving voyeur who creates a sensuous, and detailed, anatomy of her physical presence and distance, an image of a seductive performance:

> She seemed to – how shall I say? – to fluctuate, as if we were engaged in an improvised dance my part in which was to stand still while she

flickered and shimmered in front of me, approaching close up and at once retreating, watching me covertly from behind that black veil which my overheated imagination has placed before her face. Then the next moment she would go limp and stand gawkily with one foot out of her shoe and pressed on the instep of the other, gazing down in a sort of stupor and holding a bit of her baby-pink lower lip between tiny, wet, almost translucent teeth. It was as if she were trying out alternative images of herself, donning them like so many slightly ill-fitting gowns and then taking them off again and dispiritedly casting them aside.[2]

Morrow's imagination is relentlessly literary and analogical, always seeing real life as a copy, or an echo, of some artistic original. While the implied metaphor above is one of compulsive display, the implied allusion is to a Salome of the senses, one played out by a precocious child. This kind of ritualised exhibition and fascination determines the subsequent relationship between A and Morrow, a 'fragile theatre of illusions', as Morrow calls it, in which his earlier crime of violence against a woman is replayed and re-enacted under A's direction.

Morrow's carefully structured letter alternates between his memories of the intense relationship with A and a sequence of studied, mock-academic reflections upon the paintings, the alternating rhythm suggesting an uncanny sense of mutual reflection between the drama of his narrative and the subjects of the paintings. The relationship with A quickly assumes a sado-masochistic character whose stylised violence is mirrored in the imagery of the collection. The erotic and violent voyeurism in *Athena*, as Banville himself has observed, recalls the classic tale of sado-masochism, *The Story of O* (1970), by Pauline Réage.[3] A and Morrow, like Beauty and the Beast, act out their sexual fantasies in the same room where the paintings are stored, thereby emphasising the claustrophobic intimacy, not just of their secret affair, but between low life and high art. What Morrow recalls, above all else, is the way his 'long-disused libido' was brought back to violent life by the carefully choreographed sexuality of their days spent in the room, with A acting out a series of voyeuristic, exhibitionistic fantasies for Morrow, a kind of ghastly therapy which culminates in her appeal to Morrow to recreate a version of his original crime. With some limited benefit of hindsight, Morrow now realises that her submission to his desire was the source of her power over him, a strategy to keep him in the same room as the paintings, and to ensure that he kept his promise to authenticate them. Morrow also concedes that, being a prisoner of

their desire, he was always playing a role, while A was 'more interested in the stage directions than the text'. For A, 'the accompanying
ceremonial', rather than the sexual act itself, consumed her remarkable theatrical talents. All of her gestures and postures encourage an
increasingly violent and brutalising sexuality, with Morrow gradually
becoming aware that she is encouraging him to act out those voyeuristic fantasies that are shared between the artistic and the pornographic
spectator. At one point, A takes Morrow from the room and brings him
to a specialist bordello run by 'Ma Murphy', where she arranges a sexual performance between them which is observed by a young prosti-
tute, Rosie. In Morrow's recollection of these seductive yet banal
perversities, analogies with exalted or profane forms of art only serve
to emphasise his remoteness from the experience, his crippling sense
of inauthenticity, his recognition of the savage within the savant:

> I saw myself towering over her like a maddened monster out of Goya,
> hirsute and bloody and irresistible, Morrow the Merciless. It was ridicu-
> lous, of course, and yet not ridiculous at all. I was monster and at the
> same time man. She would thrash under my blows with her face
> screwed up and fiercely biting her own arm and I would not stop, no, I
> would not stop. And all the time something was falling away from me,
> the accretion of years, flakes of it shaking free and falling with each
> stylised flow that I struck. Afterwards I kissed the marks the tethers had
> left on her wrists and ankles and wrapped her gently in the old grey rug
> and sat on the floor with my head close to hers and watched over her
> while she lay with her eyes closed, sleeping sometimes, her breath on
> my cheek, her hand twitching in mine like something dying. (175)

There is a disturbing stylisation of violence here, achieved through a
lyrical, almost tender rendition of cruelty. At the end of *The Book of
Evidence*, Freddie Montgomery concludes that 'failure of imagination'
was his real crime, 'the one that made the others possible'. He seems
to have meant that his obsessive fixation on a fantasy woman in a
painting occluded his recognition of the reality of Josie Bell. Yet in
Athena, despite the narrative's fixation on the physical reality, the sensuous presence, of A, Morrow is always reaching for artistic fantasies
which might best render her more real to his imagination, seeing her
now as 'poor Justine', now as 'Bernini's St Theresa', either a Sadean
victim, a 'devotee of pain', or an enraptured mystic, a martyr of sensuality. This paradoxical quality in Morrow's account of their ritualised
sexuality is remarked upon by Nicci Gerrard, who suggests that
'orgasm and death writhe together' in A's 'pain-obsessed imagination',

and sees in Morrow a fetishist 'like a pornographer or an artist', a connoisseur of the revolted senses.[4]

Perhaps Morrow's choice of name for his new love was more than fanciful or arbitrary, more than a sign of anonymity. As a token for Athena, her name conjures up a Greek myth which has a dramatic similarity to the fundamental motif of Banville's trilogy. This postmodern novel adopts a myth about violence and fantasy, highlights the correspondence of significant detail in both, and suggests a structural parallel between the epic and the ordinary. In the original myth, Athena was born when the god Hephaestus split open the head of Zeus with an axe, emerging as a warrior-woman, possessed of a strength which the imagination of Zeus had feared might surpass his own. In mythical terms, Athena is the imagination made flesh, the shocking revelation of a supreme womanhood. She is also the subject of the eighth and final picture in the stolen collection. The story of A, as related by Morrow, is simultaneously the story of Art.

The seven mythological paintings which punctuate the narrative's progress suggest an archetypal world in which Morrow's affair with A is represented in heroic, tragic forms. The dramas depicted in these paintings create a kind of parallel narrative within Morrow's memoir, illustrating his own tale with mythical images of violent passion from another world, another time. The titles of the paintings, which in themselves suggest the brutality of the action, are as follows:

> *Pursuit of Daphne*
> *The Rape of Prosperpine*
> *Pygmalion (called Pygmalion and Galatea)*
> *Syrinx Delivered*
> *Capture of Ganymede*
> *Revenge of Diana*
> *Acis and Galatea*

In the novel, the description of each painting is prefaced by fictional details of authorship and period, in effect a realistic copy of a catalogue entry. All of the paintings are said to be seventeenth-century Dutch works; all of the artists' names are anagrams of John Banville. In a novel about the search for authenticity, such playful imitation of authenticity is part of the fictional game. Even within these fictionalised descriptions, as we shall see, the 'real' world of art history makes several guest appearances, further complicating the already uncertain distinctions between fact and fiction.[5] The tone of the descriptive guide, especially in the early entries, is scholarly, objective and critical, almost wholly controlled by the image under scrutiny. Gradually, however, Morrow's self-identification with the emotions suggested by these images begins to enter into his descriptions, finally blending the epic and the everyday worlds of violence and passion, doing so in a way which suggests that life, Morrow's life, is an impoverished imitation of the art he envies.

Even before Morrow breaks the rules of objectivity which ought to control his accounts of the paintings, he seizes upon details which seem to speak to his own condition and situation. With the first painting, for example, *Pursuit of Daphne* by 'Johann Livelb' (the pseudonym adopted by Gabriel in *Birchwood*), Morrow describes the scene of a mythical drama in which Apollo pursues the fleeing goddess. The pursuit is observed by Cupid, a 'gloating satyr' who eagerly anticipates 'the spectacle of the rape that he believes he is about to witness'. Ironically, this dark piece of epic voyeurism focuses on a distinctly unathletic Apollo, 'slack-limbed, thick-waisted, breathing hard, no longer fit for amorous pursuit'. To further deflate the heroic pretensions of the image, and to suggest the kind of artistic self-inscription already at work in the novel, Morrow cites anonymous speculation which argues that the figure of Apollo is a self-portrait by Johann Livelb. Daphne, in accordance with the myth, remains beyond Apollo's reach, and is transformed before his eyes into a laurel tree. Morrow's critical sympathy, and artistic identification, is with the frustrated god, especially that expression in his eyes, 'the desperation and dawning anguish of one about to experience loss'. Finally, the literary critic Erich Auerbach is quoted, 'writing in a different context', and is borrowed to confirm Morrow's suspicion that the classical integrity of the work has been compromised and devalued by its stylistic concessions to a vulgar realism.[6] The factual and the fictional, the objective and the subjective, are held together here in a blatant piece of fictional artifice which conveys Morrow's anguish and awe in an elaborately stylised form.

The dramatic interplay and parallel between life and art, classical and contemporary, original and copy, does not always preserve these distinctions as clearly as Morrow had planned and, towards the end of his seven descriptions, the commentary is overtaken by his subjective projections and fantasies. The reflections upon the paintings begin to signal a corresponding crisis in the narrative proper, as when Morrow records his understanding of the sixth painting in the series, *Revenge of Diana*. In this well-known mythological drama, the goddess Diana is enraged to find herself being spied upon by Actaeon while taking her bath. In one of the several Ovidian metamorphoses which characterise the series of paintings, Actaeon is transformed into a stag and then torn to pieces by his own hounds. Morrow's version of this work, painted by 'J. van Hollbein', shows the moment of Diana's shocked realisation of being observed, the moment of voyeurism which ensures terrible retribution. In the countenance of the goddess, Morrow confesses to seeing only his A:

> She looks a little like you: those odd-shaped breasts, that slender neck, the downturned mouth. But then, they all look like you; I paint you over them, like a boy scrawling his fantasies on the smirking model in an advertising hoarding. (168)

Morrow's self-confessed 'besetting sin' of solipsism prevents him from seeing what he is looking at, and forces him, instead, to observe his private fears and fantasies in the paintings, played out by the gods. The imminent violence promised by the mythological drama coincides with Morrow's revelation that A pleads with him to beat her in the way he had once beaten another woman. He is shocked to discover that his past has been discovered by A, who now demands its re-enactment in a violent simulation of its original brutality, one in which she will play the willing part of his victim and his love. Morrow realises that he is not the only one doing the watching, that the deluded voyeur has been observed all along.

This humiliating, foolish sense of having been both profoundly misled and utterly deceived by appearances brings together the worlds of art and experience, and is the ironic moral of the final painting in the series, *Birth of Athena*, the only one which remains without a commentary. Instead of a commentary, the painting is finally introduced in the form of yet another duplicate, a colour postcard of the work, sent from abroad by Morden to Inspector Hackett, who informs Morrow that only *Birth of Athena* was genuine, that all of the others were fakes. With this painting, and the fictional details of its authenticity, Banville re-enters the artistic world of *Ghosts*. The artist of *Birth of Athena*, 'Jean Vaublin (1684–1721)', is that Watteauesque creator of *Le Monde d'or*, a canvas which, in that earlier fiction, turned out to be a consummate copy of a missing, elusive original. Morrow's search for authenticity, in life as in art, yields only a parallel series of deceptive but enthralling fictions about that authenticity. This is the maze of self-reflecting mirrors which so many of Banville's narrators confess to be the culmination of their confused and yet necessary quest for the truth. Fiction, of a supreme kind, a kind which may even be superior to the truth, is their only consolation.

This theme, of necessary and complete invention, is also the defining characteristic of the novel's most fully realised invention, Aunt Corky, who serves as a richly ironic counterpoint to the mythical aura of A. Aunt Corky is the 'realistic' alternative to A, an object of Morrow's horrified fascination. One of those Gothic eccentrics, like Granny Godkin in *Birchwood*, or Kepler's mother in *Kepler*, who provide a comic, subversive foil to the dreamy pretensions of so many of Banville's narrators, Aunt Corky is also the result of pure self-invention, a condition which Morrow naturally admires. Not an aunt, after all, but a cousin on Morrow's maternal side, claiming to be of Dutch or Flemish origin, cultivating a foreign accent which seems to confirm her ancestral claim, Aunt Corky is one of the great performers in *Athena*, a wholly invented life. Morrow, having been forced to reinvent himself several times, reserves a special regard for this chameleon in his family:

> I am still not sure which one of Aunt Corky's many versions of her gaudy life was true, if any of them was. Her papers, I have discovered, tell another story, but papers can be falsified, as I know well. She lied with such simplicity and sincere conviction that really it was not lying at all but a sort of continuing reinvention of the self. At her enraptured best she had all the passion and rich inventiveness of an *improvvisatrice* and could hold an audience in a trance of mingled wonder and embarrassment for a quarter of an hour or more without interruption. (22–3)

Unlike A, Aunt Corky is no work of art, but her ugliness and her stoicism invite comparison in Morrow's imagination with 'Dürer's dauntless drawing of his mother', and her theatrical facial gestures conjure up 'a Roualt face'. Morrow's account of his brief reunion with her highlights his farcical visits to see her in a nursing home, and later her life and accidental death in his house, after he had reluctantly agreed to look after her himself. Only once does the narrative concerning A and the paintings cross over into the largely separate narrative concerning Aunt Corky, in a bizarre episode where 'The Da' visits Morrow's home, keeping an eye on his art specialist's movements. 'The Da', another master of artifice, now dressed as a lady 'in a dark-blue felt toque with a black veil', sits having afternoon tea with Aunt Corky, discussing art and unbiddable children. Aunt Corky is wholly innocent of the sinister intrigue surrounding her nephew. When she dies, Morrow searches through her papers, and discovers the full extent of her self-invention.

His admiration for this complete fiction – 'What an actress!' – cancels out any surprise at her inauthenticity: the identity she invented for herself was much more interesting than the one she concealed.

Self-invention is perhaps the single issue which eventually brings together the various layers of narrative and speculation in *Athena*. Invention brings release, but also confusion, a refuge from reality but also a barrier between the self and that reality. Morrow, as is his custom, reaches for an analogy drawn from everyday life to try and suggest the necessity and the effect of escapism – the interior world of 'the afternoon cinema':

> What we see up there are not these tawdry scenes made to divert and pacify just such as we: it is ourselves reflected that we behold, the mad dream of ourselves, of what we might have been as well as what we have become, the familiar story that has gone strange, the plot that at first seemed so promising and now has fascinatingly unravelled. Out of these images we manufacture selves wholly improbable that yet sustain us for an hour or two, then we stumble out blinking into the light and are again what we always were, and weep inwardly for all that we never had yet feel convinced we have lost. (227)

This sense of nostalgic yearning is perhaps what attracts Morrow to his paintings, where he can see, in heroic form, prefigurations of his own violent and doomed life. He can admire what he calls 'the quality of its silence', but these monstrous fictions only remind him of his lost innocence or, worse still, of an innocence he never possessed.

Morrow's sense of his own ineradicable corruption is forced upon him by his ambiguous sense of sexuality, one which leaves him stranded between real and ideal forms of womanhood. This, in fact, seems to be a thematic pattern of the trilogy, one which begins with *The Book of Evidence* and closes with *Athena*, a pattern of intense reflection upon irreconcilable opposites. In *The Book of Evidence*, Freddie Montgomery is torn between his love for the Dutch portrait and that for Anna and Daphne; in *Ghosts*, his imaginative fascination with *Le Monde d'or* is contrasted with his troubled contemplation of both Flora and the Dutch woman, Mrs Vanden; and here in *Athena*, a similar 'troilism' is played out between the paintings and the two women, A and Aunt Corky. In each novel, the realm of art both liberates and distracts the narrator from the reality of these women, sometimes, as with Josie Bell in *The Book of Evidence*, blinding him to her presence, sometimes, as with A in *Athena*, seeming to explain that presence. In a remarkable piece of self-conscious self-analysis, Morrow reflects upon his repeated misreadings of women, as if they, like the art which reflects upon them, represented a kind of mystery beyond male comprehension:

> I do not understand women, I mean I understand them even less than the rest of my sex seems to do. There are times when I think this failure of comprehension is the prime underlying fact of my life, a blank region of unknowing which in others is a lighted, well-signposted place. Here, in me, in this Bermuda Triangle of the soul, the fine discriminations that are a prerequisite for moral health disappear into empty air and silence and are never heard of again. I could blame the women I have consorted with – my mother, for instance – and of course my sometime wife, could accuse them of not having educated me properly, of not inducting me into at least the minor mysteries of their sorority, but to what avail? None. The lack was in me from the start. Maybe a chromosome went missing in the small bang out of which I was formed. Perhaps that's it, perhaps that's what I am, a spoilt woman, in the way that there used to be spoilt priests. (46)

7 Albrecht Dürer, *Dürer's Mother* (1514)

Morrow, like Freddie before him, is a strong believer in genetic fate. Unable or unwilling simply to attribute his personal confusion and incompetence to morality or character, he likes to believe that some primal flaw, or accident, is the supreme cause of his violent rapture with women. The trilogy rests upon, and cultivates, a personalised myth of lost, or forever elusive, innocence, a myth which sustains a fragile faith in the ability of art to restore some kind of prelapsarian recognition and understanding of the real and the authentic. The consistent sense of a deviant or unnatural gaze upon the sensuous world, of women as well as of art, holds together the successive dramas of the trilogy.[7]

Only art and its fictions give Freddie/Morrow some sense of the lost distinctions between the natural and the contrived, the authentic and the inauthentic. Whether it is the art of serenity, as in *Ghosts*, or the art of violent passion, as in *Athena*, the narrator accepts his confusion and helplessness in the face of art's innocent remove from the real world, its enviable order and stasis, its contrived authenticity. Like *Ghosts* before it, *Athena* is best read, and perhaps best understood, in relation to the primal action of *The Book of Evidence*, as part and culmination of what Patrick McGrath calls 'an ongoing Banvillean philosophical investigation, less to do this time with morality, with murder and its aftermath, than with obsessive sexual love and its melancholy fallout'.[8] One of the several stylistic achievements of *Athena* is its ability to sustain its philosophical quest for knowledge about perception and authenticity in a form which dramatises and poeticises a personal, felt sense of loss and bereavement.

II

The Untouchable

It is the spectator, and not life, that art really mirrors.
Oscar Wilde, Preface to *The Portrait of Dorian Gray*

ANVILLE's long-established fascination with forms of knowledge
and illusion achieves a remarkable kind of imaginative synthesis in
The Untouchable, a novel which explores multiple shades of duplicity
through a central character and a period which, in turn, combine the
realms of politics, painting and sexuality. The novel is based upon the
life and times of Anthony Blunt, spy, art historian and homosexual.[1]
Although there is much here which recalls, and refines, the artistic
themes introduced by *The Book of Evidence*, this novel shares the ambitious, and deeply researched, historical design of Banville's astronomical tetralogy, suggesting that the most revealing fictions of all are
those which are lodged within, and sustain, our understanding of the
past. This is a supreme fiction about a supreme actor.

George Steiner, who has written his own account of Blunt, 'The
cleric of treason' (an account which he believes inspired, but which
remains unacknowledged by, Banville), suggests that this figure was
almost waiting to be reinvented:

> If ever there was a subject hand-crafted for John Banville, it is that of
> Anthony Blunt's treason, of the web of duplicities – intellectual, ideo-
> logical, professional, sexual – in which this eminently gifted mandarin
> chose to enmesh himself. Here, at the most vivid pitch, are the themes
> Banville has long cultivated: the authenticity of Renaissance and
> Baroque painting, the shadowlands of compulsive yet clandestine
> homoeroticism, the Byzantine ferocities of the academic, and the
> seductions of crime and of violence as these play on cloistered intellect.
> What could be nearer to a Banville invention than a man transmitting

to his students the most rigorous ideals of scholarship, of documentary integrity in the morning lecture, and expending the remainder of the day in forgery, betrayal and mendacity?[2]

Blunt's own fictional provenance appears in an earlier novel by Banville, suggesting that the novelist had an eye on his imaginative potential for several years. In *Ghosts*, the reconstructed Freddie is working with Professor Kreutznaer, who was, we are told, 'co-author with the late Keeper of the Queen's Pictures of that controversial monograph on Poussin'. That version of Freddie is a firm believer in the value and the necessity of disguise:

> To thine own self be true, they tell you; well, I allowed myself that luxury just once and look what happened. No, no, give me the mask any day, I'll settle for inauthenticity and bad faith, those things that only corrode the self and leave the world at large unmolested.[3]

The original Freddie, in *The Book of Evidence*, formulated his own paradoxical faith in the superior reality of appearances and false fronts – 'To place all faith in the mask, that seems to me now the true stamp of refined humanity.' Anyone following the progress of Banville's fiction, especially the evolution of Freddie, will recognise the part which this motif of the mask plays in these parables about invented lives and identities. The essential point about such figures is their belief in the subjective truth of a fiction. *The Untouchable* extends this aesthetic into the world of political espionage and sexual intrigue, where the idea of a simple fiction is deeply and imaginatively complicated by questions of moral betrayal. Banville's version of Blunt is a character called Victor Maskell, whose very name highlights those elements of arrogance and falsehood which distinguish the artistic performance of a master-spy.[4]

What is remarkable, and inventive, then, about Banville's version of this character and this history? To a great extent Banville keeps to, and respects, the major outlines of the story of the Cambridge spies – Blunt, Guy Burgess, Donald Maclean, Kim Philby and John Cairncross – and the significant details of their intrigues and friendships over several decades, from the days of their ideological conversion in the 1920s to the eventual exposure of their activities, whereupon Burgess and Maclean defected to Russia and, in 1979, Margaret Thatcher informed a stunned House of Commons at Westminster that Sir Anthony Blunt, Keeper of the Queen's Pictures, had been a lifelong Soviet spy.[5] After this parliamentary denunciation, Blunt gave a carefully prepared interview to the British newspapers *The Times* and *The Guardian*, in which he explained and defended his past actions.[6] Banville's novel adopts this retrospective stance for what Maskell describes as his 'last testament', a solipsistic submission which resembles Freddie Montgomery's book of evidence, one to be placed alongside, in his words, 'the other, official fictions'. Maskell's memoir disputes the authority of these 'official fictions' while acknowledging the fiction of a story told by a virtuoso of deceit. William Trevor sees *The Untouchable* as a remarkable work of 'faction', a genre well suited to Banville's love of conjuring with versions of authenticity and truth, one which allows him to push his epistemological riddles to the limits of fiction.[7]

In his creation of Victor Maskell, Banville takes two major intertextual liberties with the biography of Blunt, both of which extend the themes of betrayal and deception. First, unlike Blunt, Maskell is married with two children. His eventual realisation that he was always gay now seems to him an inevitable kind of personal betrayal which only intensifies his sense of sexual duplicity. His sexuality, like his politics, is an illicit practice which requires constant caution. Homosexuality, like spying, is a crime under law, both activities requiring infinite and exquisite public camouflage. Second, unlike Blunt, Maskell is an Irishman, son of an Ulster clergyman. For this conversion of the quintessential Englishman into an Irishman who reinvents himself as an Englishman, Banville borrows elements from the biography of the Irish poet Louis MacNeice, who went to school at Marlborough College with Blunt but who never shared Blunt's sexual or political tastes.[8] One of the most significant elements in this borrowing is the figure of a younger, mentally disturbed brother, who now appears as Freddie in *The Untouchable*.[9] Making Maskell an Irishman adds to the character's constant sense of being an outsider on the inside, someone whose treacherous and traitorous career might just be explained by his roots. Betrayal now assumes a racial as well as a purely political character: Maskell spends most of his life acting the role of an English dilettante, yet he remains aware of the denial and the deceit required for such a performance. These two invented layers of identity, sexual and racial, reshape the historical figure of Blunt into that kind of fictional character much loved by Banville, one who finds himself torn in two, always regarding another self, another life. This motif of the divided self gives *The Untouchable* its distinctive sense of a displaced identity, and of a consciousness fascinated by its own protean fictions.

The novel opens on the day when Maskell, now aged 71, has just concluded his carefully stage-managed interview with the press, fending off questions about his loyalties and motives. He has returned to his apartment and has decided, for reasons he cares not to explore fully, to write his own version of the past, summoning up ghosts from two lives, his Irish childhood and his English adulthood, the interplay between these two intensely recollected landscapes providing an alternating rhythm to the structure of his story. For someone who spent most of his life carefully avoiding any textual evidence which might have betrayed him, the act of writing strikes him as particularly radical and daring, the decision of a man who knows he is dying, finally free to compose and create a self-portrait which satisfies an imaginative understanding of himself. At the same time as he begins his autobiography, he agrees to be interviewed by a young woman, Serena Vandeleur, a journalist who wishes to write his biography. A lifetime spent contemplating works of art makes Maskell regard those around him in artistic terms, as if their type had already been represented and fixed by some great artist, or by some low comedy, from the past. This way of seeing the world is, he confesses, 'another of my besetting weaknesses, to see people always as caricatures. Including myself.' Vandeleur, he reflects, has 'the drawn look of a Carracci madonna'. Anticipating her questions about his faith and motivation, he leads her into his study and shows her a painting, his most prized possession, which he likes to believe will answer all such queries. The picture, *Death of Seneca*, by Poussin, is central to Maskell's self-image and to the development of that image throughout the novel.[10] Maskell tries to explain the inspirational significance of the image to Vandeleur:

> 'The subject', I said, in what I think of as my Expounding Voice, 'is the suicide of Seneca the Younger in the year AD 65. See his grieving friends and family about him as his life's blood drips into the golden bowl … Seneca fell foul of Claudius's successor, the aforementioned Nero, whose tutor he had been. He was accused of conspiracy, and was ordered to commit suicide, which he did, with great fortitude and dignity.[11]

Maskell would have Vandeleur, and his readers, believe that this image might be read in his favour, an image which tells of heroic sacrifice and service rewarded by disloyalty and ignorance. Seneca the Stoic provides Maskell the Machiavelian with an ennobling and exemplary precedent for an honourable death. Maskell likes to believe (the extent of his self-delusion is not so evident at this early stage in the novel) that the analogy between the classical and the contemporary worlds is free of any sense of incongruity or parody, that his own motives and principles may be identified with Poussin's idealisation of ancient virtue hounded to death by a corrupt system.

Political commitment is both a challenge and an anathema to an aesthete like Maskell, and he repeatedly returns to this dilemma in his conversations with the sceptical Vandeleur, trying to explain and illustrate the intolerable contradictions between a love for art and the academy and, on the other hand, a fascination with the certainties of Marxist ideology. In retrospect, he now believes that he never really believed in anything, that his seeming commitment to Marxism was a form of impetuous escapism, an escape from intellect:

> I suppose that is what I meant when, at the outset, Miss Vandeleur asked me why I became a spy and I answered, before I had given myself time to think, that it was essentially a frivolous impulse: a flight from ennui and a search for diversion. The life of action, heedless, mind-numbing action, that is what I had always hankered after. (138)

Maskell now realises that his imagination had betrayed him, since his experience of the real world of revolutionary socialism left him aghast at its vulgar immediacy, and intellectually contemptuous of the kinds of self-deception required of those converts from the cloisters of Cambridge. (The scholar Copernicus is marked by a similar envy of the world of action, only to find it repulsive.) One of the most characteristic effects of his memoir is that of grotesque bathos, an effect realised when he contrasts the fanciful expectations of a brave new world generated by rhetoric, propaganda and spy-novels with the sinister and brutal realities of Civil War Spain and revolutionary Russia. His narrative includes a series of intensely evocative, often quite farcical, journeys undertaken as part of his new mission to discover the reality of the alternative political order to which he has devoted himself. Maskell is in his imaginative element during these many sea-voyages, a traveller caught between contrasting worlds, usually intoxicated by fantasies of anticipation. He recalls a visit to Spain in 1936, 'a hateful country', in which the horrors of street violence were only slightly relieved by visits to the Prado museum, where the art of Goya and El Greco reflected a similar kind of madness, but one which could be studied and enjoyed from a safe, contemplative distance.[12] One of the most memorable, and most surreal, journeys was that to Stalin's Russia, 'a horrible place', recalls Maskell, where he experienced yet again the split between revulsion and attraction.[13] His account of meetings with his Soviet handlers at the Kremlin, stocked with a gallery of bizarre stereotypes, and told with an overwhelming sense of the comic absurdity of the entire expedition, is one of the descriptive and narrative highlights of the novel. In Moscow, as in Madrid, Maskell's new ideology tries to reconcile itself with his old faith:

> And there was art. Here, I told myself, here, for the first time since the Italian Renaissance, art had become a public medium, available to all, a lamp to illumine even the humblest of lives. By art, I need not tell you, I meant the art of the past: socialist-realism I passed over in tastful silence. (An aphorism: *Kitsch is to art as physics is to mathematics – its technology.*) But can you imagine my excitement at the possibilities that seemed to open before me in Russia? Art liberated for the populace – Poussin for the Proletariat! Here was being built a society which would apply to its own workings the rules of order and harmony by which art operates; a society in which the artist would no longer be dilettante or romantic rebel, pariah or parasite; a society whose art would be more deeply rooted in ordinary life than any since medieval times. What a prospect, for a sensibility as hungry for certainties as mine was! (123–4)

One of the pleasures, and defining effects, of Maskell's narrative is the reproduction of his earlier postures, their forced idealism captured to perfection, and the whole being subjected to a kind of pitiful irony. Yet he realises, and confesses, that he found the totalitarian state quite congenial, and for similar, conservative reasons admires Poussin's versions of imperial Rome. Much as he envies Russia's collection of priceless, largely unseen, art works, the theatrical demands which permanent residence would make upon his personality, even one so gifted in that department, seem intolerable. (Maskell, like Blunt, chooses not to defect because he would no longer be free to visit Europe's art galleries.)[14]

Any reservations which Maskell felt about placing his faith in Marxism are dramatically justified when he recalls the most spectacular betrayal of all, the Hitler–Stalin pact. For Maskell, this consummate piece of ideological absurdity confirms his belief that nobody is to be trusted, that the confidently drawn distinction between good and evil, Marxism and Fascism, has vanished. (Even the British royal family is implicated in duplicity, as Maskell discovers when he is asked by the King to retrieve secret documents which might expose sympathy for the family's Nazi relatives. Maskell's journey to seek out these documents, based on an identical mission undertaken by Blunt, is one of the comic highlights of the novel.) Old certainties no longer console, and the world of politics is one which recognises no limit to deception or contradiction, no end to delusion. With the Hitler–Stalin pact, even the traitors feel betrayed. Robbed and cheated of any political certainty or faith, Maskell reverts to type, that of the pleasure-seeker. In his more innocent days, Maskell liked to believe that his disloyalty to England was really a form of loyalty to Russia; after the shameful discovery that masters as well as servants ca:¹ betray a cause, his secret life as spy and homosexual is free of any need for intellectual rationale. Now he can lead a double existence for its own, thrilling sake.

Most of Maskell's narrative is an attempt to deny, or explain away, an ideological motive for his treachery (as if that would be too dull-witted), and to replace that pointless kind of approach with one based on personality (as if that would do him justice). To the scandal of the investigator, one such as Miss Vandeleur, Maskell suggests that pleasure rather than principle may be the key to the investigation. Always the dilettante, Maskell explains that his line in criminality has an aesthetic as well as a political imperative, the latter being the object of conventional interest, the former an affront to conventional morality:

> Espionage has something of the quality of a dream. In the spy's world, as in dreams, the terrain is always uncertain. You put your foot on what looks like solid ground and it gives way under you and you go into a kind of free fall, turning slowly tail over tip and clutching on to things that are themselves falling. This instability, this myriadness that the world takes on, is both the attraction and the terror of being a spy. Attraction, because in the midst of such uncertainty you are never required to *be yourself*; whatever you do, there is another, alternative you standing invisibly to one side, observing, evaluating, remembering. This is the secret power of the spy, different from the power that orders armies into battle; it is purely personal; it is the power to be and not be, to detach oneself from oneself, to be oneself and at the same time another. (143)

Like most of Banville's narrators, Maskell is too much a solipsist, too extreme an individualist, to entertain a shared faith. The only time he can entertain others is when they provide him with an audience. Espionage, as he explains it here, is an oxymoronic state of being, a pleasurable fear, a terrifying delight, a Gothic pursuit. Contrary to received opinion and the fictions of the thriller genre, the secret life of a spy is a special, unimaginable kind of freedom. For the spy who is also a homosexual, it is a forbidden pleasure, another form of necessary invisibility which intensifies that sense, so marked in Maskell, of view-ing civil society as if it constituted an alien species. Being an intimate of the royal family, and one of England's leading art historians, gives Maskell the sweetest possible sensation of respectable subversion; being an Irishman completes his sense of mischievous power.

Maskell's narrative, ironic, narcissistic and sensuous in its style, is an attempt at an *apologia pro vita sua* which also includes a variety of characters – friends and family, homosexuals and heterosexuals – who help him to understand the roles he has played. Unlike the trilogy cen-tred on the equally solipsistic Freddie Montgomery, *The Untouchable* marks a return to a narrative which opens itself up to modern history, offering its readers a detailed and atmospheric series of sketches of Maskell's social world over several decades. One of the more obvious ironies about Maskell's individualist career is that he was part of a team, a conspiratorial fraternity linked as often by shared sexual inter-ests as by a common ideological ambition. Most, but not all, of the his-torical associates of Blunt appear in the novel, and each is given a new pseudonym – Guy Burgess is 'Boy', Donald Maclean becomes Philip MacLeish and, most controversially, Graham Greene becomes 'Querell', a sinister Judas-figure who eventually betrays Maskell. Most of Maskell's friendships originate from his Cambridge days, and his memory of these individuals is one marked by nostalgia as well as bit-terness, for he now realises that he was not the only one wearing a mask. His greatest delusion, perhaps, was to have believed that some private lives could remain exempt from the lure of betrayal.

Maskell's social world was that of the English upper classes, a circle of intelligent, adventurous and decadent individuals who delighted in shocking those whom they saw, or preferred to see, as the guardians of that very privilege which they enjoyed. That circle became part of the Bloomsbury set, leading a self-indulgent, hedonistic life dominated by endless parties, erotic self-dramatisation and exhibitionism, and relentless exchanges of opinion about politics and art. (Set a few decades earlier, *The Untouchable* could have been read as a tale about Oscar Wilde.) Some figures from the era are not granted a fictional dis-guise, thereby adding to the authentic gloss of the memoir, as with the figure of T. S. Eliot, whom Maskell remembers meeting at a Palace function, and recognising in the poet 'the lifelong, obsessive dissem-bler', another foreigner acting the part of an English gentleman.

The one figure from the past who dominates Maskell's memory is Nick Brevoort, son of a wealthy Dutch Jewish family, whose father,

Max, publishes books on art, and whose sister, Vivienne, impulsively and fatally, marries Maskell. From their first encounter, on a day when Maskell comes to discuss his art essays with Max Brevoort, Nick becomes the object of Victor's love and admiration, a young man he now recalls as 'pale as ivory, his black hair standing on end, all eyes and angles, a figure out of Schiele'. A kind of latter-day Adonis, Nick seems an unlikely convert to Marxism, a reluctant, unconvinced follower of the revolution. He also keeps a safe sexual distance from the Cambridge network, and is decisively heterosexual. Maskell's infatuation with Nick leads him to take a decision which brings together those two worlds – England and Ireland – which he had hoped would remain forever apart, resulting in one of the most telling, and most poignant, episodes in the novel. Nick expresses an interest in visiting Maskell's home, in Carrickdrum, County Antrim. Yet another sea-voyage, grim and surreal, ensues. For the first time in his life, Maskell feels that he is being spied upon, and he does not like what he imagines Nick sees. His family gathers to greet the two men – his sad and bewildered father, his over-excited and embarrassed stepmother, and his simpleton brother, Freddie, his 'Quasimodo' – and the occasion is one which makes Maskell feel only shame. This is the first time that his mask of Englishness slips, and he is horrified to see the shabby provincialism of his background, which claims him as one of its own.

That background reveals even deeper layers of deception in Maskell, as we learn (but Nick does not) of how the family had changed their Gaelic name and Catholic religion during the Famine in order to survive the catastrophe. Maskell's present incarnation as an Englishman is only the latest in a history of constructed identities. He remembers his decision never to share this knowledge with Nick:

> I had no wish to introduce Nick to these legends, and much less to walk with him through the sites where had stood the stone cottages of my forebears and the base beds from which they had sprung. In these matters he and I observed a decorous silence: he did not speak of his Jewishness, nor I of my Catholic blood. We were both, in our own ways, self-made men. (77)

As the Yeatsian allusion suggests, Maskell is determined to deny class and race, and to assert a wholly fictional lineage, one which is born out of ambition rather than loyalty.

This humiliating visit to Ireland is also Maskell's initiation into a betrayal of his family. Freddie, a true innocent, more child than man, unnerves Maskell with his dumb-show antics, and seems to mock his older brother's recognition of a shared origin. Years later, when his father dies, Maskell pays one more visit to his home, this time to place Freddie in a home, where he soon dies. Nick was the kind of brother he would have preferred, or would have chosen, but at the end of the novel he discovers that the seemingly non-committal Nick has helped betray him to the authorities. Nick lived the biggest lie of all, becoming a Tory grandee, while secretly continuing his work as a Soviet spy. Nobody, not even the godlike Nick, is above the world of infinite, unimaginable deception. In one final, pathetic gesture, Maskell tells Nick that he will bequeath his beloved *Death of Seneca* to him. The traitor, Maskell seems to suggest, best deserves this tribute to a man betrayed.

While Maskell was deceived by Nick, he was always sure that another character in the company did not belie his true nature, and that he was probably the one who urged Nick to proceed with public exposure and humiliation. That character turns out to be Querell. Whereas Maskell looks back on Nick with nostalgia as well as disillusion, his portrait of Querell is one of pitiless contempt. Querell is portrayed as the supreme traitor in *The Untouchable*, in Chris Petit's view 'a gleeful hatchet job and act of cold revenge' on Graham Greene.[15] The savagery of this portrait makes perfect fictional, but little historical, sense. Greene, like Blunt, worked for British Intelligence in MI6, but they were never close, and Greene's interest in spying was itself largely literary.[16] He had once worked with Kim Philby, and had even visited him in Moscow when he defected, using Philby as the basis for the character of a lonely spy-in-exile in *The Human Factor* (1978), one of his many political thrillers.[17]

Maskell's narrative opens and concludes with paranoid reflections upon Querell. The irony of searching for a traitor in his midst is not lost upon Maskell, but Querell, unlike Nick, deceived him by not wearing a mask. Maskell now recalls those many parties where the Cambridge set gathered:

> Sometimes Querell would come round, tall, thin, sardonic, standing with his back against the wall and smoking a cigarette, somehow crooked, like the villain in a cautionary tale, one eyebrow arched and the corners of his mouth turned down, and a hand in the pocket of his tightly buttoned jacket that I always thought could be holding a gun. He had the look of a man who knew something damaging about everyone in the room. (33)

Unlike most people in Maskell's circle, Querell was always what he appeared to be – that was the paradoxical secret of his deception. Convinced that everyone wore some kind of contradictory disguise, Maskell never suspected that behind the appearance of this villain lay a villain. He remembers hating Querell for a number of reasons, his hypocritical Catholicism, his anti-Semitism and his paedophilia, but most of all for his writing, 'his bleak little novels', which to Maskell did no more than capture 'the spiritual exhaustion of the times'. With a daring double irony, Banville's high priest of neo-Stoicism derides Querell's realism, 'the sure mark of the second-rate novelist': the inveterate, incurable snob, Maskell sees no artistic merit or justification in these popular fictions about espionage. A dedicated defender of a classical aesthetic, he takes his values from the frozen, 'timeless' world of ancient Rome and Greece, with its more elevated forms of deception and intrigue. As William Trevor suggests, his artistic preferences, like his hatred of Querell, probably reveal more about his own defective personality than they do about the object of his loathing.[18]

At the end of the novel, Maskell is directed to Nick by Querell. In a superbly crafted episode, Maskell and Querell meet in a gloomy London pub, full of skinheads and pinball machines, for a final reckoning. (How many of Banville's most revelatory moments take place in such dives!) Like a 'pair of sad old withered eunuchs', stranded in an unrecognisably modern London, they exchange versions of betrayal. That Querell had betrayed him comes as no surprise, but another, unexpected, more intimate treachery is revealed – Querell's affair with Maskell's wife, Vivienne, and, to a shocked Maskell, the sudden possibility that he is not even the father of his own children. There is a kind of sadistic retribution at work here, with Querell having punished as well as outwitted an increasingly isolated and bewildered Maskell. The former pleasure of a political double existence gives way to the fear of a sexual betrayal.

The Untouchable is the first novel by Banville in which a voyeuristic, or contemplative male fantasy about women is displaced by its seeming opposite, homoerotic desire. Maskell's postmarital realisation that he prefers homosexual adventures to a more conventional form of love seems consistent with his preference for the exclusively male world of espionage, a fraternity dedicated to secrecy in everything, including sexuality. 'Boy', the most outrageous and flamboyant of all the gay figures in the novel, understands this collusion between sexuality and secrecy better than most, and comes up with his own witty neologism for this group of Marxist gays, the 'Homintern', although their Soviet handlers maintain an embarrassed silence on the radical sexuality of their British agents. Politics and sexuality, especially when their form is forbidden, provide a special kind of pleasure, not least the sense, or the illusion, of powerful and radical transgression, the feeling that the body, as well as the intelligence, is constantly alert and sensitive to adventure and risk. Maskell recalls post-war England as a kind of golden age for gays:

> The fifties was the last great age of queerdom. All the talk now is of freedom and pride (pride!), but these young hotheads in their pink bell-bottoms, clamouring for the right to do it in the streets if they feel like it, do not seem to appreciate, or at least seem to wish to deny, the aphrodisiac properties of secrecy and fear. At night before I went out cottaging I would have to spend an hour downing jorums of gin to steady my nerves and steel myself for the perils that lay ahead. The possibility of being beaten up, robbed, infected with disease, was as nothing compared with the prospect of arrest and public disgrace. And the higher one had climbed in society, the farther one would fall. (353-4)

Both politically and sexually, Maskell and Boy experience an additional thrill which is implied in that fear of a fall from elevated places, namely, playing with the working class. Academic Marxists, like Cambridge gays, enjoy the idea, if not always the reality, of betraying their own class in favour of one they despise, but one which serves their appetite. Boy and Blunt enjoy the crude sexual vitality of a young Welsh guardsman, Danny Perkins, but secretly deplore his lack of refinement. Blunt's later lover, Patrick Quilly, an ex-soldier and a fellow Irishman, whom he recalls as his 'quondam catamite', is a wonderful housekeeper and lover, but Blunt is terrified at the prospect of Quilly embarrassing him through any attempt to discuss art in front of his friends.[19] Such patrician sensitivity to the tastelessness of working-class lovers, a philistine 'bit of rough', is not something Maskell seeks to defend: rather, he accepts it as yet another mark of his contradictory, often absurd, behaviour. In his reflections on Quilly, Maskell recalls their relationship as the perfect alternative to marriage with a woman, since his partner 'was neither female, nor fertile', and wonders 'if women fully realize how deeply, viscerally, *sorrowfully*, men hate them'. This suggests that Maskell turns to men because he turns away, regretfully, from women. Like so many of Banville's 'high, cold heroes', Maskell both fears and envies women, is scared of their fertility, their sexuality, but desires their apparent harmony, their self-composure. Grand interpreter of Poussin, Maskell is less theoretical about sexuality, but he offers one tentative generalisation about homosexual types – 'queers seem to come in only two varieties, the sloven, like Boy, or the monk, like me'. The monk leads us to the world of the Stoic, both figures dedicated to forms of self-denial, sexual and political, leading lives based on principled retirement.

Banville has chosen carefully in identifying Maskell with the supremely male character of Poussin's images of Stoic virtue. Here is a very different artist, a very different world, from Watteau or Vermeer, with their sensuous studies of the female gaze or dream landscapes in which the guiding spirit is Venus or Pan. Whereas their art seems to reveal or explain nothing, being simply an object of enigmatic and seductive beauty, the art of Poussin, as Anthony Blunt himself noted, quoting Poussin's contemporaries, is that of *'le peintre philosophe'*.[20] Blunt's classic monograph on Poussin (still regarded as an authoritative, definitive work) provides Maskell with a rationale and Banville with a sub-text. According to Blunt, Poussin was deeply read in the lives and works of the ancient Stoics, Plutarch, Valerius Maximus, Livy and Tacitus, and enjoyed expressing his own values through quoting those of Seneca.[21] He never painted a *Death of Seneca*, but some of his greatest work represented his understanding of Stoic dignity in the face of misfortune and tragedy, such as the monumental *Death of Germanicus*, painted for Cardinal Francesco Barberini, nephew of Pope Urban VIII, or *Landscape with Diogenes*, or *Landscape with the Body of Phocion Carried out of Athens*. He also drew sketches of his Stoic heroes, such as *The Death of Cato the Younger* (held by the Royal Library, Windsor Castle, where Blunt worked as Keeper of the Queen's Pictures). Poussin's patrons, notably Cardinal Richelieu, often commissioned such works in order to see the reflected glory and dignity of their own regime. Poussin's service to the French royal court and to the papacy is the result of deep ideological sympathy with the conservative powers of the day, a conviction that these allegories of heroic virtue enact a kind of parallel history, where past and present civilisations regard each other.

Banville's version of this source of inspiration suggests a very similar identification between ideology and art, but in the self-regarding account given by Maskell the intertextual analogy becomes strained, to the point of near parody. Towards the end of his story, Maskell defends his life through his work, citing his 'definitive monograph on

Nicholas Poussin'. Like a cornered man, in defiance of his pursuers, he declares his work to be that of a singular genius, an envied and incomparable achievement:

> One might say, I have invented Poussin ... After me, Poussin is not, cannot be, what he was before me. This is my power. I am wholly conscious of it. From the start, from the time at Cambridge when I knew I could not be a mathematician, I saw in Poussin a paradigm of myself: the stoical bent, the rage for calm, the unshakeable belief in the transformative power of art. I *understood* him, as no one else understood him, and, for that matter, as I understood no one else. (343)

This is the voice of genius at its most arrogant, its least imaginative (a voice not heard in Blunt). To try to judge Banville's intention here, it is perhaps worthwhile to recall and compare those other scholars in his work who once thought, or were told, that they had produced a similar *magnum opus,* Copernicus, Kepler or the biographer in *The Newton Letter.* None of these writers dares to trust the 'truth' of his text, or the accuracy of his perception. Ironically, Maskell admits that he always despised the ideological certainties of Marxist aesthetics, declaring that Poussin's art has a purely formal existence but no extractable meaning. Conversely, Blunt declared that Poussin's Stoic paintings 'cannot be properly understood if they are considered in formal terms only'.[22] At one point, Maskell quotes Blunt quoting Poussin, in a revelatory statement by the French artist which Maskell believes may best express his own understanding of the proper stance of the intellectual in times of political crisis:

> In a letter to his friend Paul Fréart de Chantelou in 1649, Poussin, referring to the execution of Charles I, makes the following observation: 'It is a true pleasure to live in a century in which such great events take place, provided that one can take shelter in some little corner and watch the play in comfort.' The remark is expressive of the quietism of the later Stoics, and of Seneca in particular. There are times when I wish I had lived more in accordance with such a principle. Yet who could have remained inactive in this ferocious century? Zeno and the earlier philosophers of his school held that the individual has a clear duty to take a hand in the events of his time and seek to mould them to the public good. This is another, more vigorous form of Stoicism. In my life I have exemplified both phases of the philosophy. When I was required to, I acted, in full knowledge of the ambiguity inherent in that verb, and now I have come to rest – or no, not rest: stillness. Yes: I have come to stillness. (198)[23]

8 Nicolas Poussin, *The Death of Cato the Younger* (c. 1638)

This calming moment of self-reassurance is overtaken and displaced by Maskell's intensifying doubt about the existence of any form of authenticity, artistic, political or sexual. Like Dorian Gray, he begins to fear the indifference of art to his anguish, and suspects that his faith may have been misplaced – 'Or have I double dealt for so long that my true self has been forfeit?' In the end, Maskell is determined on suicide, the classic gesture of the Stoic, citing Baudelaire's belief that suicide is the only sacrament in the religion of Stoicism. It is hard to share Maskell's belief that he, like Seneca, is a reformed servant of power and corruption, an honourable man who finally discovers the consolation of philosophy. His belief, or hope, that he can imitate and re-enact the drama of his favourite painting is perhaps his most damning delusion of all.[24] If one were to look for a true Stoic in Banville, it would be Kepler, not Maskell: the wandering scholar-astronomer, we may recall, is also inspired by a work of art, a copy of Dürer's engraving of *Knight with Death and the Devil*, 'an image of stoic grandeur & fortitude', as he describes it, and from which he derives great solace in times of tribulation.

The story of Blunt and the Cambridge spies offers Banville an ingenious plot through which he can dramatise the many kinds of betrayal, political, personal, ethical and artistic, which preoccupy his imagination. His very first novel, *Nightspawn*, is founded on the anxiety of betrayal. A quarter of a century after that intense, but rather crude, thriller, Banville has discovered a story, and achieved a stylistic precision, which show how the motif of treachery can be made to work in the service of a richly philosophical fiction, a drama of the self torn between individual and political loyalties. The range and synthesis of meanings made possible through this motif are what make *The Untouchable* such an adventurous and stylish achievement. The many-layered conceit of illusion and deception also implicates, of course, the necessary fictional strategies of narrative and recollection, the textual process of writing itself. Blunt's account reveals a history of betrayal, while simultaneously showing us the kind of fictional performances which that history required. Espionage becomes yet another supreme fiction, the activity, the fatal talent, of a tragic, perhaps a merely pathetic, actor. If there is any redemption in *The Untouchable*, it can only lie with the quality of that deluded imagination.

12

Two dramatic pieces:
The Broken Jug and *Seachange*

The novels and the plays make a sort of broken Ark of the Covenant,
wherein we find preserved the jumbled remnants of our culture: a
snatch of Schubert, a memory of Milton's cosmology, a night, tem-
pestuous and bright, such as Kaspar David Friedrich loved. This is
the shattered song of our time.

> John Banville, 'Samuel Beckett dies in Paris aged 83'
> (*The Irish Times*), 27 December 1989

WRITERS WHO have made their reputation in a single genre often
find it difficult to achieve recognition for creative work which
falls outside that genre. Poetry by Beckett, or by Joyce, might be an
example of this critical tendency to relegate what is seen as somehow
a pursuit secondary in interest and value to the primary defining form.
Major writers nearly always experiment in a variety of forms, if only to
see how their imagination is reshaped by the demands and the discipline of alternative forms of expression. Sometimes the experiment is
what we might see as a sporting interlude between major enterprises,
a relaxation of the major creative design.

Banville's two plays, *The Broken Jug (1994)*, written for the theatre,
and *Seachange* (1994), written for television, are interesting digressions from novel-writing, both appearing between *Ghosts* (1993) and
Athena (1995). The plays give Banville a chance to exercise those
dramatic skills so evident in the fiction.

The Broken Jug[1] is an adaptation of a classic German comedy, *Der
zerbrochene Krug* (1807) by Heinrich von Kleist (1777–1811), a choice
which confirms Banville's well-established regard for German literature, a regard reflected in the many and varied forms of reference in
the novels to writers such as Mann, Rilke and Goethe. Writing his own

version of Kleist was, according to Banville himself, the culmination of a long and fruitless attempt to get some other Irish writer to do it.[2]

Banville's version of Kleist is a short two-act play which retains most features of the original plot and characterisation, but which changes the location from early-nineteenth-century Holland to Ireland at the height of the Famine, from Utrecht to 'Ballybog', a stereotypical West of Ireland village like Friel's Ballybeg. In terms of language, character-isation and setting, this is a distinctively Irish version of the German *Lustspiel*. 'You could describe it as a case of "mad sub-editor re-writes Kleist"', Banville has remarked.[3] Banville's own comedy is based on a plot which revolves around the deception and confusion provoked by a farcical court case in which a broken jug provides the only material evidence for a crime whose perpetrator turns out to be the judge him-self. Judge Adam, prosecutor and culprit, represents a chaotic version of British justice in Ireland, a devious and utterly corrupt local tyrant who has to endure an official visitation by Sir Walter Peel, the Lord Lieutenant's inspector of courts. This is as much a comedy of class as one of culture. The case of the day, the conduct of which Sir Walter observes with rising disbelief, involves charges brought by the widow Reck, against persons as yet unknown, of destruction of her precious jug, and of interference with the virtue of her beloved daughter, Eve. The accused, and the defendant, is Eve's suitor, Robert Temple, whose family has been involved in a bitter sectarian struggle with the Reck family over land. As the chaotic proceedings develop, with Sir Walter being fed copious amounts of poteen to distract him from the parody of justice taking place before his eyes, the finger is eventually pointed at Judge Adam, who is exposed and detained by his own court. His position will now pass to Lynch, his clerk, a mocking figure who seems to have been waiting in the wings for such an opportunity to outwit and depose his master. Justice is finally done, with little thanks to Law and Order. The play, as Fintan O'Toole has remarked, uses a court-room farce to highlight the tragic reality of the Famine outside the court-room.[4]

This parallel between the absurd and the grotesque, between domestic and political chaos, recalls the demented world of *Birchwood*, especially its ancient quarrel over land and title. *The Broken Jug* gives Banville an opportunity to replay some of those fictional stereotypes, and to do so through a borrowed drama whose satirical vision of order coincides with his own. Many of Banville's novelistic themes, such as betrayal and corruption, find an echo in this distilled piece of demotic theatre, one which, yet again, shows his ability to graft classic texts onto his own creative design and purpose.

The Broken Jug was first produced in the Peacock Theatre, Dublin, in June 1994, and met with an enthusiastic popular and critical reception. Banville himself seemed surprised and amused by its success, and noticed that the tragic side of his play seemed to be quickly overwhelmed by its comic energy, turning the event into what he described, happily, as 'an Ealing comedy'.[5]

If *The Broken Jug* shows Banville's ability and willingness to adapt a classic comedy to the theatre, then his other play, *Seachange*, written for a television series,[6] shows his determination to confront this most popular medium of all with uncompromising severity. *Seachange* may be seen as Banville's tribute to Beckett, a short intense drama about unspeakable grief which recalls the lyricism and the loneliness of the early Beckett, such as *All That Fall* or *Embers*. This thirty-minute play has the elemental simplicity of setting, situation and conflict of those haunting early pieces in which Beckett employed the Irish landscape and an Irish idiom to intensify the sense of strangeness and loss felt by the characters.

On a day in late spring, a man and a woman chance to sit together on a bench at the foot of a pier by the open sea. The man, well-spoken and dressed in a neat three-piece suit, with starched white shirt (but no tie), tells of having been found on the rocks behind them three months ago, having miraculously and mysteriously survived drowning. On that same day, he tells her, a child was found drowned at the same spot. For the rest of the play, he persists in recounting his story to a speechless and clearly grief-stricken woman, lamenting the failure of his memory to help him remember and understand his close encounter with death. In a rhetorical style which recalls Beckett's Krapp, his story is delivered with a pompous, rather forced breeziness which seems to suppress some deep torment. All through his monologue, the camera faces the couple squarely, revealing the incoming tide behind them, and the occasional figures, including a couple with a child, who walk along the pier. The woman scarcely responds to his delirious tale; indeed she only looks at him once, as if she cannot believe his inability or unwillingness to imagine who she might be. At one point, the man quotes Yeats's lines from 'The Stolen Child', 'Come away, O human child! / To the waters and the wild', hypnotised by the strange coincidence of the child's death and his own survival.

Finally, he notices the woman staring at something in the sea, and they rise together to discover a seal staring at them from the water. The woman then utters her solitary line of the play – 'Doesn't it look like a child's head?' Here is the mother of the drowned child, come to remember and to lament her loss. The play ends, as it began, with a tender, plaintive song by Schubert, one of Beckett's favourite composers.[7]

Seachange is a finely worked dramatisation of pain and confusion, simple, understated and concentrated, using Banville's skill with intensely related monologue, and making full dramatic use of the stark contrast between volubility and silence to create a terrible kind of tension which always threatens to reveal its source, but never does so explicitly. Seen the second time, the identity of the woman known, the play assumes a most poignant irony.

Conclusion

Qui dit romantisme dit art moderne.
Charles Baudelaire, *Salon de 1846*

A T THE outset of this study I proposed the idea that a single story underlies Banville's fiction, that the novels continue to open up new perspectives on a recurrent source of obsessive fascination – the imaginative consciousness of a divided self. Banville's formal habit of writing in a series, whether a tetralogy or a trilogy, strengthens this impression of a writer for whom each novel is only an episode, an intense moment, in a story of many parts. Even the typology of his narrators suggests that we are always listening to a single voice, one which is renamed in each text, but whose narrative mission is inherited from his fictional predecessor, to be passed on to the succeeding incarnation of that stylish, haunted voice. One narrative effect of this sequential design is that certain, if not most, of these novels only complete themselves within a series; individually, they remain partial, provisional tales. Novels such as *Mefisto* or *Ghosts* need their companion-texts to make full sense, being deeply dependent upon earlier, shaping dramas for their fictional justification and dramatic resolution. We can read Banville *à la carte*, but the most rewarding approach, one which I think Banville requires, is to stay the full course.

To propose that a single story unifies, or underlies, Banville's work is merely to emphasise that work's carefully crafted sense of purpose and design, its philosophical interests, and perhaps something of its sense of narrative direction; it is not to suggest that a single story somehow explains, miraculously, a complex, and often unpredictable, body of fiction. There is no 'key' to Banville's mythologies. The fictions themselves, as a reading of any individual novel suggests, challenge and undermine any sense of simple, confident self-sufficiency. Banville's work is a kind of metanarrative which, unlike most meta-narratives, repeatedly questions its own coherence. What sustains that work, throughout its multiple versions of the self, is its creative dependency on the major intellectual and artistic issues of the modern age, the Copernican revolutions in language as well as in science: most of the narrators are survivors of those revolutions, whose solipsistic tales draw all their imaginative strength from their contact and their fascination with mythologies of former days and other arts. Part of Banville's remarkable fictional achievement comes from his ability to construct and sustain his own mythology about the past, investing each of his narrators with a rich literary, artistic and intellectual imagination, one which is energised by its store of images. Banville's distinctive postmodernity owes a great deal to its love of premodernity.

The figure and practice of Samuel Beckett offer a suggestive analogy with Banville's aesthetic. Banville has repeatedly pointed to Beckett as one of his exemplary writers, emphasising what he believes are the distinctive marks of his modernity – impersonality, classicism, and a poetic voice.[1] (We might also note, in passing, the sequential nature of Beckett's fiction.) I think Banville shares with Beckett that curiosity about the workings of the nostalgic mind, its grief over lost love, lost opportunity, lost self, which often finds expression in versions of Irish pastoral, Banville's Wexford providing him with the landscape of childhood as do the Dublin mountains for Beckett.[2] James Mays believes that Banville is Beckett's true inheritor, a writer who 'transposes the epistemological questions raised in Beckett's trilogy into a world of espionage and deception', and whose 'paradigm of the writer is measured in relation to issues of personal trust and political allegiance.'[3] There are certainly many incontestable similarities between the two writers, formally and philosophically. Stylistically, however, the two seem worlds apart, as if Banville had absorbed the idea of Beckett, but translated it into a style which is positively baroque when seen alongside Beckett. After *Murphy*, Beckett's novels never display the kind of intellectual and literary exhibitionism which marks so much of Banville's art. And yet both writers have created a body of fiction which depends utterly on the drama of a voice, a consciousness which feeds off its own imagination and memory, and which consoles itself with its own fictions.

This is where Beckett and Banville, however, part company, the former writing himself out of literature, the latter displaying an insatiable appetite for more. The crucial difference between these two kindred writers turns, I believe, on Banville's faith in the humanist, and humanising, character of great art. If the possibility of such faith seems very limited in Beckett, it appears limitless in Banville. This kind of idealism, sometimes associated with the aesthetic of modernism[4] and its celebration of art for art's sake, recalls and reveals the romantic theory of the imagination which I believe is fundamental to Banville's own aesthetic. This idealism is always presented in Banville's fiction as a fragile, but necessary, kind of faith, and is usually subjected to extremes of violence and confusion. Each novel, as I have tried to show, constructs a situation and a landscape which threaten the extinction of such an ideal. The originality, and the continuity, of Banville's fiction lies in the variety of ways in which he is able to dramatise this recurrent conflict within a single voice, a single, solitary personality, one which is distinguished by a richly poetic, intensely visual imagination. That originality and continuity, and the suggestion of a single voice throughout the fiction, are stylistic effects, even illusions, which draw deeply, and ironically, upon the art of mimicry, the skilful imitation of a whole range of discourses, poetic, philosophical, historical, even journalistic. This is what I mean by 'creative dependency', an artistic strategy which creates its own distinctive mythology through the imaginative impersonation of other voices and narratives, shaping them into unprecedented fictional designs. One of the many pleasures for the reader of Banville is to observe and recognise the elements of this compositional performance, a kind of rhetorical ventriloquism in which the artist only speaks through borrowed voices, thereby concealing his own. This is an impersonal art which foregrounds subjectivity.

Despite his irritation at not being acknowledged as a probable source of inspiration for *The Untouchable*, George Steiner has paid one of the best-informed and most perceptive tributes to Banville's achievement as a novelist. Comparing Banville to John Updike (on the basis of their experimentation with trilogies, 'a genre relatively rare, and indeed suspect, in recent English fiction', according to Steiner), he declares the Irish writer to be 'the most intelligent and stylish novelist currently at work in English' on this side of the Atlantic.[5] He notes, and applauds, Banville's deliberate cultivation of links, through quotation, allusion and reference, with the European tradition of the novel, links which resonate throughout his work and which advertise its modernist pedigree. He also draws attention to the demands which that work makes upon its readers, suggesting that its intricate and sophisticated pattern of learned intertextuality defines and limits its readership, one which he believes is required to be 'mentally adult, literate in the arts and the sciences and prepared to read closely'.' Steiner responds to what he regards as the thinking person's novelist, a writer who assumes a degree of literary and cultural training in his readers – in effect, a student of the humanities. Leaving aside the wistful conservatism behind this assessment (which completes Banville's own fiction of belonging, not to the vulgar present, but to a Golden Age of the novel), I think Steiner has seized upon the very design which makes Banville's fiction so traditional in such a postmodernist way – its absorption of other forms of knowledge and expression, what we might call its interdisciplinary passion. The ideal, or at least the committed, reader of Banville is forced to contemplate ways of seeing and imagining which are beyond, but always mediated through, the language of literature. The symbolism of the sciences, or of painting, is regarded enviously by most of Banville's narrators, who see in it a form of elegance and clarity which their own linguistic disquiet never permits or achieves. Banville's fiction suffers from divided loyalties: it constantly yearns to be something else, something which dispenses with language; the sensuous beauty of its reflective idiom, however, suggests that this kind of literature can live with its own longing, and make a poetic virtue out of that sense of deficiency. This, perhaps, is how we might best appreciate Banville's surpreme fictions.

Notes

Introduction

1   See Patricia Waugh, *Practising Postmodernism: Reading Modernism* (London, Edward Arnold, 1992), pp. 3–24.

2   See Fredric Jameson, 'Postmodernism, or the cultural logic of late capitalism', *New Left Review*, 146 (1984), 53–93.

3   See my *John Banville*: A Critical Study (Dublin, Gill & Macmillan, 1991), pp. 2–3.

4   Waugh, *Practising Postmodernism*, pp. 130–2 (p.130) .

5   For a comprehensive account of Banville's interest in, and use of, Stevens's art, see Gary Ferguson, *Modernist Influences on the Fiction of John Banville* unpublished D.Phil., (University of Ulster, Jordanstown, 1997), pp. 197–268. Banville's views on Stevens are recorded in several interviews, notably in the *South Bank Show* interview with Melvyn Bragg (London Weekend Television, 1993), a transcript of which may be consulted in Ferguson, pp. 316–25. See also Banville's essay 'Making little monsters walk', in Clare Boylan (ed.), *The Agony and the Ego: The Art and Strategy of Fiction Writing Explored* (London, Penguin, 1993), pp. 105–13. The other great modernist poet whose celebration of the imagination attracts Banville is Rainer Maria Rilke, especially his *Duino Elegies*. See Rüdiger Imhof, *John Banville: A Critical Introduction* (Dublin, Wolfhound, 1997), pp. 18–19.

6   Harold Bloom, *Wallace Stevens: The Poems of our Climate* (Ithaca and London, Cornell University, 1977), p. 173.

7   Denis Donoghue, *The Sovereign Ghost: Studies in the Imagination* (London, Faber & Faber, 1978), pp. 1–34 (p.24). The definitive statement by Coleridge on this version of the imagination is to be found in chapter 13 of his *Biographia literaria* (1817).

8   Denis Donoghue, The *Ordinary Universe: Soundings in Modern Literature* (London, Faber & Faber, 1968), p. 268.

9   John Banville, *Birchwood* (London, Granda, 1984) p.12.

10 Seamus Deane, '"Be assured I am inventing": the fiction of John Banville', in Patrick Rafroidi and Maurice Harmon (eds), *The Irish Novel in our Time* (Lille,

Université de Lille, 1975), pp. 329–39 (p.333)

11 Linda Hutcheon, *A Poetics of Postmodernism* (London, Routledge, 1988), pp. 106–23.

12 Georg Lukács, *The Historical Novel* (Harmondsworth, Penguin, 1969).

13 Hutcheon, *A Poetics of Postmodernism*, p. 114.

14 This is why I would suggest that, while Banville's fiction seems written in sympathy with the deconstructionist spirit of postmodernist thought, it shows, especially in the astronomical tetralogy, equal sympathy for a scientific mind which believes in truth, empirical method and objectivity. The current theoretical fashion to dismiss all such facts as fictions is satirised and contested in Alan Sokal and Jean Bricmont, *Intellectual Impostures* (London, Profile, 1998).

15 Donoghue, *The Sovereign Ghost*, pp. 10–11.

16 As part of his construction of a literary persona, a man of letters who has risen above the supposed insularity of Irish writing, à la Joyce or Beckett, Banville has regularly dismissed any Irish influence on his work. In this simplistic and wilful opposition of the national and the international, the modern and the traditional, the aesthetic and the ideological, he has been followed by several critics, notably Imhof. In the last few years, however, this mask of indifference has been exchanged for a more generous and tolerant regard for the Irish presence in his work, and the corresponding sophistication of Irish realism in writers such as John MacGahern. See my articles, 'Stereotypical images of Ireland in John Banville's fiction', *Eire–Ireland*, 23:3 (1988), 94–102, and 'Versions of Banville: versions of modernism', in L. Harte and M. Parker (eds), *Contemporary Irish Fictions* (Basingstoke, Macmillan, forthcoming).

17 Richard Kearney, *Transitions: Narratives in Modern Irish Culture* (Dublin, Wolfhound, 1987), pp. 91–100 (pp. 91, 98-9).

18 Deane, '"Be assured I am inventing"', p. 334.

19 John Banville, *The Book of Evidence* (London, Secker &Warburg,1989), p. 65.

20 John Banville, *The Newton Letter* (London, Granada, 1984), p. 53.

21 Banville's choice of Watteau and Poussin as artists who embody opposed forms and ideals of desire, the one 'feminine', the other 'masculine', coincides with, and reflects, the conventional judgement of the art historian Kenneth Clark (who preceded Anthony Blunt as Surveyor of the King's Pictures). Clark sees Poussin's representations of women as 'aloof', due to what he calls 'a less intense personal involvement with feminine beauty'. Watteau, on the other hand, he considers the epitome of the artist who captures the essence of that beauty. Clark's account of the history of the representation of beauty and women is blissfully undisturbed by contemporary theory. See his *Feminine Beauty* (London, George Weidenfeld & Nicolson, 1980), pp. 24–5. For those interested in how poststructuralist and psychoanalytical theory might be applied to the relation between literature and art, see Julia Kristeva, *Desire in Language: A Semiotic Approach to Literature and Art*, ed. by Leon S. Roudiez (Oxford, Basil Blackwell, 1980), especially her essays on Giotto and Bellini, pp. 210–70. A more elementary, and much more accessible, introduction to these questions (although it says little about the version of high art visible in Banville) may be found in Rosemary Betterton (ed.), *Looking on: Images of Fem-*

ininity in the Visual Arts and Media (London, Pandora, 1987).

22 Banville, *The Book of Evidence*, p. 179

23 John Banville, *Athena* (London, Secker & Warburg, 1995), p. 7.

24 Declan Kiberd, *Inventing Ireland* (London, Jonathan Cape, 1995), p. 635.

25 Banville, *Birchwood*, p. 175.

26 John Banville, *The Untouchable* (London, Picador 1997), p. 103.

27 See Imhof, *John Banville*, pp. 158–61.

28 Joseph N. Riddel, *The Clairvoyant Eye: The Poetry and Poetics of Wallace Stevens* (Baton Rouge, Louisiana State University, 1967), p. 11.

1 *Long Lankin*

1 For the complete text, see R. V. Williams and A. L. Lloyd (eds), *The Penguin Book of English Folk Songs* (London, Penguin, 1976), pp. 60–1.

2 R. Imhof, 'An interview with John Banville', *Irish University Review*, 11:1 (1981), 5–12 (p.9)

3 A point made by Imhof in his article 'Banville's supreme fiction', *Irish University Review*, 11:1 52–86 (p. 55). But the stories are not, as Imhof argues, arranged along the same lines as Joyce's *Dubliners*.

4 John Banville, *Long Lankin* (London, Secker & Warburg, 1970), p. 99. All subsequent page references will be given parenthetically in the text.

5 Imhof, 'An interview with John Banville', p. 8.

6 John Banville *Long Lankin* (Dublin, Gallery, 1984).

7 Lucretius, Roman poet and philosopher, wrote his lengthy poem in praise of Epicurus, arguing that the pleasures offered to the senses by the natural world were the only proper aim of human existence.

8 F. O'Toole, 'Stepping into the limelight – and the chaos', *The Irish Times*, 21 October 1989.

2 *Nightspawn*

1 Michael Denning, *Cover Stories* (London, Routledge & Kegan Paul, 1987), p. 2.

2 John Banville, *Nightspawn*, (London, Secker & Warburg, 1971), p. 7. All subequent page references will be given parenthetically in the text.

3 The passage recalls the opening lines of Dostoyevsky's *Notes from Underground*, and alludes to Keats's verse tragedy *Isabella*, or *The Pot of Basil*, a version of the story from Boccaccio.

4 Imhof, 'An interview with John Banville', p. 5.

5 Deane, '"Be assured I am inventing"', p. 334.

6 Imhof, 'An interview with John Banville', p. 6.

7 *Ibid.*, pp. 6–7.

8 John Banville, 'Greece wasn't the word: second thoughts", *The Independent*, 28 March 1994.

9 In the Greek myth, out of the blood of the slain youth Hyacinthus grew a beautiful flower; hence the name, and its association here with 'Flora'.

3 *Birchwood*

1 Imhof, 'An interview with John Banville', p. 11.

2 See Imhof, *John Banville*, pp. 62–71, for detailed discussion of genres. Imhof emphasises the formal intricacy of the novel, what he calls its 'wheels-within-wheels' design. On Banville's use of the Big House genre, see also Susanne Burgstaller, '"This Lawless house" – John Banville's post-modernist treatment of the Big-House motif in *Birchwood* and *The Newton Letter*', in Otto Rauchbauer (ed.), *Ancestral Voices: The Big House in Anglo-Irish Literature* (Hildesheim, Georg Olms, 1992), pp. 239–56; Geardóid Cronin, 'John Banville and the subversion of the Big House novel', in Jacqueline Genet (ed.), *The Big House in Ireland: Reality and Representation* (Dingle, Brandon, 1991), pp. 215–30.

3 Banville, *Birchwood*, p. 12. All subsequent page references will be given parenthetically in the text.

4 For the background to this myth, see A. J. Spencer, *Death in Ancient Egypt* (London, Penguin, 1982), pp. 142–51.

5 This anagram of 'John Banville' reappears as the name of the fictional painter of *Pursuit of Daphne*, the first of a series of paintings in the text of Banville's later novel, *Athena* (1995).

6 'Aire and Angels', from which the following lines suggest something of the exalted quality which Banville tries to create in this section of the novel:

> Then as an Angell, face and wings
> Of aire, not pure as it, yet pure doth weare,
> So thy love may be my loves spheare;
> Just such disparities
> As is twixt Aire and Angells puritie,
> 'Twixt womens love, and mens will ever be.

See John Donne, *Selected Poems*, ed. John Hayward (London, Penguin, 1977), p. 36. Note also Donne's use of astronomical metaphor to suggest the mysteries of love: in its inventiveness and daring, Banville's use of this kind of imagery often seems 'metaphysical'.

7 Nabokov's *Ada* is a strong presence in *Birchwood*. Subtitled *A Family Chronicle*, its central characters are also twins. Nabokov's equally self-conscious narrator is fascinated, like Gabriel, by the fictions of time, saying, 'I am also aware that Time is a fluid medium for the culture of metaphors' (Vladimir Nabokov, *Ada* (Harmondsworth, Penguin, 1970), pp. 420ff.) See also Imhof, *John Banville* p. 76.

8 David Lodge finds that sexual ambiguity is a favourite and recurrent motif in much of this kind of writing: 'One of the most emotively powerful emblems of contradiction, one that affronts the most fundamental binary system of all, is the hermaphrodite; and it is not surprising that the characters of post-modernist fiction are often sexually ambivalent.' See Lodge's *Modes of Modern Writing* (London, Edward Arnold, 1977), p. 229.

9 Geert Lernout, 'Looking for pure visions', *Graph*, 1 (1986), 14–15.

10 Deane, '"Be Assured I Am Inventing"', p. 333.

11 See Kearney, *Transitions*, pp. 91–3. Kearney discusses the epistemological

questions raised by these two 'philosophers of modern European doubt', as he calls them. The line from Wittgenstein is taken from the *Tractatus logico-philosophicus*, 5:6.

12 Imhof, 'An interview with John Banville', p. 11.

4 *Doctor Copernicus*

1 Arthur Koestler, *The Sleepwalkers* (London, Hutchinson, 1979); Thomas Kuhn, *The Copernican Revolution* (Cambridge, Mass., Harvard University, 1976). While both books deal with astronomical theory and history, Koestler is more concerned with the individual personality's creative dimension.

2 Koestler, *The Sleepwalkers*, p. 124.

3 *Ibid.*, pp. 191–5.

4 Kuhn, *The Copernican Revolution*, p. 135.

5 For Koestler, this fear seems as much a question of personality as of conviction. See *The Sleepwalkers*, pp. 153–65.

6 Kuhn, *The Copernican Revolution*, p. 136.

7 Especially Goethe's *Faust*, in its description of ambition and corruption through Faust and Mephistopheles, a relationship echoed in that between Copernicus and his brother, Andreas. But Thomas Mann's version of the myth, *Doktor Faustus*, seems to me just as important: it is a novel which provides many references and allusions in Banville's tetralogy, and whose protagonist, the musician Adrian, in his obsession with the symbolic language of musical harmonies, offers an interesting comparison with Banville's astronomer. On Goethe, see Rüdiger Imhof, 'German influences on John Banville and Aidan Higgins', in Wolfgang Zach and Heinz Kosok (eds), *Literary Interrelations – Ireland, England and the World*, 3 vols (Tübingen, Gunter Narr, 1987), vol. 2, pp. 335–47. Banville himself has spoken of Mann's novel as 'a presence behind all four books in the series'. See Imhof, 'Q. & A. with John Banville', *Irish Literary Supplement*, Spring 1987, p. 13.

8 John Banville, *Doctor Copernicus* (London, Granada, 1980), p. 13. All subsequent page references will be given parenthetically in the text.

9 Banville, *Birchwood*, p. 11

10 On the orthodoxy of such fictions, see P. Machamer, 'Fictionalism and realism in sixteenth-century astronomy', in R. Westman (ed.) *The Copernican Achievement* (London, University of California, 1975), pp. 346–53.

11 On the centrality of language to *Doctor Copernicus*, see Imhof, *John Banville*, pp. 78–83.

12 Koestler, *The Sleepwalkers*, p. 132. The image of Andreas as a 'leper' accords well with Banville's motif of the outsider in *Long Lankin*.

13 Banville's Copernicus and Mann's Adrian seem to share this kind of physical revulsion, an aloofness from contact with others epitomised in Adrian's Latin motto, *Noli me tangere*, 'Let no one touch me'.

14 The idea that suffering, especially that associated with serious illness, deepens and strengthens the character may be inspired by Nietzsche: see *Thus Spoke Zarathustra*, R. J. Hollingdale (London, Penguin, 1961), p. 18.

15 For the story of Rheticus's historical role, see Koestler, *The Sleepwalkers*, pp. 153–90.

16 For details of this crucial transfer of authorial control, and the possibility of Copernicus's connivance in the affair, see Koestler, *ibid.*,pp. 166ff. and Kuhn, *The Copernican Revolution*, pp. 187ff.

17 Koestler, *The Sleepwalkers*, p. 167.

18 See Kuhn, *The Copernican Revolution* pp. 196–7, for the background to these political and religious issues, and how it shaped the public reception of the heliocentric theory.

19 Quoted here from R. Porter (ed.), *Rewriting the Self: Histories from the Renaissance to the Present* (London, Routledge, 1997), p. 10.

20 Mann's *Doktor Faustus* also begins and ends with the childhood image of the linden tree.

21 Wallace Stevens, *Selected Poems* (London, Faber, 1980), p. 99. Banville's novel is rich in allusion to and quotation from *Notes toward a Supreme Fiction*.

22 See my article 'Naming the world: language and experience in John Banville's fiction', *Irish University Review*, 23:2 (1993), 183–96.

5 *Kepler*

1 For an account of Kepler's scientific discoveries, see Kuhn, *The Copernican Revolution*, pp. 209–19.

2 For a detailed analysis of the novel's formal structure, see Imhof, *John Banville*, pp. 134–41.

3 John Banville, *Kepler* (London, Granada, 1985), p. 11. All subsequent page references will be given parenthetically in the text.

4 Koestler contrasts Kepler, 'who came from a family of misfits', with Brahe, 'a grand seigneur from the Hamlet country'. See *The Sleepwalkers*,p. 283.

5 *Ibid.*, p. 266. Koestler also characterises Kepler as a man who 'always remained a waif and a stray' (p. 307).

6 When Kepler's *Mysterium cosmographicum* was first published, he added Rheticus's *Narratio prima*, the summary of Copernicus's theory, as an appendix to his book in order to save readers from what he feared would be unreadable and unintelligible. See Koestler, *The Sleepwalkers*, p. 254.

7 For details of the original incident, and Kepler's comments, see Koestler, *ibid.*, pp. 247–8. Kepler remarked, 'I believe Divine Providence arranged matters in such a way that what I could not obtain with all my efforts was given to me through chance.'

8 See Kuhn, *The Copernican Revolution*, pp. 214–19. For Kepler, as Kuhn puts it, 'God's nature is mathematical.'

9 That imperative and suppliant voice is from the 'Ninth Elegy' of Rilke's *Duino Elegies*. The key passage, which also supplies the novel's epigraph, is one of Banville's most quoted sources:

> Praise this world to the Angel, not the untellable: you
> can't impress him with the splendour you've felt; in the
>   cosmos

where he more feelingly feels you're only a novice. So show
  him
some simple thing, refashioned by age after age,
till it lives in our hands and eyes as a part of ourselves.
Tell him *things*.
R.M. Rilke, *Duino Elegies*, ed. J. B. Leishman and Stephen Spender, 4th edn (London, Chatto & Windus, 1981), p. 87.

10 From the 'Türmerlied' in Goethe's *Faust*:
Dear eyes, you so happy,
Whatever you've seen,
No matter its nature,
  So fair has it been!
For the fuller context, see J. W. von Goethe, *Faust*, Part II, ed. and tr. Philip Wayne (London, Penguin, 1967), pp. 259–61.

11 See Koestler, *The Sleepwalkers*, p. 241.

12 In Mann's *Doktor Faustus*, Dürer is Adrian's exemplary hero, especially his drawings of *Melancholia* and *Apocalypse*.

13 See Koestler's commentary on this autobiographical fantasy: *The Sleepwalkers*, pp. 415–19.

6 *The Newton Letter*

1 Banville himself described *The Newton Letter* as 'very much an interlude in the tetralogy'. See Imhof, 'An interview with John Banville', pp. 5–12.

2 The full background to this incident can be read in R. S. Westfall, *Never at Rest: A Biography of Isaac Newton* (Cambridge, Cambridge University, 1980), pp. 532–41.

3 For the complete text, see Hofmannsthal, *Selected Prose*, ed. H. Broch (London, Routledge & Kegan Paul, 1952), pp. 129–41.

4 See Geert Lernout, 'Banville and being: *The Newton Letter* and history', in J. Duytschaever and G. Lernout (eds), *History and Violence in Anglo-Irish Literature* (Amsterdam, Rodopi, 1988), pp. 67–77. Imhof stresses the influence of Goethe's *Elective Affinities* on the novella. See his *John Banville*, pp. 148–50, and his article 'German influences on John Banville and Aidan Higgins'.

5 Banville, *The Newton Letter*, p. 10. All subsequent page references will be given parenthetically in the text. A film version of the novella, by Courthouse Film Productions, entitled *Reflections*, was shown in the Channel Four series, *Film on Four: Take Two*, in 1986, with screenplay by Banville and directed by Kevin Billington. Gabriel Byrne played the part of the biographer of Newton.

6 Just as Gabriel, in *Birchwood*, faced with Justin and Juliette, those 'doubles in body and spirit', invents a composite fiction which he names 'Justinette'.

7 Almost word for word from Hofmannsthal's original text: see *Selected Prose*, pp. 140–1.

8 From the last line of the 'Ninth Elegy' in Rilke's *Duino Elegies*, the same section of the poem which appears in *Kepler*. See above, Ch. 5, n.9.

9 Apparently based on an anecdotal remark made by Newton to a friend, shortly

before his death. See Westfall, *Never at Rest*, p. 863.

10 Lernout, 'Looking for pure visions'; Brian McIlroy, 'Reconstructing artistic and scientific paradigms: John Banville's *The Newton Letter*', *Mosaic*, 25:1 (1992), 121–33.

11 Georg Lukács, The Theory of the Novel (London, Merlin, 1971), p. 88.

7 *Mefisto*

1 Banville has disclaimed any realistic intent in the early part of the tetralogy, saying that 'these astronomers were merely a means for me to speak of certain ideas, and to speak of them in *certain ways*. They also, of course, supplied readymade plots, which was handy.' See Imhof, 'Q. & A. with John Banville', p. 13.

2 See Imhof, *John Banville*, pp. 162–87, for detailed comparison between Goethe's *Faust* and *Mefisto*. This analysis was first published in Imhof's article 'Swan's way, or Goethe, Einstein, Banville – the eternal recurrence', *Etudes Irlandaises*, 12:2 (1987) 113–29.

3 Pressed on the correspondences between *Mefisto* and *Birchwood*, Banville says that this final novel of the series 'was returning to what one might call the realm of pure imagination out of which *Birchwood* was produced. No more history, no more facts!' See Imhof, 'Q. & A. with John Banville', p. 13.

4 In an interview on the eve of *Mefisto*'s publication, Banville mentioned this recurrent motif: 'There are things in fiction you do consciously and things you do because you couldn't help doing them. The notion of the lost self is something I can't help because I come back to it again and again.' See Ciaran Carty, 'Out of chaos comes order', *The Sunday Tribune*, 14 September 1986.

5 *Mefisto* (London, Secker & Warburg, 1986), p. 8. All subsequent page references will be given parenthetically in the text.

6 See my 'Naming the world', 183–96.

7 O'Toole, 'Stepping into the limelight'.

8 *The Book of Evidence*

1 For a comprehensive account of the Macarthur incident, see Joe Joyce and Peter Murtagh, *The Boss: Charles J. Haughey in Government* (Dublin, Poolbeg, 1983), pp. 211–36.

2 Seamus Deane, 'Witness for the defence', *The Irish Times* , 25 March 1989.

3 On the question of male fantasies about women, Imhof suggests that Nabokov's *Lolita* is an instructive parallel text for *The Book of Evidence*. See his *John Banville*, pp. 181–5.

4 *The Book of Evidence*, p. 16. All subsequent page references will be given parenthetically in the text.

5 *Human, All Too Human* (1878), here quoted from R. J. Hollingdale (ed. and tr.), *A Nietzsche Reader* (London, Penguin, 1977), pp. 76–7.

6 Freddie's description of the work is taken almost, but not quite, verbatim from the official guidebook , *The Budapest Museum of Fine Arts*, prefaced and edited

by Ágnes Czobor (Budapest, 1981), p. 59. The painting in question is therein entitled *Portrait of a Woman*, and is doubtfully attributed to Jan Vermeer Van Delft (1632–75). Rüdiger Imhof first identified the Budapest Museum as the location for this painting. See his *John Banville*, p. 256.

9 Ghosts

1 Thomas Kilroy, 'This isle is full of noises', *The Irish Times*, 27 March 1993. See also Imhof, *John Banville*, pp. 194–5.
2 The line is from 'Large Red Man Reading'. See Stevens, *Selected Poems*, p. 130.
3 This famous phrase comes from Rimbaud's poetic manifesto in his letter 'À Paul Demeny', 15 May 1871. For a commentary on the phrase's application to *Le Bateau ivre*, see Wallace Fowlie, *Rimbaud* (Chicago and London, University of Chicago, 1966), pp. 33–4. In 1932 Beckett wrote a translation of this extraordinary poem, a translation only discovered some forty years later. See James Knowlson and Felix Leahey (eds), *Drunken Boat* (Reading, Whiteknight, 1976). Of related interest is the series of poems written by Rimbaud's friend Verlaine under the title *Fêtes Galantes*, a series largely inspired by Watteau's paintings. Trying to explain the inspiration behind this series of reflections, Verlaine emphasised their 'sentiments costumés en personnages, de la comédie italienne et de féeries à la Watteau'. See Paul Verlaine, *Selected Poems*, ed. R. C. D. Perman (Oxford, Oxford University, 1969), pp. 12–13, 37–47.
4 Marianne Roland Michel, *Watteau* (London, Trefoil, 1984), p. 171.
5 For a detailed comparison of *Ghosts* and *The Tempest*, see Hedwig Schwall, 'Banville's Caliban as a prestidigitator', in Nadia Lie and Theo D'haen (eds), *Constellation Caliban: Figurations of a Character* (Amsterdam and Atlanta, Ga, Rodopi, 1997), pp. 291–311. Both texts, she argues, may be read as an 'erudite joke'.
6 John Banville, *Ghosts* (London, Secker & Warburg, 1993), p. 147. All subsequent page references are given parenthetically in the text.
7 *Gilles* and the first version of *Cythera* now hang in the Louvre, in Paris, while the second version of *Cythera* is in the Charlottenburg Palace, in Berlin. For a comprehensive scholarly account of these paintings, and their biographical and historical contexts, see Donald Posner, *Antoine Watteau* (London, Weidenfeld & Nicolson, 1984), pp. 116–277, especially pp. 182–95, 266–77. See also Imhof's comments on Watteau, *John Banville*, pp. 203–4. Banville's regard for Watteau, expressed in an interview, is worth noting:

> I love Watteau, but I don't really like him as an artist: technically he is not very interesting. His pictures are rather wan; yet I love the way Watteau's figures seem to have their own light. There is an extraordinary picture, it is in the Wallace collection in London – people sitting in a woodland scene at night, and they are like glow-worms. I love that, I find a pathos in that. These glowing figures are very very moving; this is poetry. Yet I wouldn't admire Watteau as a painter, whereas I admire Cézanne. You can love things without admiring them and you can admire things without loving them.

See Hedwig Schwall, 'An interview with John Banville', *The European English*

Messenger, 6:1 (1997), 13–19 (p.18). (The painting which Banville refers to in this extract seems to be Watteau's *Rendez-vous de chasse* (*Halt during the Hunt*), yet the painting reveals a daytime, not a night-time, scene.) In this interview, Banville has several interesting things to say about his interest in painting, especially his admiration for Cézanne and Velázquez.

8   Posner reminds us that the eighteenth-century Pierrots 'were reprehensible in morals, obscene in language and gross in social behaviour'. The nineteenth century excised this 'lunatic' and dangerous element from the character, and invented a much more sentimental version of 'the sad clown'. See Posner, *Antoine Watteau*, p. 267.

9   *Ibid*, p. 181.

10 Banville reviewed P. N. Furbank, *Diderot: A Critical Biography* (London, Secker & Warburg, 1992), in *The Irish Times*, 13 June 1992.

11 Michael Fried, *Absorption and Theatricality: Painting and Beholder in the Age of Diderot* (London, University of California, 1980), p. 99. The chapter in Fried most relevant to these ideas about the 'theatricality' of art is entitled 'Toward a supreme fiction', pp. 71–105.

12 Fried, *Absorption and Theatricality*, p. 101.

13 See my 'Naming the world', p. 190.

10 *Athena*

1   For a detailed and dramatic account of 'The General' and his notorious career, see Paul Williams, *The General: Godfather of Crime* (Dublin, O'Brien, 1995). Most of the paintings stolen from Beit, including Vermeer's *Lady Writing a Letter*, were eventually recovered. In August 1994, 'The General' was assassinated by the IRA. In 1997, these events were made into a film entitled *The General*, based on Williams's book, and directed by John Boorman.

2   *Athena*, p. 48. All subsequent page references are given parenthetically in the text.

3   See Joe Jackson's interview with Banville, 'Hitler, Stalin, Bob Dylan, Roddy Doyle … and me', *Hot Press*, 18:19 (1994), 14–16. In the interview, Banville confesses that, at one point, he had thought of naming the woman in *Athena* as 'O', 'which would have been too obvious'.

4   Nicci Gerrard, 'The Midas touch', *The Observer*, 19 February 1995.

5   As, for example, in the commentary on the third painting, *Pygmalion*, by 'Giovanni Belli', which quotes directly from Gombrich on the influence of Guido Reni upon mythological art. See Gombrich, *The Story of Art*, 15th edn (London, Phaidon, 1995), pp. 393–4.

6   The spirit, if not the letter, of the 'quotation' is from Auerbach's modern classic, *Mimesis: The Representation of Reality in Western Literature* (Princeton, Princeton University, 1953).

7   Banville himself has commented upon this kind of thematic continuity in the trilogy, remarking that 'all three books are about images, in Freddie's imagination'. See Hedwig Schwall, 'An interview with John Banville', p. 14.

8   Patrick McGrath, 'An elegiac love letter', *The Irish Times*, 11 February 1995.

11 *The Untouchable*

1 In a postscript to the novel, Banville acknowledges the major help of three books on the subject of the Cambridge spies: Barrie Penrose and Simon Freeman, *Conspiracy of Silence* (London, Grafton, 1986); John Costello, *Mask of Treachery* (New York, William Morrow, 1988); and Yuri Modin, *My Five Cambridge Friends* (London, Headline, 1994).

2 George Steiner, 'To be perfectly Blunt', *The Observer*, 4 May 1997. In the opening lines of this review, Steiner writes:

> I had best declare an interest. A number of motifs in this novel would appear to be based on my brief study of Anthony Blunt, *The Cleric of Treason*. This source is passed under silence. It is, however, a privilege to be of service to John Banville.

There is an implied charge of plagiarism here, or at least one of discourtesy. The problem lies, perhaps, in knowing, or guessing, what those 'motifs' are, and then whether or not they are exclusive to Steiner's essay, or available in those sources which Banville does acknowledge in the postscript to his novel. (Steiner's essay is itself quoted and acknowledged regularly in Costello's *Mask of Treachery*, one of Banville's sources.) A 'motif' suggests an interpretation rather than a body of evidence, an image rather than a fact. Reading Steiner's essay, which offers an incisive, subtle and utterly convincing psychological portrait of Blunt, one which analyses the emotional link between his sexuality and his scholarship, the only motif which suggests a borrowing not evident or available in Banville's given sources is that of the obsessive scholar who sees treason as an ideal form of action denied by scholarship, a fantasy of engagement with a reality which is held at a necessary distance by the demands of academic research. This interpretation of Blunt is certainly very close to Banville's representation of Maskell, but Banville did not necessarily depend on Steiner for this aspect of his fictional character. Furthermore, versions of this kind of motivation can be seen in some of the earliest figures in Banville's work, such as Copernicus, over a quarter of a century ago. While I don't think the implied charge of plagiarism can be upheld with any comparative textual precision, the possibility that Banville was unaware of Steiner's essay is very remote. That such a charge is raised at all almost seems an inevitable consequence of a fiction which chooses to declare its factual sources, calling into question, as the novel itself does, the boundaries between an original and a subsequent tale, between history and fable. Steiner's study, 'The cleric of treason', was first published in *The New Yorker*, 8 December 1980, 158–95. It was later reprinted in *George Steiner: A Reader* (Harmondsworth, Penguin, 1984), pp. 178–204.

3 Ghosts, p. 198.

4 Several of Banville's named sources see Blunt's character in terms of a masterly impersonator. Costello argues that 'Blunt's impassive masklike countenance was his primary asset' (*Mask of Treachery*, p. 20); and Modin, Blunt's Soviet handler in England, writes that Blunt's 'gentlemanly mask was … impenetrable' (*My Five Cambridge Friends*, p. 222).

5 See Costello, *Mask of Treachery*, p. 35.

6 See Penrose and Freeman, *Conspiracy of Silence*, pp. 505–18.

7 William Trevor, 'Surfaces beneath surfaces', *The Irish Times*, 26 April 1997.

8 In the 'Acknowledgements' to *The Untouchable*, Banville cites as his source Jon Stallworthy, *Louis MacNeice* (London, Faber & Faber, 1995). In an interview published a few months before the appearance of the novel, Banville commented on the link between Blunt and MacNeice:

> I gave Blunt the poet Louis MacNeice's life. They were very good friends at school, Blunt and MacNeice. Blunt was an expert on the painting of Poussin and, when I was doing research I opened up Louis MacNeice's *Selected Poems* and the first poem was called 'Poussin', so I thought, this is a good omen.

See Hedwig Schwall, 'An interview with John Banville', p. 13.

9 MacNeice's younger brother, Willie, suffered from Down's syndrome, and for a while was sent away to a mental hospital in Scotland. For an account of MacNeice's childhood and his relations with Willie, see Stallworthy, *Louis MacNeice*, pp. 23–71.

10 *Death of Seneca* is Banville's invention, a fiction which bears a studied resemblance to related subjects represented by Poussin. Blunt did own a Poussin, *Eliezer and Rebecca at the Well*, 'his pride and joy' according to Costello. It was purchased for him by his friend Victor Rothschild, who appears as Leo Rothenstein in *The Untouchable*. See Costello, *Mask of Treachery*, p. 209. Various galleries in Britain declined the offer of a painting associated with the notorious Blunt, until it was eventually accepted by the Fitzwilliam Museum at Cambridge.

11 Banville, *The Untouchable*, p. 27. All subsequent page references are given parenthetically in the text.

12 Blunt and MacNeice journeyed to Spain in 1936, in the early optimistic days of the Civil War, at a time when many left-wing writers and artists supported the new Republic and opposed Franco's rebellion. See Stallworthy, *Louis MacNeice*, pp. 178–82. For an account of the involvement of writers in the Spanish Civil War, including several of MacNeice's friends, such as W. H. Auden, see Frederick R. Benson, *Writers in Arms* (London, University of London, 1967), pp. 3–50.

13 The historical inspiration for this episode seems to come from an equally bizarre journey undertaken in 1935 by Blunt, then a Cambridge don, with a party of Soviet sympathisers who saw it as a visit to 'the promised land' of socialism. Blunt seems to have spent most of his visit viewing the rich collection of work by Poussin at the Hermitage Museum. See Costello, *Mask of Treachery*, pp. 251–4.

14 See Modin, *My Five Cambridge Friends*, p. 222.

15 Chris Petit, 'It's Cliveden, actually', *The Guardian*, 1 May 1997. Why Banville should select Graham Greene as the basis for this savage characterisation is not easy to understand. Whether it is, as Petit declares, 'an act of cold revenge', begs the question of original provocation. To the best of my knowledge, the only time that Greene and Banville crossed paths was during the Guinness Peat Aviation Awards in Dublin in November 1989, when Graham Greene acted as

adjudicator. Acting on the recommendation of the international panel of assessors, Greene declared Banville the recipient of the prestigious award, for his *The Book of Evidence*. However, Greene then announced an unprecedented award to Vincent McDonnell, who received a special prize for his first work of fiction, *The Broken Commandment*, a work which had not even been shortlisted. The simultaneous award to McDonnell caused quite a stir, and seemed like a snub to the assessors as well as to Banville.

16 See Costello, *Mask of Treachery*, pp. 415–16.

17 See Modin, *My Five Cambridge Friends*, p. 267. In a preliminary note to *The Human Factor*, Greene reflected on the intimate relation between fact and fiction in this kind of thriller, in terms which seem quite apposite to Banville's own novel:

> A novel based on life in any Secret Service must necessarily contain a large element of fantasy, for a realistic description would almost certainly infringe some clause or other in some official secrets Act. Operation Uncle Remus is purely a product of the author's imagination (and I trust it will remain so), as are all the characters, whether English, African, Russian or Polish. All the same, to quote Hans Andersen, a wise author who also deals in fantasy, 'out of reality are our tales of imagination fashioned'.

Graham Greene, *The Human Factor* (London, Bodley Head, 1978), p. 4. Very much Banville's sentiments, I would suspect.

18 Trevor, 'Surfaces beneath surfaces'. He writes, 'The sleaziness and failure with which Blunt, or Maskell, so bitterly imbues him are in fact Blunt's own, the coinage of a twilight realm where nothing is what it seems to be.'

19 Quilly is based on the figure of William John Gaskin, a former Irish guardsman who lived with Blunt for nearly thirty years. See Costello, *Mask of Treachery*, pp. 24–8.

20 Anthony Blunt, *Nicolas Poussin*, 2 vols (London, Phaidon, 1967), vol. 1, p. 160. Blunt's study was based on the Mellon Lectures in the Fine Arts, delivered at the National Gallery of Art, Washington, DC, in 1958.

21 See 'Poussin and Stoicism', chapter 4 in Blunt, *Poussin*, 1, pp. 157–76.

22 *Ibid.* 1, p. 160.

23 For Blunt's version of this passage, see his *Poussin*, vol. 1, p. 169.

24 Blunt died, not from suicide, but from a heart attack in 1983, three weeks after Donald Maclean had died in Moscow. See Costello, *Mask of Treachery*, pp. 602–4.

12 Two dramatic pieces

1 John Banville, *The Broken Jug* (Oldcastle, Gallery, 1994).

2 See Eileen Battersby, 'Comedy in a time of famine', *The Irish Times*, 24 May 1994.

3 Battersby, *ibid.*

4 Fintan O'Toole, 'Vigour meets rigour', *The Irish Times*, 8 June 1994.

5 In conversation with the present author.

6 John Banville, *Seachange*, (Radio Telefís Éireann, 1994). The play was one of

several in a series entitled *Two Lives*, produced by Michael Colgan. Each play was restricted to two characters. Other writers who contributed to the series included Patrick McCabe, with *A Mother's Love's a Blessing*, Anne Enright, with *Revenge*, and Dermot Bolger, with *In High Germany*. See Luke Clancy, 'TV for two', *The Irish Times*, 10 September 1994.

7 The play opens with Schubert's 'Der Einsame' ('The lonely one'), and closes with his 'Du bist die Ruh' ('You are rest'). I am grateful to Monika McCurdy for help in identifying these songs. Beckett's love of Schubert has been well documented by James Knowlson in his biography, *Damned to Fame: The Life of Samuel Beckett* (London, Bloomsbury, 1996). See especially pp. 626, 681–3.

Conclusion

1 See, for example, Banville's tributes in the wake of Beckett's death 'Writing for the last word', *The Observer*, 31 December 1989; and 'Samuel Beckett dies in Paris aged 83', *The Irish Times*, 27 December 1989.

2 The relation between biography and fiction in Banville remains to be explored. His recollections of a Wexford childhood are always worth reading, if only to appreciate its transformation in a novel such as *Birchwood*. See 'Lupins and moth-laden nights in Rosslare', *The Irish Times*, 18 July 1989. Of related interest is the memoir of their shared childhood by Banville's sister, Vonnie Banville Evans, *The House in the Faythe* (Dublin, Poolbeg, 1994).

3 J. C. C. Mays, 'Biographies in limbo', *The Irish Review*, 21 (1997), 134–6.

4 See Gene H. Bell-Villada, *Art for Art's Sake and Literary Life* (London, University of Nebraska, 1996), pp.1–13, 161–201.

5 Steiner, 'To be perfectly Blunt'.

Bibliography

Works by John Banville

Short stories

Long Lankin (London, Secker & Warburg, 1970).

Long Lankin (Dublin, Gallery, 1984).

Novels

Nightspawn (London, Granada, 1971).

Birchwood (1973; London, Granada, 1984).

Doctor Copernicus (1976; London, Granada, 1980).

Kepler (1981; London, Granada, 1985)

The Newton Letter (1982; London, Granada, 1984).

Mefisto (London, Secker & Warburg, 1986).

The Book of Evidence (London, Secker & Warburg, 1989).

Ghosts (London, Secker & Warburg, 1993).

Athena (London, Secker & Warburg, 1995).

The Untouchable (London, Picador, 1997).

Plays

The Broken Jug (Oldcastle, Gallery, 1994).

Seachange (Radio Telefís Éireann, 1994).

Backgound works

Auerbach, E. *Mimesis: The Representation of Reality in Western Literature* (Princeton, Princeton University, 1953).

Banville, J. 'Lupins and moth-laden nights in Rosslare', *The Irish Times*, 18 July 1989.

Banville, J. 'Samuel Beckett dies in Paris aged 83', *The Irish Times*, 27 December 1989.

Banville, J. 'Writing for the last word', *The Observer*, 31 December 1989.

Banville, J. 'Making little monsters walk'. In C. Boylan (ed.), *The Agony and the Ego: The Art and Strategy of Fiction Writing Explored* (London, Penguin, 1993).

Banville, J. 'Greece wasn't the word: second thoughts', *The Independent*, 28 March 1994.

Banville Evans, V. *The House in the Faythe* (Dublin, Poolbeg, 1994).

Battersby, E. 'Comedy in a time of famine', *The Irish Times*, 24 May 1994.

Bell-Villada, G. H. *Art for Art's Sake and Literary Life* (London, University of Nebraska, 1996).

Benson, F. R. *Writers in Arms* (London, University of London, 1967).

Betterton, R. (ed.) *Looking on: Images of Femininity in the Visual Arts and Media* (London, Pandora, 1987).

Bloom, H. *Wallace Stevens: The Poems of our Climate* (Ithaca and London, Cornell University, 1977).

Blunt, A. *Nicolas Poussin*, 2 vols (London, Phaidon, 1967).

Boylan, C. (ed.) *The Agony and the Ego: The Art and Strategy of Fiction Writing Explored* (London, Penguin, 1993).

Burgstaller, S. '"This Lawless house" – John Banville's post-modernist treatment of the Big-House motif in *Birchwood* and *The Newton Letter*', in O. Rauchbauer (ed.), *Ancestral Voices: The Big House in Anglo-Irish Literature* (Hildesheim, Georg Olms, 1992).

Carty, C. 'Out of chaos comes order', *The Sunday Tribune*, 14 September 1986.

Clancy, L. 'TV for two', *The Irish Times*, 10 September 1994.

Clark, K. *Feminine Beauty* (London, George Weidenfeld & Nicolson, 1980).

Costello, J. *Mask of Treachery* (New York, William Morrow, 1988).

Cronin, G. 'John Banville and the subversion of the Big House novel', in J. Genet (ed.), *The Big House in Ireland: Reality and Representation* (Dingle, Brandon, 1991).

Czobor, Á. (ed.) *The Budapest Museum of Fine Arts* (Budapest, 1981).

Deane, S. '"Be assured I am inventing": the fiction of John Banville', in P. Rafroidi and M. Harmon, (eds.), *The Irish Novel in our Time* (Lille, Université de Lille, 1975).

Deane, S. 'Witness for the defence', *The Irish Times*, 25 March 1989.

Denning, M. *Cover Stories* (London, Routledge & Kegan Paul, 1987).

Donoghue, D. *The Ordinary Universe: Soundings in Modern Literature* (London, Faber & Faber, 1968).

Donoghue, D. *The Sovereign Ghost: Studies in the Imagination* (London, Faber & Faber, 1978).

Donne, J. *Selected Poems*, ed. J. Hayward (London, Penguin, 1977).

Ferguson, G. *Modernist Influences on the Fiction of John Banville*, unpublished D. Phil. thesis (University of Ulster, Jordanstown, 1997).

Fowlie, W. *Rimbaud* (Chicago and London, University of Chicago, 1966).

Fried, M. *Absorption and Theatricality: Painting and Beholder in the Age of Diderot* (London, University of California, 1980).

Furbank, P. N. *Diderot: A Critical Biography* (London, Secker & Warburg, 1992).

Gerrard, N. 'The Midas touch', *The Observer*, 19 February 1995.

Goethe, J. W. von. *Faust*, Part II ed. and tr. P. Wayne (London Penguin, 1967).

Gombrich, E. H. *The Story of Art*, 15th edn (London, Phaidon, 1995).

Greene, G. *The Human Factor* (London, Bodley Head, 1978).

Hofmannsthal, Hugo von. *Selected Prose*, ed. H. Broch (London, Routledge & Kegan Paul, 1952).

Hollingdale, R. J. (ed. and tr.) *A Nietzsche Reader* (London, Penguin, 1977).

Hutcheon, L. *A Poetics of Postmodernism* (London, Routledge, 1988).

Imhof, R. 'An interview with John Banville', *Irish University Review*, 11:1 (1981).

Imhof, R. 'Banville's supreme fiction', *Irish University Review*, 11:1 (1981).

Imhof, R. 'Q. & A. with John Banville', *Irish Literary Supplement*, Spring 1987.

Imhof, R. 'German influences on John Banville and Aidan Higgins', in W. Zach and H. Kosok (eds) *Literary Interrelations – Ireland, England and the World*, 3 vols (Tübingen, Gunter Narr, 1987).

Imhof, R. 'Swan's way, or Goethe, Einstein, Banville – the eternal recurrence', *Etudes Irlandaises*, 12:2 (1987).

Imhof, R. *John Banville: A Critical Introduction* (Dublin, Wolfhound, 1997).

Jackson, J. 'Hitler, Stalin, Bob Dylan, Roddy Doyle … and me', *Hot Press*, 18:19 (1994).

Jameson, F. 'Postmodernism, or the cultural logic of late capitalism', *New Left Review*, 146 (1984).

Joyce, J. and Murtagh, P. *The Boss: Charles J. Haughey in Government* (Dublin, Poolbeg, 1983).

Kearney, R. *Transitions: Narratives in Modern Irish Culture* (Dublin, Wolfhound, 1987).

Kiberd, D. *Inventing Ireland* (London, Jonathan Cape, 1995).

Kilroy, T. 'This isle is full of noises', *The Irish Times*, 27 March 1993.

Knowlson, J. *Damned to Fame: The Life of Samuel Beckett* (London, Bloomsbury, 1996).

Knowlson, J. and Leahey, F. (eds) *Drunken Boat* (Reading, Whiteknight, 1976).

Koestler, A. *The Sleepwalkers* (London, Hutchinson, 1979).

Kristeva, J. *Desire in Language: A Semiotic Approach to Literature and Art*, ed. L. S. Roudiez (Oxford, Basil Blackwell, 1980).

Kuhn, T. The *Copernican Revolution* (Cambridge, Mass., Harvard University, 1976).

Lernout, G. 'Looking for pure visions', *Graph*, 1 (1986).

Lernout, G. 'Banville and being: *The Newton Letter* and history', in J. Duytschaever and G. Lernout (eds), *History and Violence in Anglo-Irish Literature* (Amsterdam, Rodopi, 1988).

Lodge, D. *Modes of Modern Writing* (London, Edward Arnold, 1977).

Lukács, G. *The Historical Novel* (Harmondsworth, Penguin, 1969).

Lukács, G. *The Theory of the Novel* (London, Merlin, 1971).

McGrath, P. 'An elegiac love letter', *The Irish Times*, 11 February 1995.

Machamer, P. 'Fictionalism and realism in sixteenth-century astronomy', in R. Westman (ed.), *The Copernican Achievement* (London, University of California, 1975).

McIlroy, B. 'Reconstructing artistic and scientific paradigms: John Banville's *The Newton Letter*', *Mosaic*, 25:1 (1992).

McMinn, J. *John Banville: A Critical Study* (Dublin, Gill & Macmillan, 1991).

McMinn, J. 'Stereotypical images of Ireland in John Banville's fiction', *Eire – Ireland*, 23:3 (1988).

McMinn, J. 'Naming the world: language and experience in John Banville's fiction', *Irish University Review*, 23:2 (1993).

McMinn, J. 'Versions of Banville: versions of modernism', in L. Harte and M. Parker (eds), *Contemporary Irish Fictions* (Basingstoke, Macmillan, forthcoming).

Mays, J. C. C. 'Biographies in limbo', *The Irish Review*, 21 (1997).

Michel, M. R. *Watteau* (London, Trefoil, 1984).

Modin, Y. *My Five Cambridge Friends* (London, Headline, 1994).

Nabokov, V. *Ada* (Harmondsworth, Penguin, 1970).

Nietzsche, F. *Thus Spoke Zarathustra*, tr. R.J. Hollingdale (London, Penguin, 1961).

O'Toole, F. 'Stepping into the limelight – and the chaos', *The Irish Times*, 21 October 1989.

O'Toole, F. 'Vigour meets rigour', *The Irish Times*, 8 June 1994.

Penrose, B. and Freeman, S. *Conspiracy of Silence* (London, Grafton, 1986).

Petit, C. 'It's Cliveden, actually', *The Guardian*, 1 May 1997.

Porter, R. (ed.). *Rewriting the Self: Histories from the Renaissance to the Present* (London, Routledge, 1997).

Posner, D. *Antoine Watteau* (London, Weidenfeld & Nicolson, 1984).

Riddel, J. N. *The Clairvoyant Eye: The Poetry and Poetics of Wallace Stevens* (Baton Rouge, Louisiana State University, 1967).

Rilke, R.M. *Duino Elegies*, ed. J.B. Leishman and S. Spender, 4th edn (London, Chatto & Windus, 1981).

Schwall, H. 'Banville's Caliban as a prestidigitator', in N. Lie and T. D'haen (eds), *Constellation Caliban: Figurations of a Character* (Amsterdam and Atlanta, Ga., Rodopi, 1997).

Schwall, H. 'An interview with John Banville', *The European English Messenger*, 6:1 (1997).

Sokal, A. and Bricmont, J. *Intellectual Impostures* (London, Profile, 1998).

Spencer, A. J. *Death in Ancient Egypt* (London, Penguin, 1982).

Stallworthy, J. *Louis MacNeice* (London, Faber & Faber, 1995).

Steiner, G. 'The cleric of treason', *The New Yorker*, 8 December 1980.

Steiner, G. 'The cleric of treason', *George Steiner: A Reader* (Harmondsworth, Penguin, 1984).

Steiner, G. 'To be perfectly Blunt', *The Observer*, 4 May 1997.

Stevens, W. *Selected Poems* (London, Faber, 1980).

Trevor, W. 'Surfaces beneath surfaces', *The Irish Times*, 26 April 1997.

Verlaine, P. *Selected Poems*, ed. R.C.D. Perman (Oxford, Oxford University, 1969).

Waugh, P. *Practising Postmodernism: Reading Modernism* (London, Edward Arnold, 1992).

Westfall, R. S., *Never at Rest: A Biography of Isaac Newton* (Cambridge, Cambridge University, 1980).

Williams, P. *The General: Godfather of Crime* (Dublin, O'Brien, 1995).

Williams, R. V. and Lloyd, A. L. (eds), *The Penguin Book of English Folk Songs* (London, Penguin, 1976).

Index

Note: page numbers in bold refer to main entries; page numbers in italic refer to illustrations; 'n' after a page reference indicates a note number on that page.